THE EXPOSED SPY

K. A. KRANTZ

The Exposed Spy; The Immortal Spy: Book 5

First Print Edition: October 2020

Cover and Formatting: Gene Mollica, LLC

Published 2020 by K.A. Krantz

www.KAKrantz.com

ISBN Print: 978-1-952293-01-6
ISBN eBook: 978-1-952293-00-9

Printed in the United States of America

Earit

For welcoming the crazy and dealing with the reality of it.

CHAPTER 1

The stench of scorched plastic permeated the two-bedroom apartment on the second floor of a town house in Southeast Washington, DC, Primary Mid World. Subfloor sneered through missing chunks in the faded parquet entryway. Blackened, gritty adhesive captured billowing lint, trapping dust bunnies in shredded orange-and-yellow floral linoleum. The leather sectional looked like it'd been mauled by a mountain lion. Numerous long gashes in drywall revealed nicked studs and allowed clumps of asbestos to spill over chipped baseboards. In the kitchen, decades of gunk belched across shattered knotty-pine cabinets, no longer hidden beneath the missing harvest gold range. The equally ancient microwave-hood combo and the slightly newer fridge were also missing in action. Anything requiring or delivering electricity had been stripped from the apartment, including the prized flat screen and next-gen VR system.

Not the sight Bix had anticipated upon receiving a summons from the youngest member of her team. It took her a moment to adjust to being corporeal and clothed, then another to acclimate to the amped-up push and pull of Mids' native magic. Judging the depth of the monstrous growl behind her, she wasn't the only one feeling the changes in magic. Seven feet of burly blond erstwhile

Berserker loomed over her. His lone hand twitched lightly on her hip, glowing hunter green as his evolving magic responded to his displeasure.

What the hell had happened in the Mids during their absence? She and Tobek hadn't been gone *that* long.

Bix signaled for Tobek to take the bedroom on the far side of the kitchen, while she headed down the short hall to the single bath and second bedroom. Narrow front windows provided a glimpse of a rosy late-summer sunset dipping behind neighboring buildings. Night didn't bode well for anyone lurking in a place stripped of light fixtures.

Picking her way across the wrecked floors, Bix moved silently toward the second bedroom. A glance in the bathroom confirmed the vanity lights and exhaust fan had been ripped out, along with all wiring. She paused in the shadows of the short hall, counting one null-space and one demigod's resonance in the eerily silent bedroom. Only humans created a null-space, and it was a human Sage who lived here, so that was a good thing. The demigod? Surprising yet welcome. She crossed the threshold, a smile of relief dawning.

A thousand watts of electricity lit her up like the Eiffel Tower on Bastille Day—then ceased almost as quickly.

"By the gods, Bix, I'm sorry. I didn't hear the clack of your damn shoes." Ashtad Ba'al, her dear friend and former team leader in the spy game, wrapped his arms around her and held her tightly. The nearly four-hundred-year-old son of a storm god, Ashtad was required to live in the Mids during his mandatory five-century trial to godhood. He could wield electricity along the gamut from a gentle illuminating flicker to a weapon of great destruction. This wasn't the first time he'd crimped her hair. Fortunately, she was immortal and nonflammable.

"Was sort of expecting that greeting after you'd decided I was persona non grata." She laughed into his sable curls amply streaked in gold. The abundance of highlights remained the only visible evidence of his recent trauma, and for that, she was grateful.

However, his linen shirt reeked of smoke, unfun smoke of the not-mind-altering sort. "Why do you smell like a war zone?"

"Long story." He released her and reached behind him, opening the closet door. "All clear, Cian. It's Bix and Chief."

A lanky ginger teen stumbled into the room, hands on knees, gasping. "Man, am I glad to see you. You too, Chief."

By Chief he meant Tobek, whose glowing dark green pupils made his otherwise bright blue eyes seem teal in the shadows of the hall.

"Rest of the apartment is clear," Tobek rumbled, bracing his arm atop the doorframe. "Either you're starting a renovation, or you pissed off someone, kid."

"Well, this place is a rental, so…" Cian shoved aside the mound of clothes, junk, and debris on his bed and motioned for Bix to sit.

"I came as soon as I got your message," Bix said, perching on the bed. "This seems more dire than you let on."

"This," Cian gestured wildly to the disaster surrounding them, "is, like, way lower on the crisis scale than the reason I asked you to come home."

"You're under twenty-four-seven watch by the Angelic Host. Your entire neighborhood is owned and occupied by angels who are charged with keeping an eye on you, so this isn't some random smash-and-grab." Bix tried to keep her patience. Not with the kid, with the situation. She didn't like ninety-three percent of angels, but she had a special arrangement with an archangel regarding Cian's welfare to prevent things exactly like this mess. "Am I snatching angels by the short feathers, or are you going to tell me there's a good reason why they let this happen?"

"We should do this briefing someplace less ventilated," Tobek suggested, not moving from the hall. He was bigger than the doorway. Moose. "Angels can hear a gnat fart, after all."

"No, no," Cian and Ashtad blurted in unison.

"I kind of need to be seen as being home," Cian hedged.

Tobek straightened. Bix narrowed her eyes.

"Because?" Bix prompted.

"I got fired from Project Resen," Cian admitted on a long sigh.

"What?" Bix cried as Tobek's inventive expletives conveyed the rest of her opinions on the matter.

Project Resen was the new defense system intended to repel, restrain, or track Other World entities across the Mids. It was the only hope the Mids had in combating advancing armies of anti-gods, who intended to consume all magic until nothing remained of the hundred-odd Mid Worlds and their inhabitants. The invaders were aptly known as Devourers, militaristic shapeshifters with forward troops already inside the Mids and feasting on prisoners. Bix and her team—along with Tobek and his battalion of Berserkers—had busted their asses to bypass political shenanigans and get Resen into development. Now Cian got fired right before Resen launched? Something smelled fishy…and it wasn't the kid's rotting takeout containers.

"Firing a system architect before the system goes live is project suicide. I'm not a techie, and even I know that." Bix crossed her ankles and clacked the heels of her mermaids-eating-sailors pumps. "What's their excuse?"

"That I abused my access to spy on ranking members of the Consortium while siphoning highly secure data for personal gain." Cian shoved his hands in his hoodie's pockets. "Bix, you've got to know it didn't go down like that. I mean, testing the system was my job. Management just didn't like what I found."

Pride warmed Bix's re-formed heart. Cian had come such a long way from an underage barback; he was almost a fully-fledged covert operative. The fact he kept getting caught was sort of a downer, but she and the rest of their team continued to train him. The kid had always been a genius; that came with being a Sage. The downside of all those book smarts was that they had turned him into an information addict with the same unquenchable thirst as a hard-core meth head, so the charges against him were totally plausible but irrelevant.

"What did you find?" she asked in a singsong way.

"I didn't think it was much of anything at first. I spotted an anomaly, I reported it, and that's when shit went stinky." Cian scratched the fractal of crystal embedded in his forearm covering an inked wilted leaf. The leaf was the mark of a failing grade from the Houses of Fate to which Sages and Oracles aspired. "If they hadn't kept erasing my tests, I wouldn't have kept digging."

"Digging into…?" Bix gestured for him to continue.

Ashtad, not Cian, reached under his shirt to the small of his back and tugged a tablet from his waistband. "As you probably noticed, the Consortium's goons took everything from this apartment that required any kind of electricity. They didn't just terminate Cian's employment, they put a clean order out on him."

Angels, dragons, gods, and Fates comprised the political and magical ruling body of the Consortium. Their job was to protect and populate the Mids, whenever they weren't stabbing each other in the face to gain personal power. Fucking politics.

"A Consortium clean order would've left this place spotless and renovated to boot to support a narrative that Cian had moved out due to rent increases." Tobek peeled a shard of wooden framing from the wall. "This much mess? This much noise? This public reckoning? This was a message to the choir of angels watching over him, and to you, sweetheart, his true employer."

"The Consortium is too chicken to come at me directly these days, so they consider my inner circle fair game. Stupid, but it excuses his babysitters, at least. They can't defy the leaders of their not so free Worlds. The question is who inside the Consortium ordered the message?" Bix took the glowing tablet from Ashtad. Other World magic tickled her palms. Any tech Ashtad owned had Other World components to enhance performance and security, while Cian's tech blended human and Mids' magic. On the screen of Ashtad's tablet, a spherical 3D topographical grid of blue, purple, and green lines formed peaks and valleys. "It's…pretty?"

"It's Resen's foundation, the repositioned ley lines woven with the Fates' threads." Cian thrust his chin at the screen. "You're looking at a simulation I ran in the staging environment, which pings the real thing to do a one-hit data grab. That's all the Mids under the blanket of Resen."

"That is so cool," she breathed, zooming in on parts of the grid. The mattress sank beside her as Tobek looked over her shoulder.

"All those intersections? They're actual ley line intersections? We've gone from a hundred to—" Tobek's magic spiked, cutting off his air. The bed warped, then collapsed in a tangle of soggy kelp. Tobek thudded to the floor, eyes wide.

Bix caught herself with an undignified squat and glared at her big blond bear. Tobek referred to these random magic flare-ups as "hiccups." Unpredictable and short-lived. He had spent his extremely long life applying magic derived from one set of rules. His recent evolution had taken those rules and chucked them. He had to relearn everything, break old habits, and be a novice again because he could now access magics that were once unimaginable, which meant his mistakes could be catastrophic. She and he had spent the last few weeks way out of the Mids, so he could get past the baby steps without inadvertently wiping out whole populations. He'd assured her he was safe for public exposure and had insisted on tagging along when Cian had summoned her. Turning Cian's bed into a bad day at the beach was less problematic than the time he'd turned their bedroom into an acidic aquarium, complete with mutant sharks. However, mortals were in the blast zone now. Mortals they both cared about.

A protracted snigger escaped Ashtad. Cian gaped.

"Still working out the kinks in the upgrade," Tobek mumbled as he gained his feet and extended a hand to Bix. "My apologies."

"At least it's seaweed this time." She offered a half smile and took his hand. She couldn't be mad at him; with her track record, it'd make her the worst hypocrite. She simply needed to be quicker on the draw to deploy protective shielding around his weird. That was on her, not him. He always had her back; it was her turn to step up for him. Didn't mean she wouldn't tease him about it when they were alone, though. Alas, they weren't, and she was way more concerned about whatever had her team concerned. "Cian, what'd you find in the data grab that freaked out someone in the Consortium?"

"This." Cian swiped his fingers over the tablet's screen, zooming in on grid lines until an anomaly came into view. "See how that ley line isn't like the others? See how that segment right there is sparkling? Like someone dumped a bunch of glitter in it?"

Tobek leaned in for a better view. Bix leaned away.

"I'm not going to break the tech. The bed was just a hiccup, nothing more." Tobek held up his hand. "Promise. I won't touch anything."

She tucked into his side and angled the screen his way. "You know more about ley lines than anyone in this room. What do you think?"

"I think ley lines should glow like the northern lights, not have clumps of whatever that is corrupting the line." He wagged his pinky over the rendering in question. "If you notice, it's only affecting the bit coming out of the World in which it's rooted. If we knew whose ley line that was, we could ask them what that's about."

"Which brings us to the actual reason I asked you here." Cian glanced at Ashtad, who gave him a nod of encouragement. "I mapped all the ley lines, their root Worlds, and which archangel and dragon queen were born alongside the ley line on those respective Worlds. The line's dragon queen died during the Renaissance, which leaves Archangel Ariel as its surviving birth mate."

Bix choked on a breath, wheezing. "Archangel *Ariel*? The Chair of the Consortium? The headest head honcho of the entire Mids? That Archangel Ariel?"

Cian and Ashtad nodded in contrapuntal time.

Tobek whistled and scratched his long beard. "You said the data grab was just a snapshot. Any chance this is an irregularity in the configuration of Resen and nothing to do with the ley line?"

"I asked him the same thing when he came to me with the

report." Ashtad crossed his arms over his chest. "This was after the first two reports he'd filed with his higher-ups went missing."

"They didn't go missing," Cian muttered. "They were *erased*. Twice, I filed a report like a good little drone, and twice, someone went in and erased not only my report but the scripts I use to pull and analyze the data. Like they thought I couldn't recreate the reports from memory? Kind of the point of being a Sage."

"Oo, I love the smell of conspiracy in the evening." Bix drummed her fingertips against the back of the tablet. "What happened when you sent it up the food chain, Ashtad?"

"They blew up my condo," he quipped flatly.

Bix's heart stopped for three extra beats. Darkness rippled along her spine. "Tell me that's a joke. Tell me that's not why you smell like a war zone."

Cian took the tablet from her, tapped the screen a few times, then handed it back. A news program played. In the background, a familiar high-rise in Rosslyn, Virginia, just a hop upriver from where they currently stood, burned in flames too blue to be natural. Most of the top floors were gone. It was a nightmare of dense smoke and balconies collapsing like cards as people fled the scene, battered and bleeding. The video cut to soot-covered first responders and stretchers of black bags amid the flash of emergency lights.

"That's when I put out the call." Cian hunched his back, probably because he couldn't hunch his shoulders anymore; they'd crystallized due to an infection. Poor kid perpetually looked like a linebacker about to take the field.

"There were humans in that building," Tobek growled. "Lots of humans."

"The Consortium didn't care." Ashtad shrugged. "I was in the elevator on my way up to the penthouse when it exploded."

"Oh, no, no, no, no," Bix sputtered as tendrils of darkness seeped from her back to answer the call of her rage. "I am going to rip Ariel's wings from her rigid spine. Slowly and with great glee."

Tobek laid a heavy hand on her shoulder. "It's a message, sweetheart. If she wanted either man dead, they would be. In an instant. It's not an accident young Ba'al survived, any more than it's an oversight neither of them has been arrested."

"She knows there is no way I'll let this pass," Bix hissed. "She and I have a history, a recent and unpleasant one. Ariel threw down the gauntlet. I'm picking it up."

"Unless you want to assume sole leadership of the Mids as Empress Bix, thus overthrowing its elected body, you must leave that gauntlet where it lies," Ashtad countered. "Ariel isn't an individual in want of cosmic justice. She is the Chair of the Consortium. What that representative body says and does governs all the Mids. She is the face of that body. This entire thing is political. Politics is your weakness. Nonetheless, you have to play her game."

"The hell I do." Bix looked to Tobek for support.

He shook his head. "Young Ba'al is absolutely right. You can't attack the sitting Chair of the Consortium without rock-solid proof of her crimes."

"It's not a crime when it's done by the government." Cian took back the tablet. "Look, the stuff going down with me and Mister Ba'al isn't the big problem."

"It's a misdirection." Ashtad wiped the edge of his mouth. "A favorite trick of magicians, politicians, and spies."

"Exactly." Cian fiddled with the tablet. "The problem is that stuff in Ariel's ley line. I ran the data grabs three times, right? So I could write new reports? Check out the changes in the line from first grab to last. Time lapse is a month."

Bix reexamined the tablet screen. Three close-ups of the sparkling ley line filled the screen, each image showing the glitter sliding farther up the line. The color of the line below the glitter was darker than that above it. "It's spreading?"

"If it hits that first intersection, it'll spread to all the ley lines." Cian looked about helplessly. "Admittedly, I don't know what that stuff is. It could be nothing, or it could be something. But if it was nothing, why is the Consortium trying to hide it?"

"It's not nothing," Tobek assured. "Ley lines shouldn't look like that."

"Until we know what it is, we have to assume the worst. Whatever this is could destabilize the foundation of Resen." Ashtad puffed a curl out of his eye. "The Mids will never launch its defense system. We'll continue to be totally exposed to the Devourers."

"Resen needs every archangel and dragon queen alive and in good health to work as designed," Cian added. "So, you killing Ariel would also screw us, Bix."

"Lucky angel," Bix muttered. "What about the dragon queen who recently died? How badly did that mess us up?"

War was a bitch, and politics was worse. Allies and enemies had suffered numerous losses over the last year. Some were keenly felt, and the repercussions were still unfolding. Like now. Damn it all.

"Not going to lie, it would've been better if she was still with us. Resen would definitely be stronger and probably more stable once it launches." Cian looked to Ashtad, who nodded in agreement. "We didn't know about Resen back then. If we had, things might've been different. There *are* lines that have only their archangel or only their dragon queen. Most have both, but there are exceptions. However, from here on out, we can't afford to lose any more dragon queens, archangels, or ley lines."

"The foundational elements have balanced the netting based on who is in play now," Ashtad elaborated. "Resen should scale as new elements are born, but any loss is bad. It's like kicking the third leg from under a tripod."

"That's why it's really, really good both you and Chief are here." Cian grinned sheepishly. "Dealing with a ley line is so far above my pay grade. Those who might know how to solve the problem aren't talking, or they're straight up trying to silence us."

"Are you saying you have a *mission* for the team, Cian?" Bix teased, sort of. If she didn't crack a joke, she would go on a Resenending rampage, and that'd be...bad. She didn't want to rule the Mids. She despised administrivia. She liked being in charge of her shit but didn't want to own that job for billions of others. No, thanks. Despite the Consortium, the Mids was a great place to call home what with the vibrancy of all the messy lives being lived with such beautiful chaos and constantly evolving order. This collective of Worlds was home to dear friends, mortal and otherwise. Those friendships gave her immortal life purpose and meaning, which was why she would let it look like she was playing Ariel's infernal game.

Cian took a deep breath and nodded slowly. "Yeah, yeah, I guess I do."

"Lay it on us," Tobek encouraged.

"We need to get samples from the ley line and its root World to a special team of scientists who might be able to identify the cause of the sparkles," Cian asked more than stated. "Before whatever it is gets to the intersection and without the Consortium erasing us from existence."

"Scientists?" Tobek arched a brow. "What kind of scientists?"

"Spe-special ones?" Cian stammered.

Tobek prided himself on the whole continuing education thing. He'd spent lifetimes as a doctor, an artist, an engineer, a linguist, and more, in addition to being a soldier. No doubt he was jonesing to join the science party. Hell, it might've been a party he'd started a century or two ago. Never could be too sure with him.

Bix patted Tobek's chest but directed her question at Cian. "A team you trust?"

"Yeah, hundred percent," Cian answered without hesitation.

"Okay. Samples for Cian's special scientists it is." Bix gave Ashtad his tablet. "Are you going to run overwatch or work the field, Ashtad?"

"I need to get Cian set up with a rig so he can run overwatch, then I'm ready for the field." Ashtad gestured to the closet door. "Don't suppose you could give us a gate to one of my bolt-holes?

Discretion is the better part of valor, what with the Consortium watching."

"Second site secure?" she asked.

"A tribute to an old spy's paranoia," Ashtad confirmed, tapping the tablet screen and holding it up for her. A picture of a high-tech nuclear fallout shelter gleamed in the evening light. "Leave the door open, if you would. We need to make it look like Cian's still here, so the goons don't go looking for him."

As long as Bix had an accurate mental image of a location, she could open a gate to said location. Huge. Dinky. Didn't matter. She didn't even have to be nearby to do it. It was one of many fabulous aspects of her gatekeeper magic.

"Alrighty then, you guys prep and get the location of our fourth musketeer while Tobek and I have a little chat with the fallen archangel who was supposed to be covering Cian's ass." Bix placed the gate to the bunker inside Cian's closet. "I want to see if the archangel will share a clue as to how we get a viable sample from a ley line without getting punted across multiple universes."

"It'd also be good to know if anyone inside the Consortium is aware of Ariel's actions and how it jeopardizes Resen." Tobek cut his finger on a piece of broken furniture and used his blood to draw wards around the closet door. A visible wave of green-and-silver blended magic surged through the room with a gust that lifted hairs and ruffled clothing. The wards shimmered around the door, then repopulated around the room like viral code, spreading into the hall and beyond. Magic retracted with a loud sucking sound. Doors and windows slammed shut. Green and silver faded into nothingness.

A breathless silence held the room.

"That should keep any unwanted visitors out of the fallout shelter." Tobek frowned at his hand, brows knitting. "Probably going to keep them out of your apartment too."

"Probably going to keep them out of the entire city quadrant," Ashtad drawled. "Might need to fine-tune potency, there, Chief."

"Noted." Tobek shoved his hand in his jeans front pocket.

"You ready, sweetheart?"

"That's it? You guys will take the mission just like that?" Cian rubbed his forearm again and stared as if everyone in the room was growing horns. "You're not going to force me to out my special scientists?"

"Aw, Cian." Bix pouted, but a smile overtook it. "Yes, that's it. You're allowed to bring a mission to the table for the team to consider. You've worked hard to earn our trust. This is one of the ways it pays out. As for your scientists? We all have assets we don't drag into the light unless it's absolutely necessary."

"You decide when it's necessary, not us," Ashtad clarified. "Protecting your assets is essential to spycraft. Welcome to the next level, kid."

Tobek gripped Cian's crystallized shoulder. "This also means you own the responsibility if things go wrong. You ready for that burden? It's heavy."

"Psht, yeah." Cian rolled his eyes, but his voice cracked.

"Come on, Tobek, before you turn Cian into a squid or something." Bix laughed and opened gates to a Mid World on the other side of the collective.

CHAPTER 2

On a Mid World of blood-red terrain where crystalline mountains formed monoliths like the hands of a butcher bound and begging for his life, criminals of every race traded the illegal and illicit in the Crimson Market. The Market was run by five syndicates, four of which were Chwedlonol—the myriad mortal magical races native to the Mids. The fifth syndicate, a choir of disavowed angels, masqueraded as long-eared, long-tailed imps to protect the Chweds from greater enemies and to exploit enterprises deemed criminal by national governments. It amused Bix no end to watch the normally imperious angels waddle around in the guise mandated by their archangel.

Tobek escorted Bix around the market square where a quartet of mermen performed in four of the ornate fountains. Scents spicy and savory wended on gentle drafts, enticing visitors to any number of stalls and cafés arranged by syndicate neighborhood. The suns were warm but not too warm, bright enough to bathe the market red, but not so bright as to cause a glare. The density of the crowds reflected commercial prosperity but not fashionable popularity. The market was clean, upscale, gentrified even. At least in the square. No doubt the alleys remained the discreet choice for settling disputes.

The unique weight of being observed by the masses settled along Bix's shoulders and tickled her nape. No one had known she was the infamous Chimera when she'd lived here for a year undercover as the right hand of a rising syndicate leader. Then events had unfolded, and now everyone knew who she was. She was getting used to being recognized. Unfortunately, she could never be sure of the reception. Bogeyman from whom folks would hide? Cosmic entity before whom people would grovel? Source of endless power to whom the greedy, the smarmy, and the stupid would try to cozen? It was never a simple passing greeting, a common social acknowledgment of coexistence, then moving along. Alas. She missed being closer to ordinary.

Of course, gamboling with Tobek brought its own kind of attention. Tobek naturally exuded a commanding presence that had nothing to do with his magic and everything to do with the way he carried himself. Walking beside him, it was possible to be figuratively overshadowed; literally overshadowed was inevitable.

"You going to be okay here, in the Mids?" she murmured, wrapping one hand around the bicep of Tobek's amputated arm. His erratic magic pinged off her like opposing shower jets turned up too high. She was the infinitely more powerful entity, so he couldn't harm her. She just worried about him…and those around him.

"It's the ley lines." He stretched and curled his fingers as green magic glowed around them like webbing, then dimmed. "Their relocation and integrations with the Fates' weave are impacting all native magic. Everyone who wields it is affected. It's not just me and my evolution."

"We knew there'd be changes once Resen was built. Didn't foresee all of them, admittedly." She leaned her head against his shoulder. Bix's magic was older, broader, and one generation removed from the origins of all existence. While she was related to the creators of Mids' magic, she couldn't tap into it without damaging it. Heck, she couldn't even exist in the Mids without Tobek being here to siphon the excess magic she expelled and convert it into something beneficial to the Mids. His continuous evolution depended on him absorbing a variety of magics, like a really big ShamWow.

"It wasn't your job. That falls wholly on the Consortium." He stopped at a cartographer's stall, where maps of various Mid Worlds detailing traveling hot spots of magic hung like sheets upon clothing lines. "Metropolises were built where ley lines crossed. Cities died and bloomed as old lines faded away and new ones were born. Humanity is unconsciously drawn to the hubs of magic in order to stabilize the magic in the areas. Chweds follow humans for economic gains. We should be seeing the start of mass migrations across the Mids. Commercial hubs will relocate, once-thriving areas will be abandoned in favor of the new centers, and regional governments will scramble to claim the new seats of power. Unless the Consortium addresses these seismic shifts in populations and resource demands, we're looking at centuries of war among the native races across the entirety of the Mids."

"Eh, make that a millennium of slaughter, easy," a phlegmy voice mewled. The breeze kicked up and native magic spiked as a leathery green imp appeared behind Bix. "Well, well, well, look who's back in town. Your boyfriend is a little different, though, eh? Stands out like a typhoon in a desert."

"And you're a little ridiculous," Tobek grumbled, casting a derisive glance at the archangel in disguise.

"Samael, it's good to see you too," Bix greeted, fighting back a grin. Samael was the only archangel she could abide. Frenemy in the beginning, he'd grown on her as a trusted ally who'd run some fugly missions at her side. Alas, to keep his cover intact, Bix's reputation required her to treat his lowly imp with disdain.

"What do you want, Chimera?" Samael twirled his finger, and the breeze coalesced into a cone of silence surrounding the three of them as Tobek resumed strolling. Wind was the angels' schtick, air their element, and atmosphere among their contributions to the Mid Worlds to which they were inexorably bound. "Come to get the name and location of one of those memory-keeping gods my choir's been tracking?"

"You found them?" Bix diverted her planned spiel, ignoring Tobek's muttering about angels meddling where they're not wanted. "The last three gods who hold my missing memories?"

One trailer full of emo baggage Bix hauled around happened to be that three-hundred-odd years ago she'd divvied up all her marbles and handed them out to seven gods to be reclaimed at some future date. It'd left her a complete amnesiac without a clue as to who she was or what she could do. Why had she done it? To save the Mids from the Devourers, supposedly. Emphasis on that last word. These days, she had a little over half her wits back in her head, which gave her access to half her magics. Being restored to her full glory meant this mission would be moot and Ariel would be cowering under her desk. Never mind that Bix's official title was High Executioner for All Worlds and that she probably had a huge backlog due to her prolonged absence. Then there was the small matter of her family, their ability to create and annihilate universes on a whim, and the marrow-deep hatred she had for certain members she couldn't recall any more than she could recall the reasons she hated them. Fun times, right? Gah.

Both Tobek and Samael had known her from the pre-memory-wipe era. Tobek couldn't talk about it due to a curse the all-powerful her had imposed on him back in the day. Samael would answer most of her questions if asked, but was way more keen to get her back to normal so she could save him and the Mids from the Devourers. Bless him.

"Yeah, we've got a list of ten who fit the description of mad gods who are Mid World guardians who developed personality quirks after you went galactically MIA." Samael plucked a pink carnation from a fairy florist's bucket and offered it to Bix with a sly leer. "Don't look so stunned. I said we'd find them, and I'm pretty sure we've narrowed the field as far as we can without tipping our hands."

"Gimme, gimme?" She smiled with more teeth than charm,

waving off the fragrant flower and laughing inside as observers bent to whispering. Imps were notoriously treacherous, spiteful, and greedy. Their magic placed them in the midlevel ranks of Chweds, but their avarice bonded their race across Mid Worlds, giving them an enviable network of thieves, traffickers, and extortionists. "I mean, I have another mission with which I need your help, but knowing which god is most likely to sidetrack my efforts to save the Mids as part of some delusional revenge plot would be inordinately helpful."

"Promise not to level a city the next time you take down one of these nuts?" Samael ripped off the head of the carnation with his yellow teeth and made a great show of chewing it like cud. "Your past performances don't instill faith."

"If only my memory keepers were amenable to scheduling a confrontation, but you know gods." She looked away as he regurgitated the flower, then chewed it again. Angels didn't need to eat. They subsisted by absorbing negative emotions. Imps, on the other hand, delighted in grotesque table manners.

"Drama queens." Samael cackled, rubbing his disproportionally long and very calloused green hands together. A small piece of inked parchment slithered from his palms. He offered the list to her, then snatched it back. "Wait. Why am I getting word that a certain Sage's apartment is warded against my kind?"

A choir of angels functioned like semiautonomous appendages of their archangel. An archangel could take over the brain of anyone in any choir, while the lesser angels could only knock on their archangel's mental door and hope for an answer.

"Because I need his apartment to be more secure than it was when Consortium guards ransacked it. Which brings me to why I'm paying you a visit." Bix snatched the list of memory keepers from Samael and glanced over the names. One or two looked familiar, but nothing tickled a memory. Damn it.

"We had to let that happen." Samael wiped his mouth with the back of his hand. "Politics. Besides, keeping the kid alive is more important than keeping his material things intact. You might want to remember I'm disavowed by the Angelic Host. No one is coming to my aid if I pick a fight with the Consortium, especially not while you're out of pocket."

"Did Cian tell you about Ariel's ley line?" Bix slowed her pace as a flurry of shouts and the pattering of feet warned of a changeling with one teacup scampering toward them, wide eyes fixed on the sloshing liquid inside the fine china. A phlegmy rebuke brought the childlike Chwed up short in front of two imps keeping curious observers at bay from their archangel and the infamous Chimera.

"I might know something about something," Samael evaded, picking his ear canal and studying the trophy retrieved from it. It was a classic imp action and one that bolstered his disguise, but if he ate the clump of wax like real imps did, she might have to walk on the other side of Tobek to block the view.

"Is it possible to take physical samples of a ley line? Better still, is it possible to do it without Ariel knowing?" she asked.

Samael sucked a long deep breath through his stained front teeth. "I know we agreed to be allies all the way through this mess with the Devourers, but asking me to betray the secrets of archangels and their ley lines? Not saying angelic culture isn't without its flaws, but there is nothing more sacred to us than our direct ties to pure native magic. Sorry. Can't. Not this truth. Not this secret. Definitely not with you. You're a detriment to the lines, always have been."

"I've literally danced with a baby ley line. It's still alive and thriving," she objected.

"Keyword there is 'baby.'" Samael scratched his nails along his palm, and an acorn appeared. He tapped the acorn twice. It sprouted. He tickled it with his hooked nail, bending the thin green shoot. "This sprout is the baby line. It's green, malleable, capable of surviving stronger forces."

"Unless it gets eaten or mowed," Tobek grumped.

"But as it grows, it develops firmer structures, eventually protective outer casings like bark," Samael continued, speeding the growth of the sprout into a twig and ignoring her blond bear. "So now, when those stronger forces show up…"

Bix flinched as the twig snapped. "I work with a team, you know. I don't have to be the one to actually touch it."

"Your team, eh? Let me think about that." Samael picked his teeth with the broken twig. "Still a no."

"Whatever is affecting the line is spreading," Tobek argued. "If we do nothing, whatever it is will defile every line, including yours. It's your duty to native magic to encourage its growth, not its decay."

"Look, let the Angelic Host…" Samael paused midsentence and sneered at the red sky, which was adopting a bluish tint.

An opening gate crackled between the fountains of the market. The sonic waves of displaced atmosphere blasted apart Samael's cyclone of silence. Through the gate, a mixed-race company of Consortium guards marched in columns of five. The black-on-black Consortium logos on their tactical gear shimmered in the pale blue light shining through the gate.

The hairs on Bix's nape prickled and her stomach clenched as visible evidence clashed with her other senses. She saw a programmable gate. She saw upper-ranking Chweds in the uniforms of the Consortium. She saw the elite team fan around the market, cornering imps and chasing them down alleyways.

She *felt* something wholly different. The instinct of a predator surged to the fore as her senses pinpointed dinner by the dozens. Two beats more and her brain finally reconciled the dichotomy. Too late. Samael was already squaring off with the captain of the guards.

"What's this?" Samael taunted, holding fast to his guise. "A visit from our lofty overlords? To what do we owe the honor?"

The captain of the guard seized Samael by the throat and lifted him to eye level. "Where is the archangel known as Samael? Give him to us."

Confusion twisted Samael's elongated triangular face. His yellow eyes cut around the square as every imp played to their role, allowing themselves to be dominated by a superior race. Unfortunately, they had no idea it really *was* a superior race.

"Devourers," Bix whispered, "Not guards. Devourers."

CHAPTER 3

"The guards are Devourers disguised down to the DNA," Bix murmured, knowing full well every angel in the market could hear her with perfect clarity. "Seek the poison in their soulless presence as proof."

The imps' chaotic retreat developed a pattern of herding gawping market vendors and fascinated customers into stalls and shops, forming a loose barrier between the Chweds and Devourers. Unlike angels, the Chweds of the market didn't embody enough magic to make them interesting to the anti-gods, but the Devourers wouldn't hesitate to slaughter anyone who interfered. Thus, while darkness thrashed against Bix's spine, eager to escape and feast on the Devourers, she bid her hunger to abide. Devourers this far into the Mids was bad. Devourers impersonating Consortium security forces hunting one of her allies? After a team of supposed guards had hit Cian's apartment? Oh, she had questions. Lots. But she was a collaborative sort of spy, so she'd let Samael have the first crack at them. This was his turf, after all.

"Who?" Samael gasped. His imp's hands feebly slapped at the captain's arms. An act for certain. He couldn't keep the cunning and hate from hardening his features.

Bix knew why Samael was maintaining his disguise, but what

was the Devourers' reason? Why frame the Consortium for kidnapping? Why not roll in here in their far more fearsome native state? What were the Devourers really up to? And why didn't the captain recognize the magic rolling off Samael was that of an archangel?

"He needs help." Tobek lurched forward. It was the ageless soldier in him that made him run toward conflict to protect and defend. It was such a deeply ingrained response that he likely didn't pause to consider that Samael was also a battle-hardened soldier or that Samael's choir was a well-trained angelic army.

Three imps stumbled into Tobek's path. Green-and-silver magic built around Tobek's arm and sparked at his fingertips as he growled, warning the imps away. They didn't move. They didn't look at him either. Matter of fact, they seemed to be shielding him.

"Hold," a strange voice softly urged on a gentle breeze curling around Bix's ear. Judging by the sudden rigidity of Tobek's spine and the muting of his magic, she wasn't the only one receiving angelic instruction. "We must learn why they want our archangel and who sent them here to get him."

"Consider the collateral damage," another airy voice cautioned. "Provocation is to be avoided. We strike only as a last resort."

Samael had to be in the minds of his choir, feeding them his plan. As much as angels were assholes, Samael's choir took their jobs as protectors of this flock seriously. She and Samael had worked together often enough that he knew she had his back. All he had to do was signal. She would wait until he did. Maybe.

Of the hundreds gathered in the market, Bix was the only one on-site who could kill the gate-crashers. Devourers fed on the magic of the Mids, so the worst Samael's choir could do was give the anti-gods a tummy ache. If things escalated, it would be on Bix to defend the market. Not that she minded one whit, but as her prey, the Devourers usually sensed her presence, an innate survival sort of thing. Yet, the normally sharp-eyed anti-gods looked everywhere but at her and her big blond bear. It was as if they weren't there.

Wait a minute.

Bix searched the market, not the stalls, but the mouths of the shadowy alleys and the windows of the monoliths. Chweds stood jam-packed shoulder to shoulder, most facing the imp and the captain. A few faced her. A few boldly met her regard and inclined their heads.

Glamours.

The syndicates must've been hiding her and Tobek behind glamours. Of what? She had no idea. Statuary? Sandwich board? The magic of lesser races flew under the radar of the anti-gods as the Chweds joined in the elaborate game of illusions. It was no secret the Consortium despised her, so the syndicates had taken it upon themselves to protect the infamous Chimera from what seemed to be Consortium guards? How novel. How lovely. How useful.

"Ai—air," Samael wheezed, flailing in the captain's hold.

The captain of the guard fractionally loosened his grip. "Where is the archangel?"

"Friend, archangels wouldn't be caught dead slumming around these parts. We're a bit feral for their liking. Whoever sent your unit must be testing you." Samael's long-muzzled grin lifted to mischievous heights. The imps guffawed. The market denizens tittered.

"I feel the magic of angels around us." The captain of the guard curled his lip and growled, drawing Samael closer until they were nose to nose. "I smell Mids' power."

"If you think an imp can truss up an archangel and deliver him to you, you don't know diddly about your target." Samael flicked a curled fingernail over the captain's shoulder. "Why don't you hop back through that gate of yours and tell your boss you got the wrong address?"

The gate.

Bix cut her attention to the gate that had delivered the Devourers to the square. Devourers had mastered portal technology, but to a gatekeeper like her, there were discernible differences between a gate and a portal. Differences of more than semantics. A *gate* had brought the anti-gods to the market. That type of gate was highly regulated, tightly controlled, and limited-quantity Mids tech. Whose gate had they hijacked? Before she could investigate, the gate snapped shut and winked out of existence.

Alas, the Devourers were far from stranded. There was a public gate behind Bix. If the Devourers could get to it, they could get to another Mid World. No way could she let that happen.

Tobek seemed to sense her thoughts as he slowly backed toward the public gate. Movement in the monoliths said the glamour moved with him, so Bix moved too. Fortunately, the Devourers seemed focused on the confrontation happening in the square's center.

"Give me the archangel, and I will let you live. Last chance, imp." The captain snapped his teeth in Samael's face and growled.

"Threatening murder is how you draw attention to your actions, *captain*," Samael whispered loudly. "Your higher-ups get word of an unsanctioned attack, and your whole unit gets put down like rabid animals."

"Who said anything about it being unsanctioned?" The captain licked Samael's face. A flicker of confusion crossed the disguised Devourer's mask. The captain sniffed Samael with one long inhalation.

Tobek cursed. A bolt of green magic shot across the square, nailing the captain in the side. Noxious stench filled the air as the Devourer screamed in shock and pain. The anti-god morphed his towheaded, diamond-faced, fair-skinned body into a towering flint-skinned and pewter-horned Devourer adorned in a bronze nipple-baring uniform.

"Archangel, show yourself," howled the Devourer captain, discarding Samael with a casual toss powered by the might equivalent to a god. Samael rocketed across the market. A collective oomph accompanied Samael's inglorious crash into a stall of enchanted dust collectors. Shelves collapsed atop the imp. Samael stayed down.

Bix glowered over her shoulder. Tobek stared back at her flatly. Not a trace of contrition. So much for staying out of it until Samael gave the signal.

"Archangel, I will not ask again." The exposed Devourer swept his smoldering side with one hand, instantly restoring himself and his uniform to flawlessness. "My men and I will consume this World organism by organism until you stand before me."

At those words, the rest of the Devourer company reverted to their natural forms. Black toxic magic flared around their talon-like fingers, crackling, threatening.

The Chweds of the market sucked in a collective breath. To their credit, not a one screamed upon seeing the heinous proof of invaders whose presence until now had been a rumor festering among the masses. The lid the Consortium had tried to keep on their colossal failure to protect the Mids from a foreign army was officially blown. Now that the criminal underbelly had witnessed the gross incompetence of the ruling races, rampant anarchy would flourish. Combine this with the consequences of relocating the ley lines? The Consortium was well and truly screwed.

Reason six thousand four hundred seventy-two why Bix did not want to rule anything but her own life.

"Denizens of this feeble World," the Devourer captain called in a voice that echoed off the monoliths. "If you want to live, point us to the archangel. You have ninety seconds to present him. Refuse and…"

Across the market, a pair of Devourers dragged a merman from the fountain as a third bit off a chunk of the singer's scaly hip. The merman screamed, then fainted. Rich crimson coated the Devourer's mouth and dribbled down his chest. The crunching of bones echoed in the silent horror of the square. A trio of angels disguised as imps ran at the offending Devourers. A struggle ensued. Three blasts of toxic magic reduced the imps to bubbling puddles of goo.

Not another soul moved as tension thickened to strangle sound.

"How do you want to handle this?" Tobek murmured, pressing his lips against Bix's temple.

"I can't kill the anti-gods here," she countered quietly, knowingly alerting the angels to the problem. "Their blood and viscera will be too much temptation to the syndicates, who will collect the aftermath to resell in some other form. These Chweds have no idea the suspended death they'll be trapped in if Devourer blood gets into their bloodstream. One paper cut, and the damage would be done."

"We need a place to hold and interrogate these assholes, to find out who sent them and what they want with me." Samael groaned on a sullen breeze from beneath the heap of the stall, hiding the speed with which his body mended, a speed imps didn't possess.

"There is no place in the Mids that can hold entities who feed on the magic constituting the walls trying to contain them, not without Resen live and at full strength." Tobek glanced at his hand as his magic sparked.

"These guys get off on pain, so torture gives us nothing but pulled further into their machinations." Bix scrambled for solutions. She couldn't drop the anti-gods into the ether where the bulk of their armies were staged. That'd be doing them a favor. She couldn't dump this many Devourers on the pantheons, who *could* contain and interrogate their old foes if they had time to prepare. There was, however, one prison that could hold them, and one prisoner who delighted in receiving unexpected company. Downside, said prisoner might not leave the Devourers sufficiently intact for her to question after she finished the ley line mission. "I could try to drain their memories. I've only gotten their emotions before, but I could try—"

"No," Tobek interjected fiercely. "The cost of that is too high, and not just to you."

A second merman screamed as a pack of Devourers fell upon him, feasting on parts both fish and man. This time, the Chweds weren't so silent in their fear.

"Twenty seconds," the Devourer captain sang out.

"Fuck it. Get them out of here," Samael cursed. "Wherever they go, make sure they suffer."

"That I can do," Bix pledged. "Minor distractions would be helpful."

"On it," Samael wheezed.

As the imps made mad dashes from their would-be captors, darkness unthreaded from Bix's spine. Bix closed her eyes and gave over her focus to stalking her prey. The Devourers had spread around the market. Picking them off onesies-twosies was risky since the Devourers were linked to each other through the tattoos running down their sides. Their retaliation would be swift once they noticed their dwindling numbers, so she had to hurry. Gates opened under or behind Devourers, and shadows shoved them through. Those anti-gods with hands on imps or Chweds found themselves skewered by darkness, then scraped off into a gate.

"Chimera? Show yourself," bellowed the Devourer captain. "Come with us, and we will heal you. Attack us, and we will be relentless. You cannot win. You are too broken."

"How the hell did they know about your status?" Tobek groused.

"The ether. I was stranded there for years, powerless. Occasionally, I ran into a few of them. Either they're choosing to ignore my progress, or the memo hasn't reached all units." Bix opened her eyes in time to see multiple blasts of toxic magic coming her way. So much for the glamour. Her magic in motion must've outed her. She braced for impact.

Tobek spun in front of her, taking the blasts squarely along his back. Denial tumbled from her lips as she clenched his shoulders and tried to throw him aside. The man was a brick house.

An *unmovable* brick house?

The blasts should've sent them both careening into a monolith. The blasts should've burned his flesh down to the bone. The blasts should've left him a bubbling pile of entrails. Instead, he simply grunted, jerking with each blow of poisonous magic. His wealth of ink brightened beneath his Henley. The stink of scorched flesh accompanied a faint sucking sound coming from his torso. A fine sheet of ice pushed up from his skin and hardened over his clothes.

Not a good time for a magic hiccup.

"Move," Bix hissed, pounding on his chest.

The strength of the shove and the snatch of his magic against hers flared. Ice melted. Water evaporated. Tobek tipped his head, brows furrowing as he held her gaze. He drew a long steady breath as incandescence built within his eyes.

How? He wasn't a Berserker anymore. He'd evolved beyond it. He shouldn't be able to invoke the rage, yet there was no questioning the hundred-watt radiance of his eyes, the angry sneer, the slowly curling fingers, or the magic sparking silver amid deep green along his arms.

"Tobek, no," she whispered. "Think of the collateral damage."

Too late. The rage that made Berserkers stronger, faster, and unable to tire was rooted within him. He was the original Berserker. The source of their ability. He was no longer bound by the Fates, and that apparently meant his battle lust was unfettered.

Oh shit.

Tobek turned on the Devourer captain with an inhuman roar that blew water from the fountains and shook the ground. To Bix's surprise, Tobek's back bore none of the expected damage. She would've questioned whether the Devourer captain had missed if not for having been standing right there smelling Tobek's cooked flesh. Even his shirt was pristine. How the heck…?

Her big blond bear fired a bolt of his unique magic, nailing the captain squarely in the chest. The Devourer doubled over, hands clawing at the wound as ice crystals formed in the hole where a heart would've been. A keen and a snarl, and the Devourer healed himself.

"You," the captain hissed, a sinister smile exposing its audacious glee. "You're not the archangel, but you'll do. Take him."

Bix redoubled her efforts to clear the other Devourers from the field as Tobek went toe to toe with the Devourer captain. If the anti-god thought it was going up against another deity, Tobek's unrelenting pummeling quickly disabused the Devourer of the notion.

When all anti-gods but the captain had been dispatched to a remote prison, Bix recalled her darkness to her body and closed the last of her gates. The imps parted to allow her inside the loose circle they'd formed around Tobek and the remaining Devourer. The Devourer captain no longer fought back. There wasn't much left of the anti-god's face. Teeth littered the ground. Toxic blood coated Tobek's chest and pooled around his boots, singeing fabric and burning skin. Still, her big blond bear knelt beside the anti-god, whaling on it with one arm as the scars of his amputated arm slithered along his bicep.

"He's blind with rage," Samael murmured, hobbling in the form of the imp to Bix's side. "I haven't seen him like this since he made his bargain with the Fates."

Bix laid her hands on Tobek's broad shoulders, mindful of the spatter eating through his clothes. "Tobek, it's done. Be done."

Tobek's fist stopped midblow. His chest heaved.

"I'm not harmed," she soothed. "Let the rage pass. You defended me. I'm okay."

The lights of his eyes dimmed along with the radiance of the magic pouring off his body. He blinked rapidly. Slowly, he pushed to his feet, flexing his fingers. His knuckles were shredded, and his entire hand was coated in tarry black blood. He faced her, head hung low, hair obscuring his features.

"Sweetheart?" he snarled softly, somewhere between a wounded animal and a heartbroken man.

A sob caught in her throat. The Eternal Knot branded above his heart that hid the piece of her he held inside him should've been dark teal, a reflection of her. No more. It was six colors, six distinct hues, none of which belonged to her. All of which belonged to her siblings. She'd asked three of her siblings for help with Tobek's evolution. Behold what that trust had gotten her. Meddling by the other three. The three she did not remember and instinctually did not like. Conspiracy by all and evidence that each of her siblings had defiled her lifeline to her Berserker. Worse? Tobek had said nothing. *Nothing.*

"What did they do to you?" She tried to keep her voice steady, but it broke as her hand hovered over the proof of perfidy.

"What was needed," he rasped, reaching for her cheek.

Steeling her will, she backed from his touch. Focus on the mission. Get samples from a possibly sick ley line to Cian and his scientists. Family shit had to wait. Emotional distractions had to be packed away. Resen was the priority. Saving the Mids from the Devourers was paramount. She opened a gate beneath the unconscious Devourer captain and cut away the stained ground too, leaving no dribbles or bits behind for the syndicates to steal.

Tobek stuffed his blistered, bloodied hand in his pocket and thrust his jaw to the side. He was covered in poisonous blood, but he had such a pain fetish that depriving him of the discomforts of victory would be an insult. Bix let him savor his burns and stings. He and she had come to the market for intel from Samael, intel they still needed.

Bix turned to Samael. "The hit was sanctioned. You heard him."

"By *his* boss," the archangel griped.

Bix pointed to where the gate had been. "A gate brought them here, not a portal. A programmable *gate*. The tech is totally different. You know it. You've experienced both."

"Who, exactly, are you trying to blame for this?" Samael stepped closer to her.

"Programming the gate to open here required someone with a lot of Mids magic at their disposal," Tobek rumbled. "It's unlikely to be a coincidence the Devourers arrived in Consortium disguises. It raises the question of whether they've infiltrated the Consortium or are retained by them."

"Could've been the rot," Samael argued. "We've cleaned most of the traitors from the Consortium's ranks, but not all."

"First Cian, then Ashtad, now you." Bix poked the imp in the broad triangle of his brow. "Why didn't they recognize your power, huh? They're expert shapeshifters accustomed to hunting gods, who also are expert shapeshifters. Do you really think appearances threw them? Or is it maybe because you didn't match up to the baseline they've already established? Because you're missing two things that would otherwise make your resonance on par with your vaunted siblings?"

Samael massaged the scar behind his shoulder, the scar where his wings had been severed. "There's no way my sister's in cahoots with them."

"Then why didn't you call on her to witness their attack? Share your brain? Why didn't you let the elected leader of the Mids see what was happening this far into the collective?" Bix challenged. "Ariel knows you're here. All your siblings do."

"I invited, she declined," Samael snapped.

"That doesn't make you at all suspicious?" Bix goaded.

"Tread carefully, Chimera. This is the Chair of the Consortium you're dragging. She's in that position because a lot of us back her. Not answering my invitation doesn't make her guilty of anything other than being busy." Samael lifted his chin and drew a circle with it. "Now, if you have proof she's done something, I'm happy to hear it, see it, smell it, whatever way it comes."

Bix put a leash on her temper and willed herself to think clearly, dispassionately. "I don't have proof."

"You don't have motive either." He stared at the spots where three of his angels had been dissolved by Devourer magic. "Without Mids' magic, we cease to exist. All of us. Including Ariel. Killing her siblings doesn't give her more power either. Just the opposite. She gains nothing by collaborating with the enemy."

He was right. Bix had allowed her strong bias against Ariel to cloud her judgment. She didn't even have circumstantial evidence Ariel was the one sending the guards, much less the Devourers. She wasn't even sure it was Devourers dressed up as guards who'd cleaned out Cian's apartment.

"Okay," she conceded. "Was your choir there when Cian's was hit?"

Samael nodded.

"Any chance those were Devourers who did the raid and not Consortium guards?"

"No," he said emphatically. "They scan for souls due to the kid's roommate not having one. Every Consortium guard at the apartment was a legit Chwed."

Tobek cleared his throat. "It can't be a coincidence the Devourers are using Consortium guards as their cover at the same time verified guards are targeting Cian and company."

"Coincidence or convenience, eh? On me to answer that since those hungry bastards are gunning for yours truly." Samael picked his teeth. "Before you go pointing fingers at my sister again, maybe consider how she made contact with an upper-ranking Devourer who'd follow her orders. Every encounter we've had with them, they're dancing to their own tune. We're just food."

"Fine." Bix held up her hands in surrender. "Let's focus on the issue for which I do have proof: her ley line. Something is up with it that may or may not impact Resen. Until I know for sure, however, I'm going to assume it's a problem. Thus, you have two choices: you tell me exactly why her line glitters, or you help me figure out the answer."

Samael huffed. His changing expressions teletyped his internal argument.

"You've made your point about me being too eager to blame Ariel for everything. I'll keep my attention on her line and not her," Bix assured. "I want the Mids to be able to defend themselves against the Devourers, regardless of whether Ariel is at the helm. This isn't an excuse for a vendetta, not for me, at least."

"Any move you make on the line, no matter how good your intention, will be taken as a move against her. She will retaliate, and you will be giving her permission to do so." He shook his head. "There's jack I can do to dissuade her. If she's not the one targeting your team, she soon will be."

"It's a political catch-22. Full force of the Consortium on me and mine if we try to inspect the line." Bix couldn't help the pity sneaking into her tone. She'd never seen Samael struggle so much with a decision before. He was usually so blasé about jumping into the thick of things. "We're clear on our risks. We've deemed them worth it."

"She's not without risk here either. If our ley lines die, we do too. When an archangel is gone, their choir vanishes with them. The balance of native magic will be borked, the Mids will go into decline, and the Devourers will run amok. This is about more than Resen, you know?" He poked her with his gnarly fingernail. "Ley lines get real unpredictable when *you* get close, which makes the magic they produce get real weird. For a ley line that's damaged, you could make it worse. You could end the line."

"You said the line is damaged," she blurted, pouncing on his words. "So the Host knows there's a problem, but you guys don't know how to fix it."

He swore through pursed lips and reluctantly nodded. Just once. One nod. One nod that cleared Cian. She had to hand it to the kid for sticking to his guns.

"The recent realignment of the lines must've triggered something in Ariel's line," Tobek mused. "That bodes ill for the other lines. It'd be a damn shame if angels covering each other's asses was the reason Resen never launches."

"I help you with this, there's a strong chance I'm the one who ends up dead at the hands of my kin. You know that, right?" Samael glowered at Tobek, then heaved a loud sigh. "Death of the Mids is worse, though, so do you know any mortals who've been touched by a ley line and survived? Actual mortals, not a behemoth pretending to be."

Bix resisted looking over her shoulder at Tobek. "I do."

Samael wrapped a breeze around her ear. "Then listen closely, because if you're going to take on Ariel, her ley line, and the godsdamned Consortium, you're going to have to start a war a little earlier than planned."

CHAPTER 4

Tobek's uncontrolled rage during the confrontation at the Crimson Market sat ill with Bix. She wanted second, third, and fourth opinions about his tantrum. Plus, he was covered in Devourer goo, which limited their landing zones. Fortunately, she knew some guys with a particular set of skills. Guys who also happened to be mortals and survivors of a ley line encounter. She didn't bother to tell Tobek where they were headed. He knew the place and the men better than she did, so when he and she stepped through gates into a stainless-steel morgue, the welcoming high-pitched squeal of delight elicited a hearty chuckle from her Berserker.

A squat, potbellied goblin leapt from a rolling stool, hurtling himself at Tobek. At the last moment, the goblin jerked hard left and avoided colliding with the Devourer gunk staining Tobek's clothes.

"Home," Gurp shrieked, clapping and bouncing on his toes to angle himself between Tobek and Bix. "Family home."

"Sorry to bring him back in shabby condition." Bix bit her lip and wagged a finger in Tobek's direction. "He was burned by Devourer magic, and it did something to him. I don't know what exactly, but something. Since you're the Tobek expert, I defer to you."

Tobek shot her a droll glance as he tossed his hair over his shoulder to expose the damage wrought by Devourer spatter. Gurp plucked a tatter of charred Henley from Tobek and nibbled on it. In addition to being Tobek's best friend and something akin to his magical familiar, Gurp was a walking forensics laboratory. Not only could his senses discern things on levels far surpassing the abilities of most mortals, but he also had the extensive knowledge to identify and apply the information he'd gleaned. Sure, his primary method of detection was to eat whatever he'd found—from plutonium to corpse lilies—and that limitless hunger gave his kind an unfair reputation. However, Gurp's greatest strength was his huge heart. Once he took a shine to someone, he knew what they needed before they did. When he was allowed to deliver on those needs, he excelled bar none.

Bix considered herself extremely fortunate Gurp had included her in his family.

"Pfft. He awake. He fine." Gurp rolled his bulging muddy-green eyes as his bulbous nose quivered, sniffing Tobek. The goblin recoiled and pointed to a corner in the back of the morgue where a bright orange drench shower and eye-wash station stood in bold contrast to the shiny gray room. "Gross. Gross. Shower. Now. Clothes there."

"I must really be fetid if a goblin finds me repulsive," Tobek joked and obediently headed to the open shower, ripping off the remains of his shirt and dropping them on a mortician's table. Bix turned her back to him as he worked the zipper of his jeans. She and he were intimate, yes, but not that kind of intimate. Yet. Again. Lately? Whatever. It was complicated.

Hissing hydraulic locks heralded the arrival of a passel of brawny Berserkers bursting through the main door with wide grins. The whirr and whiz of machines in the body-modification shop next door echoed along the connecting corridor on the ground floor of the renovated coal plant serving as the battalion's base of operations on the riverfront of Old Town Alexandria, Virginia, Primary Mid World. The Potomac River separated the Berserkers' base from the Consortium's chambers in Washington, DC. They were less than ten miles downriver from where Ashtad's condo had exploded. For a short while, Bix had shared the modern-industrial basement of this building with Tobek and Gurp, back before her presence had made things too dangerous for the guys.

"Chief," the men cheered, filing into the chamber that was one part science lab, one part medical clinic, and one part morgue. Ribald comments mixed with rounds of "Whoa, put that away," and "Damn, my eyes," as Tobek stripped and showered in the open corner. Bix didn't need to look to know there were dude gestures happening out of her line of sight. The snickers gave them away. These guys had lived together for centuries, sometimes in buildings, sometimes on battlefields. No family was as close-knit as the Berserkers. For Bix, it was an unadulterated delight to be allowed to share moments with this brotherhood. Relationships like these—the ones that included her and even the ones that didn't—they were the reason she fought so hard to save the Mids.

"Chief, when you come back from medical sabbatical, you're supposed to return whole and healed." Runjit, the lead medic, snapped on a pair of latex gloves and worked the bands of a face mask over his turban. "It's in the manual. The one you wrote?"

"First day back in the Mids and things got a little unpredictable," Tobek havered.

"Hey, I recognize the funk of this brand of unpredictable." Hywl, one of Tobek's lieutenants, grabbed a purple hazmat bag and a pair of heavy-duty gloves from a drawer. The bag radiated Other World magic. "You pick a fight with those tarry-teeth bastards and not invite us? I think I'm offended. Nope. Definitely offended."

"Where's Xipil?" Tobek asked, grabbing a towel from a cabinet.

A ceiling-mounted monitor blipped. A broad nose, cognac skin, and old eyes in a permanently youthful face appeared. Xipil, Tobek's second-in-command. Based on the background of computer terminals manned by more Berserkers, he was upstairs in the operations center for the base. "Chief, it's good to see you."

Jovial variations of agreement from the dozen guys filling the clinic and from the guys behind Xipil added to the consensus.

"I feel the lockdown wards are activated. Anything I should know?" Tobek wrapped the towel around his waist, then hopped up onto one of the four mortician's tables, wincing.

"The MWA heads want you to check in with them before you're allowed to return to active duty." Xipil leaned back in his chair and laced his hands on his chest.

The Berserkers were one branch of the Mid World Army. The muckety-mucks of the MWA reported up to a Consortium security committee. Tobek's evolution had effectively ended his commission with the MWA when it had ended the Fates' ability to keep him yoked. That "check-in" wasn't going to be with MWA leadership, it was going to be with the Consortium. After his confrontation with the Devourers in the market, he'd likely be meeting with way more than the security committee…and all that assumed he wanted to re-up. He'd been cagey on the topic.

"It's too soon to put on the uniform yet, so consider me a useful field asset." Tobek flinched as Runjit swabbed his bleeding knuckles.

A bit of joy drained from the room.

"That's too bad. Now's the time we could really use some top cover." Hywl punched Tobek's stained clothes into the bio bag, yanked off the heavy-duty gloves, and stuffed those inside too before zipping the bag. "Xipil's getting dragged for shit we didn't do. They're trying to strip him of command and put some cake eater in charge."

More mutters, these decidedly less friendly.

"Hywl," Runjit hissed and shook his head.

"What? Xipil's solid, and I'm not taking a hit to the battalion's honor lying down." Hywl's outrage thickened his Welsh accent to nigh on unintelligible. He turned to the monitor. The dawning of Berserker's rage lit his vibrant blue eyes, a unique color that identified a Berserker better than any shoulder patch could. "That's not right. Fuck that shit."

Consensus again from the guys making themselves comfortable by holding up walls and crossing arms in front of their broad chests. Gurp went off next, an indecipherable tirade in a language only he and Tobek seemed to understand. The goblin's body language was quite clear, however. Clear enough that Bix backed up a few steps to dodge the fervid gesticulations.

Tobek clapped his hand on Gurp's shoulder and jostled him lightly. "Xipil, tell me what you can."

"Technically, you haven't been stripped of your clearances and Bix's classification hasn't changed either, so…" Xipil clacked a few keys on the board in front of him, and an adjacent monitor in the clinic displayed thumbnails of videos. "We're on lockdown while our battalion is being investigated for going merc with high civilian casualties."

The tone of the consensus this time dropped to truck-down-gravel-road grumbling. More than one pair of blue eyes glowed.

There were a lot of insults that could be hurled at the Berserkers, but questioning their integrity? When every man in the battalion had traded his finite human life for the burden of endless soldiering to protect and defend the Mids from domestic threats? Ho, ho, ho, someone was estupido.

"Apparently, without your leadership, we've lost our moral compass," Runjit drawled, taking samples of Tobek's injuries and putting the bits of flesh into petri dishes.

"Bullshit," Tobek groused.

The first video played in high-def black and white, showing big bodies in Berserker combat uniforms and respirator masks raiding an elven government center. Innocents were dragged by their limbs and dumped in piles, while others were walked at gunpoint off-screen.

"That's not how we take a civilian post." Tobek slid off the table and ambled closer to the monitor. "This is staging for a cop show. How were these not instantly debunked by the MWA Tribunal?"

"Wait for it." Hywl sighed, scratching his black muttonchops.

Video one rolled into videos two and three. By video four, Runjit had tied off Tobek's arm and was drawing blood while his fearless leader stared at the clips, rapt.

"What kind of gun training do these idiots have? No man in this battalion keeps his finger on the trigger when not actively engaged. It's how you shoot your buddy in the ass." Tobek waved his amputated arm at the monitor.

"Best part's coming," Runjit assured, untying the rubber cord from around Tobek's arm and capping the vial of blood.

Sure enough, by video six, the guys had taken to removing their respirators. Well, only some of the guys. Eight of them, one being Hywl. He looked directly at the camera, flipped it the bird, then ripped it off the wall. By video twelve, Xipil stopped playing the evidence.

"There's hours of footage." Xipil sighed over the connection. "The only reason we haven't been batch retired is that we can prove we were deployed elsewhere during some of the hours recorded. But only some. Records of our orders have been erased from MWA servers. Those who signed the orders are denying our deployments."

Berserkers didn't retire. The only way out of the service was in a body bag. It was written into the contracts they'd signed that had modified their mortality and made them Berserkers. Lifetime commitment meant lifetime. Yet another reason Tobek's evolution was freaking out the Consortium—he'd found a loophole in his contract.

"It's obvious to anyone who's worked with us those guys aren't us." Tobek flexed his arm. "Birdie, you carry your left shoulder too high when firing automatic weapons. Hywl keeps two unsanctioned knives in his right boot. Jin is a leftie. Taiwo goes nowhere without his lucky charms."

As Tobek rattled off the names, said guys got nudged by their peers. The flashes of relief across their faces spoke volumes about the situation, more than Xipil was letting on for sure.

"Not the first report we've had of data being erased from proprietary systems," Bix mentioned into the rumbles of commiseration, careful not to bring Ariel's name into the conversation.

"Not the first higher-up playing stupid either." Tobek glanced at the hazmat bag on one of the mortician's tables. "Consortium guards are trained better than what we just saw. You don't think…?"

"Same eight guys take off their masks in the videos," Bix pointed out. "What are the odds those eight also faced off against Devourers?"

"Aye, we all did." Hywl jerked his chin at the guys along the back wall. "Same unit. Danced with them more than once. Lost some of our boys each time too."

"You didn't always have your faces covered, did you?" Bix asked.

"Nah, only when we know air's going to be a problem," one of the guys along the wall answered.

"That's their reference." Tobek cursed. "Earlier today, we ran into a company of Devourers impersonating Consortium guards. I recognized a few of the boyos until they shifted forms. When did these merc attacks start?"

"About two weeks after you left on sabbatical," Xipil answered.

"Xipil, can you ping Cian and see when Resen's foundation was completed?" Bix kept her anger in check as suspicions multiplied. The Devourers had been impersonating spies and soldiers for a while, stealing Mids' tech and intel to further their advancement into this collective of Worlds. The Consortium knew about the impersonations, so did the MWA, so there was no excuse for the higher-ups not to give the Berserkers the benefit of the doubt… unless they were ordered not to.

"You don't want me to do that." Xipil glanced over his shoulder and lowered his voice. "All our outside communications are being monitored by the Consortium. Word is, the kid's been targeted by someone over there. Dragging him into our mess isn't going to do him any favors."

"Okay, let's come at this a different way." Bix paced in front of the wall of freezer doors. "We're going to clear the battalion of suspicion, but to do that, we need incontrovertible proof. That starts with a list of sites that were hit, along with the dates and times."

"Sending that list to the clinic printer now." Xipil hit a few keys, and the printer on the back wall hummed in answer.

"You're after the patterns." Runjit pulled the paper and scanned it before handing it to Bix. "We've already done that. Nothing popped."

Some of the sites were places Ashtad and his demigods had hit over the years, and a few were places the spy guild had run covert ops, but not enough to tie the list to her or her team. Good news, actually. The Devourers might not be targeting her team.

"The Devourers came to the Mids looking for something in addition to a good meal. We have yet to figure out what it is," Bix mused. "Xipil, you said the team had gone merc. That implies they took more than lives."

"Yes. Quite the haul from each location." Xipil reached somewhere off-screen. Rustling papers. He held up a stack. "MWA investigators brought the complete list when they turned the base inside out."

"Found nothing, of course," Hywl harrumphed.

"Compare that list against items that were once under our control going back five thousand years. Discoveries, secure transport, trophies, the works." Tobek raked his hand through his damp hair. "There's a reason they're running around in our skins. It could be an item that keys off one of us. Gurp can help with archive searches."

"Yes, yes." Gurp bobbed his head.

"On a potentially related note, there's a problem with Resen, and I need a few good men who've encountered a ley line up close and real personal to help fix it." Bix batted her lashes.

"Same squad that intercepted the Devourers plus two more," Xipil answered. "But we're on lockdown. The Consortium dropped a force field over us. They'll know the moment the perimeter is breached and by whom."

"Unless we travel with Our Lady of Darkness." Hywl doffed a nonexistent cap in Bix's direction. "I'm already drowning in shit's creek thanks to those videos. Nothing I do can make it worse, so count me in."

Every man in the clinic piped up in agreement, including Gurp.

"This is the moment I sign off, so I can maintain plausible deniability when the MWA investigators return. We'll work the thefts and frame-up angle from here. Good luck, men." Xipil saluted, and his monitor went dark.

"I've neither faced a Devourer nor a ley line, but you idiots always need someone to patch you up after you have, so I'm in too." Runjit pulled supplies from cabinets, and the guys in the room helped load stuff into medics' bags.

"We'll get our gear and the other squads. Meet back here in, what, five?" Hywl asked. The eager grin plastered across his face was mirrored by the rest of the men.

"Make it thirty minutes. Gurp and I have to pull some equipment." Tobek waved off the dirty comments that poor choice of words provoked.

Snickering, Bix opened a tiny gate to the uninhabited World she called home and retrieved four silver ear cuffs and a smartwatch from a shelf Gurp had built for her. She clipped one comm piece to her ear and tapped it twice. "Knock, knock."

A crackle, and Ashtad's voice answered, "Line secure."

"Reinforcements on their way in thirty. Do you have a location for our lost lamb?" Bix handed the three other comm pieces to Tobek, Gurp, and Hywl. Cian had piggybacked their team's encrypted communication system on the ley lines, and Ashtad had enhanced the security in his Other Worldly way. Whatever trawling was happening on the MWA network didn't affect Bix's team.

Apparently, neither had the disappearance of Cian's electronics from his apartment.

"Bring them in as laborers. We've got two teams of Consortium guards patrolling the block," Ashtad cautioned.

"Devourers are disguising themselves as guards and Berserkers, so you and the kid stay inside. Tobek's wards should keep you safeish," Bix cautioned.

"Devourers? Here? Are you kidding me?" Ashtad swore in multiple languages as Bix's watch flashed with an image of an airport terminal followed by an inflight selfie of a woman in her sixties with two inches of silver roots in an otherwise burgundy mane loosely coiled in a topknot. Also in the picture was a white pig wearing a blue tutu and service-animal vest. "Flight landed fifteen minutes ago. Should be coming through customs in five."

"Am I picking up the woman or the pig?" Bix asked.

"Beats me." Ashtad chuckled.

"All right, men, get in your civvies. To anyone who cares, we're helping the kid renovate that shithole he calls an apartment." Tobek winked at Bix as she opened a gate. "I'll call when we're ready to move."

"Thanks, boys. See you soon." With that, Bix was off to collect the missing member of her team, who was either wearing a human or a pig. She was betting on the one in a tutu.

CHAPTER 5

Both wore tutus. The woman wore a blue-and-black floof of tulle over black leggings and half-laced black combat boots. Late morning's bright sunlight dazzled off the crystals on her beaded black denim jacket. The blue lips of a corpse peeked through the faded lipstick in the same deep burgundy as the woman's hair. The pig trotted glumly at her side as they stepped off the escalator in Terminal B, Reagan National Airport, Virginia, a sneeze away from the coal plant.

"Bixie, babe," the woman screeched, propelling herself into Bix's open arms.

"Drew." Laughing, Bix hugged her best friend so tightly that had the draugr inside the woman's body been able to feel everything as acutely as the original owner of said body, Drew would've been gasping for air. Instead, Bix was the one nearly crushed by the innate strength of the draugr as Drew danced her around in a tight circle while both of them squealed with ridiculous glee. It never mattered the body Drew wore, her bestie's presence always gave Bix a good grounding dose of what really mattered in life: relationships. A body thief of sorts, Drew *could* coexist inside a living body, but the maintenance and contending with the soul made a live suit less than ideal. Plus, Drew found digestive systems understandably revolting, thus she preferred the very recently deceased. And hoo boy did she love playing the part of whomever she occupied—soulless or no—Drew could ace any EGOT entertainer.

"Aw, Bixie, you haven't been gone that long, yet I still need my bestie fix." Drew sighed happily. "So much crazy you've missed while out there offing divine traitors. How's our big blond Berserker doing? Is he going to pick up the battle-ax again?"

"Too soon to know about Tobek." Bix set her best friend at arm's length and tipped her head at the pig. "Spare suit?"

"Oh, honey, honey, this precious sow is a Consortium goon who ran afoul of the Chimera Fan Club. After your little stunt in Blackpool, it's gone cross-World, don't you know?" Drew tugged the pig's blue leash and looped her arm through Bix's as they headed for the covered walkway to the parking garage. "With the ley lines moving, some Chweds are discovering they have more potent connections to Mids' magic. The caste system is getting reshuffled. Those who were bougie before the shift are waking up to find themselves totes hoi polloi."

"How the prideful suffer." Bix winced, imagining the culture wars. The strength of one's magic defined one's caste. Like it or not, those who could manifest living, breathing people had more status than a dual-form shapeshifter. That's what put dragons and angels at the top of the food chain for Mids' native races.

"The turf wars among the guilds are all kinds of cray-cray now. Those naturally imbued with powers are fighting with those who rely on spell casting." Drew tossed a handful of large marshmallows on the ground. The pig pounced on them and swallowed them whole. "So, when the Consortium's elite used their magic to break into your fan club's HQ, they got turned into genus Sus and sold at market. I kept this gal in case I need a hostage to exchange for one of our boys."

Bix stopped. "You're sure they were all actual Consortium guards who broke in? No Devourers in the mix?"

"Uh, yeah," Drew scoffed. "Hello, Primary Mid World. The

anti-gods haven't made it this far into the collective. At least, not that I've heard."

"They hit the Crimson Market, so we can't assume this World is still safe." Bix crouched in front of the pig. It stared back at her with flagrant hostility. "Did you read the pig's soul?"

"What was there. She's missing chunks." Drew waved to a pair of human children smiling and thumping on the windows of a van parked in the passenger-pickup lane. "Enough left to know she's got connections that would be beneficial should the occasion arise."

"You didn't have to fly with her, you know. I would've come to get you." Bix led them toward the parking garage, where an elevator would allow Bix to discreetly open a gate that would fool the eye without confounding any of the security folks watching the many cameras around the airport.

"We were already in the air when Cian alerted me to your return. Second leg, because there was no way I was letting my widdle herb nerd face off with the Consortium without proper backup. This is an all-hands-on-deck sitch, so I brought extras." Drew giggled and dropped her head on Bix's shoulder. "Ah, babe, I've missed you. You don't know how much."

They lingered on the curb as traffic slowed to gawp at the pig while cars maneuvered in and out of parking spaces. Bix let the crush of humans rush past them to the elevator banks. When the last traveler got in the last elevator, she stepped off the curb.

A black Hummer limo screeched to a halt, its front tire a smidge away from her peep-toe pump.

"Oy," Drew yelled. "Walkin' here."

The rear passenger door popped open in front of Drew and the pig. No one stepped out. No one leaned out. No one rolled down a window to explain.

No one needed to. The pendant of a shrunken dragon wing soldered to a shrunken angel wing burned Bix's décolletage. Bix hunched forward and waved Drew into the limo. Drew's pencil-drawn brows lifted, but she didn't argue. Drew clucked for the pig to get in the vehicle, then clambered in behind. Bix glanced around the garage as danger prickled her nape. Danger she hadn't noticed sooner. Three black SUVs idled in the corners of the parking garage. A fourth on the ramp down. A fifth on the ramp up. A closer look at the nearest front grille revealed the colored lights hidden behind the mesh.

Couldn't be. Not waiting for her. Surely?

Regardless, Bix slid into the back of the limo. The door slammed shut the moment her foot cleared the frame. The engine revved, and the limo turned to the down ramp. The black SUV pulled forward to block. Bix relocated it with a pair of well-placed gates. Her limo sped down the remaining winding ramps with the other black SUVs in pursuit, sirens blaring and lights flashing. Her driver bypassed the queue for the pay booth and exited via the entrance as other drivers mistook the chase for an escort. The logjam of cars, trucks, and construction vehicles parted. Traffic lights flipped to green, then flipped to red the instant the limo passed beneath, trapping the SUVs. Horns sounded behind them. Loud and furious. The Hummer sailed around the sharp bend of an on-ramp and seamlessly merged onto the George Washington Memorial Parkway, give or take a few potholes. Their speed slowed as they zippered into a pack of other black Hummer limos. More decoy limos filled in around them.

Bix didn't travel by car often, but even she had to snicker at the flawless escape.

The bulletproof blacked-out window separating the driver from the passengers rolled down with a soft whirr. Apple-red hair flowed in feathered lengths over a swimmer's broad shoulders. A chauffeur's cap sat low over winged brows. Mirrored aviators slid down a sharp nose. A pair of aquamarine eyes met Bix's in the rearview mirror.

"Feng," Bix drawled. "Thanks for the lift?"

Feng the Phoenix was the living welfare gauge of native magic, the lone dragon-angel hybrid, and the only mortal who outranked a dragon queen and an archangel. According to Mids' tradition, he was also Bix's greatest nemesis, slated to die at her hands every five hundred years so he could reincarnate and wait to die all over again. However, in this iteration of their lives, they were both broken mockeries of their previous selves. In their fractured states, they'd managed to form an unlikely friendship, caused in great part by the arrival of the Devourers and the traitors within the Consortium.

"Ester," Feng called, his gaze shifting to the pig. "Naughty girl."

The pig squealed repeatedly in undeniable panic and leapt off the seat, scrambling to the corner farthest from Feng. Feng snapped his fingers. The pig went up in smoke. No fire. No flame. No ashes. Just. Poof. Gone. The shimmering blob of a soul no longer sewn into a body drifted out the car to linger in the middle of the road, awaiting its psychopomp.

"Hey," Drew squawked. "That was my hostage, Big Bird."

"You may want to remember I was the Consortium's lead investigator for quite a long time before they forsook me." Feng's European polyglot accent made the depth of his hatred for the Consortium sound ever so civilized. The twitching jaw muscle at the edge of his perfectly groomed Van Dyke beard, however, gave him away. "Ester and her twin were on my team."

Drew slapped a hand over her face and groaned. "Twin? How did I not pick up on a twin?"

"Ester and her twin are psychically linked. They alternate who stays at base and who goes into the field." Feng pushed up his glasses. "The one who goes into the field is meant to be captured to gather and relay intel on the inside workings of the enemy to the one who remains at base. Rest assured, the Consortium knows everything you've said, done, and seen since Ester entered your life. Every contact you've made, every asset you've met, everyone and everything."

Drew threw her head back and groaned as the limo rumbled over railroad tracks. "But I read her soul. Nothing came up about any part of this."

"You're dealing with the Consortium." Feng peeled right with four other limos, heading into the residential streets of Old Town Alexandria. "Gods are part of the Consortium. Depending on the risk of the mission, a god will drain parts of an operative's soul to delete any classified intel."

"If the operative dies on a mission, the god who owns their soul can't learn whatever the Consortium's up to." Drew sighed with disgust. "I can't believe the other gods tolerate that kind of skimming. The whole point of creating a life-form who is recruited into the Consortium's elite is to have a nice juicy soul on which to feed when that life is over."

"The cars in the garage, there to intercept Drew or Ester?" Bix asked as the continued attacks on her team fed the malice living within her.

"Drew is my guess." Feng slowed to coast through a Stop sign on the tail of the limo in front of him. "Since she changes bodies on the regular, she's hard to nail down. Ester was the beacon that outed her."

"Bacon beacon," Drew muttered, turning in her seat at the growing whine of crotch rockets zippering through traffic. "Should've left her to the angry mob."

"They didn't expect you, Bix; otherwise, they'd have moved to intercept when she disembarked instead of waiting for the garage." Feng studied his side mirrors as motorcycles approached on the dotted line. Modified tommy guns took aim at the back windows of each limo in the motorcade.

"Consortium-issued weapons. Magazines loaded with alternating magic-nullifying and magic-piercing bullets." Drew knocked her knuckle against the glass. "We once raided a warehouse filled with those things, remember, Bixie?"

"More interested in why these goons are aiming them at you." Bix suspected it was another message from Ariel or whoever wanted Bix to think it was Ariel. A bullet of any type couldn't kill Drew. It'd just damage her suit. But why order another obscenely obvious attack right in front of humans who weren't supposed to know that magic was real according to Consortium laws? Laws Ariel was supposed to enforce.

"Consortium security members recently infiltrated my therapy group, which alerted me to the coordinated efforts against your team. Naturally, I couldn't let that lie." Feng twitched his finger, and the motorcycles exited existence in a flare of sunlight amid a rash of honking horns.

"You too? Ariel's either lost her mind or someone is setting her up. She can't possibly be this stupid." Bix cut off the quip forming on Drew's puckering lips. "Not and still be the Chair of the Consortium. Too many political enemies."

"Unless whatever is affecting her ley line is also affecting her," Drew rushed to say before blowing a kiss at Bix. "Magical cooties. Magically contagious."

"She wouldn't be the first of us with a sickness of the mind," Feng admitted.

"Feng, you reported to her directly, right?" Bix asked.

"Yes, for more than a century."

"If she wanted to silence members of our team, is this how she'd do it? Would she be this obvious about it?" Bix had to examine both sides of the coin when it came to Ariel. Yes, her gut said Ariel was guilty, but, as Samael had said, Bix had neither proof nor motive.

"The attacks are only obvious because they're failing." Drew wrapped the untethered leash around her hand. "Our team is a special brand of pain in the ass. We're exceptionally hard to intimidate or erase."

"Ariel likely handed a list of names to her chief of security and told them to deliver a message. The ineptitude of Consortium security is a reflection of their superiority complex. It doesn't occur to the guards that someone told to 'shut up or else' would recruit bigger guns." Feng flashed a smile. "The last time they had to fight you, Bix, they had me to do their dirty work. They don't comprehend how things have changed over the last year. They haven't faced Devourers. They haven't watched an angel be eaten alive in front of them. They haven't seen a dragon carved up like rotisserie chicken and shared among the troop that caught it. They haven't seen a god's skin peel off their bones from one blast of a Devourer's magic. The enemy isn't real to them. Consortium guards are just high-powered school bullies sold on their own hype."

"Gotta agree with the expert here, Bixie. The goons who came after me were legit Consortium guards." Drew clacked the clip of the leash. "Do we really think Devourers know enough about wiring in dilapidated town houses to steal the electrical and leave everything else intact?"

"The bombing of Ashtad's place was inexcusable overkill," Bix argued. "The kind that doesn't care about collateral damage."

"Ley lines moved. Magic wonky. Boom boom bigger than intended." Drew grinned. "Gimme another one. I like playing devil's advocate."

"Ashtad and Drew aren't of the Mids, so the guards would feel justified in going big against them. Cian's human. He can't fight back against lesser Chweds, much less the upper caste who comprise the Consortium's elite guard. Going too hard against him would be embarrassing to the guards, hence a simple wrecking of his home." Feng followed the motorcade onto the outer loop of I-495, across the Woodrow Wilson Bridge, heading toward Maryland. "Now, if you're asking if I think Ariel is responsible for what's happening with the Berserkers and Samael's choir, I do not. No motive. No means. No opportunity to call the shots with Devourer troops like she has with Consortium troops."

"I take it you've been eavesdropping since I got back?" Bix tapped her pendant. Inside those seemingly metallic wings was one of Feng's dewclaws, miniaturized, of course. As long as she wore the pendant, she maintained a connection with him. That connection allowed him to listen in whenever she was in the Mids. It also allowed him to help in times of crisis, and help her he had, on more than one occasion, so she didn't get her nose out of joint whenever he decided to tune in. In their line of work, having a lifeline on standby was a good thing.

This ridiculous car chase was a case in point.

"The response of native magic to Chief's return to the Mids overrode the privacy I attempted to afford you. Sorry." Feng blushed and adjusted his sun visor. "I've been trying to track down who erased Cian's reports from Resen. Records have been doctored and logs falsified. Whoever did it knows the proprietary system."

"Yeah, well, whoever it is pulled the same stunt in the MWA's system too. We should look into any staffing overlap." Bix stiffened as the comm on her ear chirped and Tobek's deep rasp requested a gate. It was a passing thought to oblige. It'd be good for Tobek to get to Cian's before she did, especially since she now had Feng in tow. There was a wee bit of hostility between her Berserker and the Phoenix.

"It's possible the Devourers are behind both," Drew suggested, rolling her eyes as a new six-pack of motorcycles gave chase across the bridge. "If they're impersonating guards, then they have access to all the sites in which Consortium networks are hosted. They don't have to know the systems, they just have to convince a coworker to do the deed, then that coworker gets replaced by another Devourer."

"Sabotaging Resen makes sense for them," Bix admitted. "Sidelining the Berserkers, the only mortal army who's gone up against them and lived? That could be plain old pride or because the Berserkers are guarding something they want."

"If Cian's reports picked up more than Ariel's glittering ley line, it makes the case that both Ariel and the Devourers would be after our extended team." Feng exited the highway, driving toward the MGM Casino at National Harbor, which was the opposite direction from Cian's apartment. The motorcycle gang closed in, hot on their tailpipes.

"Let me get these idiots," Bix interjected as the chase team split left and right around the motorcade.

"Happy to share the fun." Feng tapped the brim of his chauffer's cap.

Bix waited until the goons in the bitch seats had their weapons aimed at all three limos. At their speeds, it took two gates and one destination to make a point. If the Chair of the Consortium was intent on sending a message, the least Ariel could do was be at work when Bix delivered her response. On the off chance Ariel was unaware of how her orders were being carried out, then Bix's reply would clarify the situation.

Bix smirked, imagining the look on Ariel's face as the bikes and bikers skidded across the minimalist ice-blue office to careen into the monstrosity Ariel called a desk. If Ariel didn't demand a face-to-face with Bix after that, then it was another tick against the archangel.

"We're going to leave the van at the casino. We should use a gate to get to Cian's apartment," Feng suggested as their assailants vanished.

"Van?" Drew pivoted from side to side in her seat. "Don't you mean limo?"

"What limo?" Feng tugged his chauffer's cap, and it reshaped into a Nats ballcap as their vehicle morphed into a panel van. His attire changed to a pale blue T-shirt and faded jeans. Bix and Drew flinched as their seats transformed from luxury leather benches to cardboard boxes plastered with pictures of DIY baby furniture. A beat later, the long shadow of the parking garage fell across the van's dashboard. The decoy limos faded out of existence as they turned down the first ramp. The panel van rocked over a speed bump, the thump-thump chased by the screech of a low-hanging muffler. "Don't worry, I'll park. Just don't exit via the doors. The Consortium's monitoring all recording devices in the Primary Mid World in an effort to track every member of our team."

"I really, really don't like the Consortium," Drew groused as Feng backed into a subbasement parking place.

"They keep delaying Resen, and the Consortium will change from a representative body to the final survivors of four dying races." Bix peered through the windshield one last time for any Consortium goons lying in wait. Nothing. With a sigh, she opened gates.

CHAPTER 6

Cian's apartment had been stripped back to the studs. Two-by-fours were stacked beneath the front windows. Sheets of plywood and rolls of foam underlayment had been piled where the kitchen had stood. Only the three-foot entry still had its chipped parquet floors. Two dozen Berserkers continued to dismantle the place in record time, piling debris where a bedroom used to be.

"Keep same for gate." Gurp pattered across exposed floor joists where walls separating a bedroom from the kitchen had once stood. A pencil balanced behind his ear, and a roll of blueprints was tucked under his arm. "Need two hours for new floor, yes?"

"Cian's the one calling the shots for this mission, so I defer to him," Bix said, her smile broadening as Tobek emerged from Cian's room in a faded Godsmack concert tee. He'd braided his beard and knotted his hair in a bun. He'd also attached one of his low-tech prostheses. High tech mixing with high magic could get a little janky, especially when facing off against a ley line. Praise to the powers that be, the man made sweaty look downright sinful.

"There is something deliciously delectable about a man covered in drywall dust," Drew purred, fluttering her fingers at Runjit as the medic hooked his hammer in his tool belt. Runjit paused, blinked rapidly at Drew, then smirked, shaking his head.

"Sweetheart, I've soundproofed the apartment and modified the wards. I'm running illusions in the windows to make it seem like Cian and a friend are working on the place." Tobek dumped two black trash bags in the pile of construction debris. "Phoenix."

"I could take care of the remodel right now," Feng offered. "Let your men save their energy for the mission."

"Sometimes the labor is the love," Tobek said flatly.

"Be practical," Feng dismissed with a tsk. "Judging by the wards, we're using this place as our base. We need solid floors at the very least, in case of crash landings. I'm sure you don't want your men breaking their spines on joists at the end of the op."

"Boys," Bix drawled. "This is Cian's home. Maybe we ask him what he wants?"

"Cian," Tobek and Feng called in unison, glaring at each other.

"Hey, the gang's all here," Cian greeted, a two-liter bottle of highly caffeinated soda in his hand. "Roomie, I thought you were in the pig."

"I leave you alone for the summer, and this is what you do to the place," Drew teased, hugging the kid. "I'm glad you're in one piece."

"Not sure how much longer that'll last once we piss off the Chair of the Consortium." Cian wriggled out of Drew's hold. "Yo, Gurp, I moved all the stuff I want to keep into the bunker. The place is yours."

Gurp saluted and went back to directing demo day.

"Cian, Feng is offering to do all, some, or none of the reno now so you can focus on the mission." Bix gestured to the Phoenix. "On the other hand, I know Gurp has been itching to rehab this place for you since you two met. How would you like to proceed?"

Bix certainly had her preferences, but Cian would soon be a newly minted adult—by human standards, at least—and had to make his own decisions. Especially about his home.

"Uh, b-both? Floors and a working bathroom would be cool. Electricity too. Pretty sure the Consortium stripped it from the whole building." The kid flapped his elbows. "Yeah. I mean doing the whole thing now makes the most sense, right, Gurp?"

The goblin toddled across the boards and handed the blueprints to Feng. "Yes, yes. Plumbing, yes? Runjit need. Kitchen too. Big sink. Small icebox."

"Please say there's a dishwasher included." Drew put her hands on her hips. "McNasty over there likes to leave science experiments lying around until they've grown small forests."

"Hey," Cian objected.

"Goblin, show me what you'd like me to do." Feng smirked and gestured to the pile of subfloor that offered a horizontal flat surface at goblin height. He paused beside Tobek to murmur, "You don't have to protect these people from me. I'm not the enemy."

"Yet," Tobek growled. "It's always *yet* with you."

Magic, green and blue, built around each man and reached for the other like thick gooey strands of bubblegum. Neither man moved during the staring match. They were of equal height, but if either of them shed their humanoid form, they were going to find themselves in a timeout on opposite Worlds. Bix was not in the mood for their crap today.

Magic sparked in a rainbow flash and abruptly contracted. Tobek grunted and stepped aside, motioning Feng through. Feng shook his head, then joined Gurp by the boards.

"Drew, Ashtad's in Cian's closet. I'm sure you want to notify the fan club that they've been compromised," Bix said before the snark bubbling on Drew's puckering lips escaped. Bix reached inside her belt and handed Drew the scrap of parchment from Samael. "Oh, and this is a list of possible memory-keeper gods. Would you and Ashtad take a gander, see if any names ring a bell?"

"Mmhmm," Drew hummed all too knowingly as she took the list, ducking between Tobek and Bix on her way to the back of the apartment.

Tobek eyed Bix, one brow arching. "Yes?"

"Get over it, especially for this mission." Bix stepped toward him, her heels striking squarely in the center of the joist. "Your magic reacts to your temper, which has been running way too close to the surface since your upgrade."

He sniffed but didn't deny it as he clapped his hands on her hips, helping her maintain her balance while she closed the distance between them.

"If you're having problems managing your own emotions, we're not doing each other any favors by allowing you to continue to filter mine." She tapped the spot above his heart where his Eternal Knot lay, the spot desecrated by her siblings. Fierce possessiveness poked and prodded the malice thriving inside her. Her Berserker. *Hers.* Her siblings would learn, possibly the hard way. "Say the word, and I'll own my own shit."

"You don't have enough of your memories to understand what you're really offering." He cupped her cheek. A trace of sorrow softened his regard. "And you have been a part of me for so long, the absence you propose would devastate me."

What she didn't understand was what had happened between him and her siblings. She didn't understand what else they'd done beyond what she'd requested of them. She didn't understand how that was affecting him. Worst of all, she didn't understand how to help him, because *he* wouldn't tell her. Was it his pride or was it something sinister one of her siblings had done to him? Pride she could understand. Pride she could work with. Siblings though… Siblings managed to twist her already complex emotions and reduce them to feral reactions. She didn't like being that uncontrolled, but she despised having her ignorance manipulated.

"What did they do to you?" she asked with a little more force than intended. "If you'd tell me, I might be able to help you through these rough patches."

"Being with you helps me. Now, focus on the mission. That's the priority, right?" He let her go as Feng approached.

"Hate to interrupt." Feng's smile was fleeting. "Bix, if you could levitate the group, I'll get this apartment redone and ready for operation."

Tobek let loose a sharp whistle. "Men, on the joists, every other, single file. Cian, that includes you."

Bix waited for the Berserkers to line up, then stacked gates to effectively lift everyone off the floor by a foot, being mindful of the ceiling and the men's unusual height. Feng held the unrolled blueprints in front of him and unfurled his wings. One gentle beat, and native magic poured down his flame-colored feathers on a stream and a song.

Crunch, crunch, crunch started a deep base tempo as demolition debris collapsed into neat piles of dust and minerals, then degraded further into nothing. A shake-shake-shake like maracas turned out to be bursts of sprayers spreading foam insulation and soundproofing between studs branded with protective wards. Slithering and hissing preceded the arrival of black, white, and copper wires sprouting from a fuse box, taking shape on vertical studs, nailing themselves into horizontal braces, and fitting themselves atop sheets of subfloor that slid off the main pile like cards in a breeze. Proper underlayment for main living fitted alongside waterproofing and in-floor heating coils as framing for the bedrooms and bath built themselves in new configurations. Plumbing pipes sprouted like plants before being closed in by drywall and covered in tile or paint. Hardwood floors went down before kitchen and entertainment-center cabinets. Black fixtures popped up from white quartz counters, and recessed lighting rotated through colors as they punched through ceiling beadboard. Doors spun into existence and hung themselves inside molding capped with tiny phoenixes stamped in the woodwork. Matte black appliances and sleek charcoal seating piled in next. Textured window coverings, bleach-white towels, a few colorful throw pillows, and framed personal photos added to the modern décor; erasing every trace of the shabby '70s that had existed before.

Naturally, cutting-edge electronics came last, provoking a loud and awed guffaw from Cian. The Berserkers hooted and cracked wise as Bix closed gates and gently set the men down in the refurbished apartment looking like something off an übertrendy urban design website.

Feng and Gurp had left no detail unattended. A squeal of delight from the newly completed back bedroom said Drew approved a full minute before Drew and Ashtad joined the rest of the group in the open living area. Drew scooped up Gurp and twirled around the apartment into the second bedroom and back out again. Drew's rapid-fire thanks caused Gurp's mud-green cheeks to flush purple.

Back slaps abounded. Close inspections of every nook and cranny had Cian being pulled from one place to another as the Berserkers eagerly showed the kid his apartment.

Feng stood in the middle of it all, a smile of satisfaction broadening as he took in the enthusiasm around him. Bix reveled in the joy filling the room.

"Bix?" Ashtad murmured at her shoulder. "What's wrong with Chief?"

"Hmm?" Bix turned to the Berserker at her other side. Tobek stood utterly immobile. His chest didn't rise or fall. His lashes didn't blink. There was a sheen around him, as though he'd been cast in Lucite. She cautiously reached for him. Ice, thick and solid, met her touch. She sucked in a deep breath.

The ice melted in a single silent sluice, like a wave crashing over him. Water evaporated as it hit the floor. Tobek inhaled a short sharp sniff and blinked. He hooked his thumb in his front pocket and smiled at the room. "All right, men, fall in. It's time for the mission briefing."

"Tobek?" she beckoned softly.

"Yes, sweetheart?" He turned his wicked grin on her.

"You okay?" She stared pointedly at his amputated arm…at the arm missing its prosthesis.

He followed her attention and scratched his jaw. "Must've forgotten the lo-fi appendage. I'll get it after the briefing."

A barrage of questions died in Bix's throat. Tobek was the master of evasions and redirects when he didn't want to talk about an issue. Magical hiccup or not, there was no way the man truly believed he'd "forgotten" his prosthesis. It was an arm and a semifunctional hand, for fuck's sake. She could push the issue right now, but if he was keeping mum about it, there had to be a reason. She respected him enough to wait until she had him alone to press for answers.

Tobek ambled in front of the big-screen TV and addressed his men. Bix glanced at Ashtad. Her friend massaged his jaw as his brow knitted. Ashtad's consternation was mirrored by Feng. Nobody was going to out Tobek in advance of a mission, that was apparent.

Didn't change the fact that something was very wrong with her big blond bear.

CHAPTER 7

"We'll split into three teams to collect the three types of samples we need." Bix leaned against the sill of a narrow front window. "Each comes with a different risk, but make no mistake, the biggest threat to all our well-being is the ley line itself."

"To understand a ley line, one must understand how a Mid World is formed." Feng held up an empty hand and twisted his wrist. A blob of bubbling putty appeared. "It begins with a planetary god creating the core with enough mass and energy to anchor itself in our constantly moving galaxy. From there, the gods begin a courtship with the dragons and the angels."

A few dirty comments from the guys rose up and died down.

"Terrestrial and water gods build upon the blob, terraforming in ways that set it apart from existing Mid Worlds. Think of this as the peacock strutting around in full plume." Feng lifted his wings and fluttered them, eliciting laughter from the gathering. "At this point, the World exists in our galaxy but is not yet part of the Mids. The gods present this provocatively wrapped World to the Consortium in a bid for inclusion in the collective."

Booing made a round or three at the mention of the Consortium.

Feng continued, unfazed, "If the politics are favorable, the Consortium brings the World into the fold, literally and figuratively. Literally, in that existing ley lines reach out and pull the World into their network. That's when Mids' magic begins to infuse the World. Dragons modify the gods' work by building mountains and trenching seas, making art out of raw materials. Angels establish atmosphere and plant the first seeds of life. They decide if a World is oxygen rich or nitrogen heavy, for example."

Comments about methane-rich Worlds resulted in good-natured ribbing. Tobek cleared his throat loudly, and the troops fell silent once again.

"From there, the Consortium populates the World and farms it." Feng spun the World on a teeny cyclone. "Questions?"

Cian raised his hand. "When does it become a root World? And who decides that? The Consortium?"

"Native magic decides both. Neither dragons nor angels—nor I—have any say in when, where, why, or which World gives birth to the newest triplets of pure native magic. A ley line is always born alongside a dragon queen and an archangel." Feng rolled the bubbling blob of a faux World on air currents between his hands. Each pass added a layer of soil or water, ridge or trench until seedlings sprouted around a thick shimmering indigo stem. "When it happens, all dragon queens and archangels are immediately aware but cannot investigate nor interfere until the ley line and its birth mates reach an age of majority."

"How long does that take?" Drew asked.

"Varies. They know the time has arrived when the nascent ley line is able to connect to the network of established ley lines." Feng set the new house plant on a shelf by the window. "At this time, the personality of the ley line becomes known. Yes, ley lines have personalities. They have feelings. They have thoughts. They have opinions. Just because they don't look like sentient entities doesn't mean they aren't. They are highly evolved and possess powers beyond that of a greater god."

"Like a titan, then?" Ashtad kneaded his thigh, the one so

heavily scarred beneath his tactical pants, he had to sit with his leg straight.

"I haven't met a titan," Feng drawled. "But, based on what I've heard of them, I'll say yes."

Low whistles and muttered expletives accompanied guffaws of adrenalized anticipation.

"Not quite a titan." Tobek hooked his thumb on his front pocket. "But the point remains salient: we're poking something that views us as maggots. It is absolutely aware of all things at all times on its root World. Anything perceived as useful will remain. Anything perceived as a threat will be quashed."

"Everyone here has been touched by a ley line and survived," Bix interjected before the notion of a suicide mission overtook the Berserkers. "That left a brand upon you, detectable by other ley lines. It marks you as a friendly, which should allow you to get close to Ariel's line regardless of its personality."

"Which brings us to team assignments. Hywl, you and green team buddy up with young Ba'al and Anudrengr." Tobek pointed to Ashtad and Drew. He had a thing about names because names held power, and because he was such an old fart that trying to keep up with whatever folks wanted to be called in this century was brain space he didn't care to spare.

"Aye, Chief." Hywl nodded once. "Where are we headed?"

"The core," Feng answered instead. "Because the ley line is rooted in the core of the World, and that core was made by a god, it is on the demigod and the creation of a god to collect those samples. Roots and soil, yeah?"

"Should I change my suit for this?" Drew gestured to her psychic's body.

"Human suit is the best one for this mission," Bix assured. "It's the least threatening because it grounds magic. Ashtad, getting to the core, you'll need the cover of the Berserkers to reassure the line. Once you hit the core, your Other World status will be subsumed, and you can move freely."

"Got it." Ashtad and Hywl exchanged thumbs-up.

"Red team, you're with me." Tobek grinned at the playful whoop-whoops. "We're taking samples from the surface down a mile. We're looking for where the corrosion starts."

"Feng and I are going after the aerial portions," Bix said. "He'll pull inside, and I'll—"

"You'll stay away from the line," Cian interjected, his cheeks turning bright red. "Sorry, but you touching a sample could contaminate it because you're...well, because of your relationship to the Mids."

Tobek snorted but stared at his feet, utterly failing to hide his grin. Cheeky bastard.

"Okay. I'll stay away from the line, however, Feng and I are also the distraction," Bix continued, steepling her fingers in front of her chest. "For all intents and purposes, Feng and I are—"

"Going to war." Feng cheered, then sobered. "In order for your teams to get far enough inside the ley line to grab useful samples, the line has to be tricked into thinking the cyclical war between the Phoenix and the Chimera has started, and that you—Mids' native children—are seeking shelter. Ley lines are, after all, most interested in preserving their creations."

"For once, our human origins are going to work in our favor against a greater magical opponent." Runjit harrumphed and motioned at the room. "We're assuming the World is populated, right? What's the take on collateral damage?"

"The population of a root World is a healthy mix of upper-caste Chweds. No mid or lesser Chweds, no humans. The ley line is too intense for lessers to withstand prolonged exposure." Feng shook his hair from his face. "Normally, the surface of the World is divided half to the archangel and half to the dragon queen."

"Normally, eh?" Runjit prodded, overemphasizing the first word.

"The dragon queen died a few centuries ago," Cian clarified. "These days, the World is wholly the domain of Archangel Ariel and her choir. It's her stronghold."

"She's making sure nobody gets near it," Ashtad added.

"She doesn't even want anyone looking at it from thousands of miles away." Cian gripped his crystallized shoulder and winced. "No digital scans, no bio scans, no records of her World at all. That's why we have to steal samples and smuggle them to a safer location."

All kinds of grunts, grumbles, and mutters rolled through the Berserkers.

"Seeing as how angels feed on negative emotions, should we expect the miserable and oppressed Chweds stuck on that World to fling themselves onto our blades?" Hywl groused. The Welshman was a hard-core angel hunter. He'd been knocking them off long before being recruited to the ranks of the Berserkers.

"Difficult to know how they've handled the changes after the dragon queen's death. Upper-caste Chweds are longer-lived than humans, so there's a good chance they remember the halcyon days." Tobek scratched his amputation scars, scars wriggling like waking serpents. "Regardless, the ley line will protect us and them from the aerial battle, but it will not protect us from the Chweds or the angels, so mind how you go."

"The battle between Bix and me should drive the angels to ground. Nobody wants to get caught between fire and night. She and I will do our best to herd them away from you." Feng tapped an empty shelf, and figurines of the Phoenix ablaze and the Chimera emerging from a starry night manifested.

"It is imperative that everyone in this room understands Feng and I aren't actually trying to kill each other. However, we have to sell the ruse to the line, so it will get ugly." Bix refused to look at Tobek grumbling beside her. "Now, logistics is going to operate a bit differently from our previous missions. Feng and I will not be on comms, simply because no tech will survive what we're going to do to each other."

"Rawr." Drew clawed the air and winked at Feng.

"Exfil will be done on relay. You get the word to me, I signal her." Tobek tipped his head toward Bix. "Allow extra time for her to find you."

"I can't use gates around a ley line. It'll interpret them as attacks. That means you guys get great big nighttime hugs on the way in and the way out." Bix opened her arms wide and wiggled her fingers. A few of the guys mimicked her, and a few blew her kisses. Man, she loved these lugs.

"Since angels control atmosphere, we're going to run this like we're in a toxic environment. Full cover. Respirators. Assume we'll engage unfriendlies the moment we touch down." Tobek grinned as his men answered with a unified "Hoo-ah."

"I've got your go bags in the bunker," Ashtad said, addressing the group as he levered up on his bum leg.

"Gear up, and remember, we need lots of samples from a variety of locations within your target area. The more information we bring the scientists, the better odds they have to figure out what's going on and how to fix it." Tobek dismissed his men and turned to Bix. "Three tugs will be for Hywl's team. Five for mine."

Bix laid her hand over her Eternal Knot as Tobek pulled on their connection. When she'd returned to the Mids after forfeiting her marbles, she'd believed those twinges and twangs were heart palpitations brought on by native magic's resistance to her presence. Now she knew it'd been Tobek trying to locate her. Funny, what she'd thought was a personal problem had turned out to be an unbreakable intimate link.

"Tobek, you know how people warn me about losing my temper and blowing up a World?" She tapped his knot. "Applies to you now. I will yank your ass out of there the moment I sense you getting overwhelmed."

He stepped close enough to kiss her temple. "You're not at a hundred percent. Every ley line in the Mids knows it. Every angel knows it, most especially Ariel. Expect her to show. Leave her to me."

"Leave her to Feng." She poked his chest. "This is politics, remember? Feng is the only one in a position to take her down without the entire Consortium turning on us."

"Sweetheart," he argued, drawing out the endearment.

"No. You focus on getting your men in and out safely with the samples. Feng and I will own the rest, including the angels." She leaned back and glared at her big bear. "When it comes to the choir, we're on a suppress-not-slaughter mission. All of them, even Ariel, must come out of this alive in order for Resen to launch. That is the bigger picture. That is our mission."

"Yes ma'am," he purred, fisting her hair in his hand. Her eyes crossed watching him lean down and brush his lips across hers. Once. Twice. On the third pass, his lips lingered.

"Tobek? What are you doing?" she whispered, her lips invariably moving against his. He *never* made the first move. He always let her come to him, let her set the tone for whatever shenanigans she wanted. Oh, he'd respond and reciprocate with tightly leashed enthusiasm every time. He made sure she knew her attentions were wanted, but at her comfort level. His limitless patience with her and her baggage was one huge reason she was trying to have a real relationship with him. She could wham-bam-shall-we-go-again-ma'am with the best of them, but she didn't invest emotionally in those partners. Anyone for whom she'd given a rat's ass had wound up mauled, maimed, or straight-up dead. Of course, Tobek had such a pain fetish that the first two options probably appealed to him.

Weirdo. Her weirdo, mind. Still, weirdo.

He kissed her once, deeply, then released her. The wickedness of his smile also shone in his eyes. "Good luck."

"Hey, before you run away?" Bix patted her whisker-chafed lips as a blush burned her cheeks. Still, she couldn't ignore the fact the man had been an overgrown popsicle before the briefing had started. "Are you sure you're good to go? Hiccups under control now?"

Confusion dulled his leer. "Sweetheart, I feel like a new man. Truly. Spending time with the troops nurtures my roots, gives me a boost I didn't realize I needed. I'll be fine."

"Okay. As long as you're sure." She forced a smile as he joined the queue of Berserkers passing gear and bags from the bunker down the hall. It was impossible to miss how his men perked up when he was near. If he'd felt depleted during his separation from them, had they been similarly affected by his absence? What about his evolution? Had it trickled down to them too? He *was* the origin of their ability. It wasn't beyond possible that every Berserker had been transformed in some way. This mission would be as good as any to spot changes…when she wasn't trying to fell Feng, scramble angels, or dodge the ley line.

This mission was Cian's first as team leader. She wanted it to go well for him for all kinds of reasons, so she had to focus. Yep. Blinders on. She could do that. No, really.

"Cian," she called. "Odds of you being able to maintain overwatch are slim. You've danced with a ley line, so you know—"

"Got it covered," Cian assured, reclaiming the center seat of the couch while the Berserkers spread out around the apartment to change into their op gear. He grabbed a keyboard from his modular coffee table and went to town. Moments later, planetary images scrolled across the big-screen TV. "You always want pics of neighboring Worlds prior to kicking off an op. These are the three nearest Ariel's root World."

"Aw, it's like you know me." Bix perched on the back of the couch and studied the pictures. She needed accurate images to open gates, but only a speck of local darkness to make a connection in her native state. She had no idea what the changes in spatial relations that came with traveling cocooned in her night would be like for the guys. She lacked the memories that could tell her if they'd done this with her before. She lacked the memories that ought to warn her if they'd suffer discomforts during transit. She lacked the memories that should confirm that they'd be safe within her darkness if shit went down bad and fast.

Was she putting them at additional risk by going cosmic? No clue. Did they trust her regardless? No. They trusted Tobek implicitly, though. They'd follow him anywhere, anytime. She had to trust her Berserker to tell her if what she'd proposed was wrong. Frankly, watching him dress in his combat uniform, seeing the ease with which he shot the breeze with his men…yeah, he acted like this was old hat. They all did, really.

Blinders. Focus. Don't go looking for more problems.

"I'd tell you to relax, but it'd be bad advice." Feng stood behind her and leaned forward. "You and I need to keep in mind the line is still grieving the loss of its dragon queen birth mate. Centuries to an old line is a nonce, and grief makes an opponent lethal."

"Plays to *our* strengths, doesn't it?" Bix glanced over her shoulder, shutting down her gnawing worry before Tobek felt it through their bond. "Ready to die today, Big Red?"

Feng sported a cocky grin and waved her on. "Bring it, you wet blanket."

She bumped him with her elbow. "I'll give you a head start. Make it look like it's an honest-to-gods chase."

"Ready, set…" He vanished in a flash of red flame.

"Time to go, boys," Bix shouted as tendrils of shadows seeped from her form, surrendering its veneer of flesh until all that remained was her native nebulous state of midnight and stars. With a disembodied chuckle, she wrapped her teams in darkness and moved out.

CHAPTER 8

Larger than the Primary Mid World, Archangel Ariel's root World was far from a thriving jewel of magical magnificence. At one time, it might've been a fecund planet, lush with wildflower prairies, deciduous forests, and algae-thickened rivers. Not anymore. It resembled a tangle of moldering salad straight from Cian's fridge. In contrast, the indigo ley line shimmered from the north and south poles like fat sparkling stems from a mutant gourd.

With all that glitter in the line, it shouldn't be hard to get samples. Assuming Bix and the team could get close enough.

Alas, the first casualty of war was the plan.

The plan called for Feng to be all supernova firebird waiting for Bix to "chase" him to this World. Yet, as Bix stretched herself along the perimeter of the planet's atmosphere, there was no sign of the Phoenix. Dude should've been hard to miss what with burning as bright, as hot, and as large as a sun on the brink of incinerating the World. That was the entire reason she, the Chimera, had to extinguish the Phoenix every five hundred years. He'd get too wild for the Mids to handle and couldn't put out his own flames. At the moment, though, there wasn't so much as a campfire visible either on the World's surface or in its sky.

So much for tricking the ley line into thinking the cyclical war had started.

The planned distraction had been necessary so she could safely deposit the ground teams. The faux battle was to help them get inside the ley line. Feng was supposed to run interference between her and the line so her presence didn't inflict further damage to it. Then there was the angel problem and the political problem.

Damn it. Damn it. Damn it.

What had happened to Feng? It wasn't like him to flake on a mission. No. Something...something wasn't right. She should return to base, taking the teams with her. Scrap this plan and devise a new one.

Yeah, but.

She knew full well if she returned to Cian's, the Berserkers would clamor to come right back regardless of Feng's absence. Tobek's blatant dislike of the Phoenix would ensure that. Plus, none of the guys would abort a mission this critical if there was a remote chance they could pull it off with minimal casualties. As long as the teams were enveloped in her darkness, they were safer than they'd be in any aircraft or tank on any other mission. Theoretically. Depended on what the ley line had in store for her.

Did she dare? Did she have any other choice, really? She was accustomed to playing the role of distraction. It was merely a matter of *what* she was distracting that was different. She could always hightail it out of here with the teams if things got too ugly. Right? Sure. Mission was still a go. Had to be. One distraction with a sidecar of deliveries coming up.

This promised to be painful.

Zooming in from the outer layers of the planet's atmosphere, Bix compelled her innate defenses to abide as Mids' magic raked over her insubstantial state with the force of a tsunami. At only half her might, she struggled to stay calm amid the onslaught born of close proximity to a full-grown ley line. It took long moments for her to adjust, to get her metaphorical head in the right place.

A tiller sprouted from the ley line at the southern pole, growing rapidly into a blade shooting straight at her. So much for not using gates. The line was already irritated, so she opened a circular gate and folded the ley line's attack back on itself. That successfully annoyed it even more. One bent blade became countless, surging from both poles. She couldn't let it touch her, for its own sake, not to mention her cargo's. Gates peppered the atmosphere. Some offshoots flew in and out, some neatly evaded. Still, the line cast more and more defenses.

Not a single angel came to its aid. Not a leaf peeled away from the rotting canopy of the World to expose the choir's stronghold or even an outpost.

Bix couldn't deposit her teams until she had a secure place to land them. If Ariel and her choir were content to let the line wage war in their stead, then maybe they needed to be more concerned about this World's welfare. Maybe they and the line needed to be reminded Bix was a cosmic entity, not a puny cloud of divine whimsy.

Time to go big or go home.

Bix enlarged her footprint of persistent night from the breadth of a two-bedroom apartment to a city block, to a city, to a county, to a state, to a continent, and still larger until she covered the World, leaving only gaps around the ley line. The ley line recoiled from her steady expansion, allowing itself to be contained within the space she defined.

There they waited, somewhere between standoff and assessment. Perhaps she'd proven she wasn't as weak as it had thought. Perhaps it was weaker than she had thought. Whatever the case, the angels had yet to show themselves. They were assholes, yes, but they didn't run away from a fight unless ordered by their archangel. Bix knew Ariel well enough to know the only time that archangel backed down was to lead her enemy into a deeper trap.

Every niggle, wriggle, and writhe of instinct said this whole situation was a trap. One that might've already claimed Feng. Yet, to get the samples to the scientists to fix this ley line to launch

Resen and save the Mids from the Devourers, Bix also had to trip the trap.

Gah.

Since immortality came with perks, Bix constricted herself around the World, bracing for the angels' first volley against her presence. When none came, she tightened her mass again, pressing into the slime-coated foliage. The acrid stench of decay drifted through her amorphous state. If she'd had a stomach, it'd probably have heaved as she continued to descend to terra firma.

Alabaster ruins of complex structures tumbled down mountain ridges and clogged brackish rivers. Glass-and-stone steeples littered valleys. Dried seabeds exposed crumbling crystalline rookeries, while blankets of decomposing vegetation hinted at sprawling, once-prosperous cities.

Not a single angel leapt from the cover of dying flora. Not a single Chwed cowered in a collapsed building. The only thing teeming with life was the ley line.

Dafuq?

With the line subdued and seemingly holding its breath, Bix coalesced around the southern pole, circling, shrinking, staying in motion as filaments within her darkness raked aside debris, clearing a landing zone at the summit of the mountain range ringing the line. Instead of heavy rock and tacky dirt, the soil resembled white sand. Not knowing how stable that would be, she tentatively set her cargo on the ground. When no one went skidding down a mountainside, she loosened her hold. Hesitantly, one by one, she revealed a Berserker to the line, feeling a bit like a wary supplicant at an altar of a voracious god.

If the men were disoriented, they gave no indication as they stood shoulder to shoulder, alternating who faced the line and who faced the landscape. Every man assumed an open, nonthreatening position. Not a weapon in hand. Not a blue eye shone brightly through a respirator mask. The line throbbed, expanding fractionally, stopping shy of the men. The men breathed, but they didn't move.

Clearly, they'd played this game with a ley line before.

Hywl, Drew, and Ashtad completed the arc of special cargo. Tobek, she held on to, gauging the reaction of the line. The last time Tobek and she had faced a line together, bodies had gone flying like buckshot. With his new and improved weird, she was more than a little concerned about how this introduction would go. She toyed with the idea of taking him skyward for the intro, but a pair of thin indigo threads peeled away from the line and slithered around Drew's legs, compelling Bix to hover around her teams.

The line continued up Drew's hips, pausing to tug on Drew's fingertips. Bix draped similarly sized threads of shadow over Drew's shoulders. She had no idea who'd be the quicker draw, but she'd yank the draugr and let the line have the psychic's suit.

"It's okay, Bixie. It's trying to reanimate the suit," Drew assured with a slight quaver. "Back away, hon. Let's not spook it."

Reluctantly, Bix did as asked. Another pair of threads parted from the line and went for Ashtad, coiling up his legs too. Around his scarred leg, it darkened in hue. He sucked in a sharp breath.

"It's okay, Bix," he rushed to say. "It's trying to hea—"

The line snatched Ashtad and Drew inside its walls. Bix didn't pause to think; her darkness morphed into talons. She reared back—

"We've got them on comms, my lady," Hywl blurted. "They're fine."

A few snickers could be heard escaping from respirators.

"Something about a visit to the proctologist," Hywl added. "The demigod is now intimately familiar with this line."

If the line was trying to heal her friends despite them being Other World entities, it...well, it didn't share Ariel's personality at all. Since that was the case, maybe she didn't have to fear what it would do to Tobek. Plus, getting everyone inside the line was kind of sort of a major milestone for the mission.

She needed to think, then act. Think. Right? Think. Breathe... or some affectation of breathing. Whoo. Yep. She could do this. *They* could do this. Team effort.

Slowly, gingerly, she set Tobek at the end of the arc with the red team. Her darkness pulled away, uncovering Tobek. His undulating green magic sparked with silver and roiled around him like contained storm clouds.

His prosthesis was gone. Again. He'd left Cian's with a replacement one firmly attached; of that she was certain. What did his new woo have against faux appendages?

Tobek extended his hand to the line as if the line was a giant domesticated dog.

A blinding flash. A thunderous boom. A violent wave of native magic rammed Bix out of the World and beyond its atmosphere into the highly destructive ether. Bix opened gates and allowed the force of the line's eviction to carry her right back to the southern pole.

Not going to lie to herself. The trip was kind of fun. Like one of those super slides at a fair. And she had to give the line credit, that was a slick counterattack. All the power without the touching. Damn thing better not have hurt her teams, though.

When Bix returned to the drop site, the Berserkers were gone and Tobek was calmly strumming on their connection. No tugging, more rhythmic reassurance. Okeydokey, then.

Without an angelic choir to corral and the guys on track to gather their samples, Bix turned her attention to finding Feng. The ley line was the most obvious culprit. If it had tried to heal Drew's dead suit and Ashtad's scarred leg, could it have tried to fix Feng too? Antagonizing the line might've triggered his PTSD, bringing forth vivid memories of the years of being brutally tortured. PTSD was a misfire of the mind, something the line could have perceived. Feng's birth, growth, and death were dictated by the wax and wane of Mids' magic. It made sense the line would know he was broken.

She wanted to believe the best of both of them, the Phoenix and the ley line. Trust but verify, though.

Pulling into a form more humanoid yet still incorporeal, Bix spiraled around the southern extension of the ley line, from ground surface to the far side of the protective layer of atmosphere. There were variances in the color of the line, darker splotches nearer the World, while the glitter was thicker in the upper atmosphere. She called out to Feng as she searched. Nothing desperate. She didn't want to harass the line now that her teams were inside. When she received no response from the line nor the pendent holding Feng's dewclaw that was tucked into her shadows, she headed for the north pole.

Here, the line protruded from a massive crater a mile below the surface. The spread of the ley line's illness marked the terrain like rings of an old tree. Some sections were darker, some lighter, but all were in varying states of decay. How the hell could Ariel ignore this? The simple answer was she couldn't. No way could any angel—the species whose blood turned to flora—not be aware that their home World, their archangel's root World, her freakin' *birthplace* was dying. But it could explain why Ariel and her choir weren't here. If Ariel knew the state of affairs, then she'd be damn sure to keep her choir far away. Not because they held a warm place in her nonexistent heart; rather, because any other archangel could inhabit a lesser angel's mind and glean what Ariel was trying to hide.

Now Bix knew. Try as she might not to be petty, Bix couldn't help it. The thicket of malice thriving inside her greedily fed on the potential for revenge. Ariel had gone to great lengths trying to break Bix physically and mentally back when Bix had believed herself to be little more than an annoyingly resilient spy. Bix had told Samael this mission wasn't an excuse for a vendetta, and it wasn't. It was, however, an opportunity.

No. Focus. Mission. Feng.

Find Feng.

Bix resumed her patrol along the ley line, calling Feng's name. She glided closer to the line, pushing reassurance its way. She wasn't there to hurt it. She just needed confirmation that Feng was here and was okay. As she coiled closer to the upper atmosphere, the line bubbled. One fat nodule. Something inside scrabbled within the blister, thinning the lining, tearing the casing.

Mammoth wings of flame ripped through the line. Talons of pure fire cupped Bix. Twin moons of bright aquamarine shone in the face taking shape amid the blaze.

"Do you trust me?" Feng demanded, his voice sonorous and echoing as it flowed up and down the line.

Bix hesitated. Yay, Feng was alive and here...and in his native state of the dragon-angel hybrid. For the record, dragons were huge. Feng was no exception. And he was fiery. Fire was pretty, but not something she liked all up in her business, especially when she was currently small and squishable in comparison. Being a roasted marshmallow? Not on her bucket list.

"Bix, do you trust me?" he asked again.

This time, she heard the urgency and desperation in his question. She nodded. It wasn't like he could kill her, right?

"We have a problem. A very big problem." He yanked her into his chest of flames and wrapped his burning wings around her, completely enclosing her in magical fire. "I will shield the line from you, but it needs your help, badly."

She shut her eyes and swallowed her keen of vehement objection as he arched back and dove into the heart of the line. Three cheers for a form of nonflammable night. They flew faster than sound, but she had to ask.

"Feng? What problem?"

Impossibly, he increased his speed. Just when she thought he wouldn't answer, he jerked to a stop and unfurled his wings. Other World magic slammed into her full force, and with it, noxious magic. Before her eyes adjusted to the change in light, she knew.

Devourers.

CHAPTER 9

Devourers by the dozens moved through a sprawling muddy cavern replete with tunnels. Stalactites and stalagmites dripped moisture into deep pools that fed into shallow streams that disappeared into pure-black pits. The roots of the ley line gleamed in fine labyrinthine networks throughout, a glow of indigo here, a hum of suckling power there. The fatter the root, the brighter the light, which made the center quite brilliant and the farther reaches usefully dim. If the structure wasn't enough of a clue, the magical resonance alone defined this space as the core of the World.

Bix had foolishly assumed the ley line was a straight path through, but not so. Two stems grew from one seed. Far, far below her, spreading for miles, was the moiré indigo and navy lakelike surface of the southern ley line, which was mirrored by the spread of the northern ley line in which she and Feng lingered. The core pulsed with the creationist power of a planetary god, providing a heartbeat for the World. That heartbeat echoed in patinaed brass chrysalises hanging like gnarled thorns from the ceiling. Hundreds of them in various sizes leeched magic from the thinner roots of the ley line and oozed toxic fumes that hovered around them in titanium clouds. Devourers wearing long metal gloves waded through the miasma and jabbed probes into the larger chrysalises.

In a far shadowed bend, two units of Devourers sparred with weapons. In the opposite curve, more Devourers practiced shapeshifting. Still more learned to use magic to form weapons from shards of broken chrysalises, while others used magic for mock guerilla warfare. A pair of Devourers bolted from a recess carrying bundles, only to disappear down a tunnel. Everywhere, Devourers were engaged in the daily life of a…military base.

"It's a camp," Bix breathed. "Just how long have these guys been here?"

"Better question, how'd they *get* here?" Feng whispered through tiny flames dancing around Bix's head. The power of the ley line darkened his innate fiery colors until he burned deep blue against her midnight. "Aren't you going to kill them? Erase the blight? Power scrub the core?"

"Is that all it would take to fix the line? If I cut out these tumors, does it stop the cancer?"

"Probably not," he admitted. "Whatever is plaguing the line feels similar, but not the same as this filth."

If Resen was operational, this infestation of anti-gods would've sounded the alarms. Hell, the infestation would never have happened. The instant the first Devourer had tried to set foot in this core, the woven magics of the foundational elements would've dropkicked the anti-god and its entire troop across the galaxy. But Resen wasn't live yet, the foundational elements were still adjusting to their interoperability, and by the looks of things, at least one of the foundational elements—Ariel's ley line—either didn't know it should've expelled these invaders or wasn't capable of doing it alone. Whatever the reason, Bix needed more intel before she did something rash and possibly detrimental to Resen.

"I'll leave the anti-gods where they are until we know more, like who put them here, if others are en route, what operations they're running out of this base, and what the hell they're growing on the line." She wasn't thrilled with the decision, but those chrysalises tugged at incomplete memories. There was something important about them, but if she went poking around, she'd have an entire camp after her. Her part of this mission was to deliver her teams home safely. Her boys were counting on her. Besides, nothing said she couldn't come back later and deal with the Devourers. "Anyway, we can't forget the political aspects of this mission. This warren is proof that Ariel is enabling the enemy, and it's more than enough evidence to have her removed as the Chair of the Consortium."

"This is enough to have her executed on the spot by the Angelic Host, which is not something we can let happen despite our personal feelings to the contrary," Feng rumbled, his anger causing flames to crackle and snap. "Ley lines don't like a solitary existence. They're happiest with high populations. To have lost its dragon queen, then its people? Compound that with its archangel abandoning it? Ariel's actions are nothing less than torture to the purest form of native magic."

Bix knew Ariel's brand of torture intimately. Shattered kneecaps and waterboarding had been the Chair's warm-up.

"At the moment, I'm more concerned about our boys," she admitted. "Green team was supposed to be down here. I don't like imagining their reception."

"The line deposited both teams here in its desperate cry for help. Last I saw them, they were swimming out of the pool below us. I supplied what distractions I could." Feng dimmed his fire slightly so she could see better. "On the other hand, the line has supplied us with copious samples from itself and the surface of the World. It couldn't get us the core samples for obvious reasons."

"Okay. That means the Berserkers are undoubtedly live-feeding this infestation to Cian. With any luck, that'll be enough to entice the right kind of witnesses to pay this place a visit. If we can pull that off, then the anti-god cleanup falls to the pantheons like it should."

"Meanwhile, I owe you an apology."

"Me? For what?" She studied the embroidery on the Devourer uniforms, searching for the most elaborate, which would indicate the anti-god in charge.

"You kept trying to tell us Ariel was in league with the Devourers. I didn't believe she'd sign a suicide pact. I should've listened to you."

"No, you were right, you and Samael. No proof. No means. No motive. No case against her. Now we have proof, but still no motive. As for means, the questions become how and when did the anti-gods contact her and what does she get from this arrangement." Bix figured rage would be her reaction to this scene, but it was essence-deep disappointment that weighed on her like cold soot. "Drew might've been on to something with the contagious cooties concept. Her World is sick. Her line is sick. Doesn't that mean she's not doing so well too?"

"Probably, which makes me wonder why Ariel is letting any of your mortal allies live. It's not like her to allow a weakness to become a problem." Feng stoked his fire, masking her resonance, as a few Devourers glanced up at the ceiling where he and Bix lingered. "I'll happily lead a damn parade of witnesses through every detail of the case, but only *after* we can prove how the enemy got here. Otherwise, Ariel will claim you planted these troops to get back at her. She'll make the personal political. More political, that is."

Unfortunately, the traitors inside the Consortium had successfully tarnished Bix's reputation enough that any evidence she presented would be considered Fake News. Even if the Berserkers were broadcasting this mission to Cian, it might not be enough because they were tainted through the smear campaign that had the battalion on lockdown. No, Feng was right. This perfect horror had to be personally experienced by bigwigs inside the Consortium and backed with unassailable evidence. Only then would Bix's motley crew of mortals be a protected group rather than a persecuted one. Only then could Cian's scientists work openly on the samples without fearing discovery. Only then would the MWA reinstate the Berserkers regardless of the other damning video evidence.

Clemency for Ariel would be up to her peers. Whether they'd choose Resen's success over Ariel's punishment, Bix couldn't say.

"Agreed. We'll dig into the how while Cian's scientists figure out the what. Meanwhile—" Bix flinched as her Eternal Knot, folded in the depths of her darkness, twanged and juddered. Dread washed through her. "Feng, brace yourself."

The World shook hard enough to dislodge Feng from the line. He plummeted toward the camp, his wings unable to gain enough of a sweep to propel him upward. Devourers stumbled and fell. Chrysalises large and small snapped from the ceiling, shattering and exposing partially formed Devourers in fetid mucoid layers. A succession of booms chased the destruction, sound after action. Plumes of deep green magic shot out tunnels in great foggy clouds, swallowing the miasma of the chrysalises and blinding the anti-gods.

Bix exploded her mass, catching Feng in a blanket of darkness thirty feet above camp as continuous and uncontrolled eruptions of Tobek's magic caused surfaces to buckle. Tremors in the ley line lakes rippled outward, blasting native magic through the hollows of the Other World core. Devourers scrambled and staggered. Some fell to their knees, heaving their guts as the magic on which they fed overwhelmed them.

"Shrink, damn it," she barked at Feng.

With a mighty roar of effort, Feng reduced from dragon to man, allowing Bix to drag him across the cavern toward the pull of Tobek's frenetic magic. The farther from the line they flew, the brighter Feng burned, until he was once again the sun in a hole of darkness.

"Smaller," Feng shouted at her. "You'll scrape a root."

She morphed from blanket to coil, permitting Feng's magic to bleed through the gaps of her presence, protecting the line from her as they sailed over the heads of armed Devourers running pell-mell toward Tobek.

Where Tobek was, his mortal team would be too.

She was the bullet; Feng was the blaze. Together, they zoomed toward Devourers and Berserkers clinging for dear life to the edge of a collapsing mud pit a mile wide. Semiconscious men and anti-gods dotted the narrow lip that was quickly dissolving beneath the waters gushing through the walls.

"Sweet mercy," Feng breathed.

Splashing and shouting warned of more anti-gods charging down the tunnel. Bix threw open gates in the passage and gates around the pit to catch the Devourers and dump them back in the main cave. The temptation to feast on their essence, then destroy the lot rode her hard, but concern for Tobek and the teams kept her focused.

"Praise to the gods who hate us," cried a Berserker, dangling by one hand as his other held tightly to the extended arm of a fellow soldier swinging dangerously in and out of a waterfall disappearing into total darkness. "Our lady of eternal night."

Breathy howls answered from Berserkers trying to save themselves and their peers. Bix's darkness picked up the boys and dropped them through gates to the safety of Cian's apartment, where Runjit and Gurp could tend to their scrapes, scratches, and dislocated joints. She counted as she went, coming up short seven bodies, three of whom were not Mids' mortals.

"Ashtad? Drew? Tobek?" she called as she banked around the upper reaches of the pit, avoiding the waterfalls for Feng's sake while casting tentacles to join the search. Being the night, she had no problem seeing in the dark via her many appendages, especially once they surged below the glow of Feng's fire. Her darkness carried her voice, a nest of shadow serpents diving here and threading there. She feared the worst and hoped for a miracle.

She'd known Tobek was on the fritz with his magic but had truly believed he'd be fine on the mission. He had an unusual bond with Mids' magic, so she'd naïvely thought the exposure to the ley line would've been good for him. Then again, it might've been. It might've been the influence of Devourer magic that had resulted in this disaster. Whatever had gone wrong, he was going to have to tell her. None of this "I'm fine" bullshit. Not on mission. Not when he'd damn near killed his men.

Bright blue electricity pulsed a beacon from the pitch-black depths. Distance made the charge barely bigger than a pinprick.

Ashtad.

Feng shot a ray of fire in answer. "Bix, they're deep. Way, way, way deep. If they fell, the draugr isn't going to be the only one in a dead body."

"I don't see souls or psychopomps, so let's keep happy thoughts." Bix dove into depths cold and wet, racing the water rushing down the walls. Her tentacles wrapped around two men treading water in a dark lake pulsing sickly green hues.

Ashtad and Hywl.

"Under the falls," Ashtad shouted. "We've got bodies under the falls."

Feng separated from Bix's darkness and unfurled his wings, stoking a fire that ignited arch to tip. Wings aflame jabbed the falls and scraped water toward the center of the lake. Bix expected a hiss and steam from flames hitting wet, but dragons owned the waters as much as the loam, so Feng's mixed heritage allowed fire to coexist with water. It was a wonderous thing to behold, fire submerging, flames swimming.

"There." Bix's voice sounded like a yelp as unmoving bodies floated from under the walls of thundering water on currents stirred by Feng.

Drew and three Berserkers floated around Tobek, a tangle of limp limbs and torn clothes. Broiled flesh bobbed in and out of the water as dented air tanks limited the bodies' movement along the surface. Sorrow crackled along the stars of Bix's night.

"What did he do?" she groaned, meeting Feng above the cluster of bad, bad, bad.

"No souls, no psychopomps," Feng repeated softly, calming his fire to a warm glow that illuminated the transition of rich reds to pale golds within his feathers. "There's still a chance."

Right. A chance. A chance Tobek hadn't killed his own men. A chance they'd come back from this. Gates to Cian's gave the fallen Berserkers a chance to survive. Drew, though…

A tentacle curled around Drew, rolling the suit of the psychic to her back. The torso was hollow. A few charred rib fragments remained of the back. The head had been obliterated.

"Drew?" Bix whispered, logic fighting with emotion. "Drew?"

"She's not in there." Ashtad sighed, relaxing into the grip of darkness pulling him from the water. "She jumped bodies when we found the prisoners."

"Prisoners?" Feng touched the bones with the tip of a feather. What remained of Drew's vacated suit dissolved into ashes that tumbled into the lake.

"Gods." Ashtad pointed up at the tunnel. "Three gods. Two seemingly husked, one damn near. Chief tried to bust them out of the cages the Devourers had stashed them in."

Gods didn't die, but they could be drained of everything except their casing and the seed of their divinity. Drew jumping into a god's body was more relief than surprise. The draugr lived for those rare opportunities. Who didn't want to be a deity for a day? However, gods imprisoned in a Devourer camp on an archangel's home World? No part of that was good.

"This pit was the result of Tobek's efforts?" Bix asked, bracing for the answer as darkness gently stripped her blond bear of his mangled air tanks.

"This pit was the result of Devourers descending on us from nowhere," Hywl panted, throwing his arms over the tentacle of darkness holding him aloft. "It was a Hail Mary. The draugr took the first hit to her front like you saw. Chief took multiples trying to shield us from the swarm."

Bix carefully flipped Tobek as she tugged on the connection that bound him to her, desperate for an answering twitch. Darkness pushed his hair from his face. Pieces of his mask had melted to his flesh and beard, boiling plastic and skin. His torso was charbroiled, but he had a pulse. Faint. As faint as the tremor he sent through their bond. If the damned man hadn't been immortal…

"Let me," Feng murmured, taking Tobek across his arms. Feng's barbed tail dipped into the lake and swung like a pendulum through the water, completing some sort of circuit. Silver and indigo ribbons of magic danced from the farthest reaches of the lake, drawn to the Phoenix and his burden. They braided up his tail, around his legs, and over his trunk where they dove into Tobek's body. Slowly, ever so slowly, ice pushed up from Tobek's ravaged body, painting a shell from shredded toe cap to singed locks.

A seizure overtook him.

Bix rushed forward, a hundred limbs of uncertainty wondering where to go, what to do, and how to help.

"Bix," Feng gently admonished as the ice melted and blended magic surged with brighter intensity over his body to bundle around Tobek. "The line is doing what it can for him. Why don't you give them a bit of breathing room, okay?"

She retreated quickly, wishing for the nth time that she could heal, could fix, could be of some use when things went this far wrong.

"He did this. He created all this water, and it's not wholly Mids in origin," Feng murmured, his tone calm, almost monotone as the icy casing once again built around Tobek. "The waterfalls protected the men's bodies during the drop. The lake softened their landing. He did his best to keep his men alive."

"Aye, that's our Chief," Hywl said with pride, double-thumping his chest. "We've followed him past the gates of different hells more than once, and we'll do it every time in the future with a godsdamned spring in our step."

Bix considered Hywl, grateful for the distraction. Fact was, Berserker or no and despite Tobek's intervention, Hywl's body should've been *wrecked* after that dive. They were an easy five skyscrapers below the surface. No lake, no matter how deep, would've broken their fall. Broken their spines? Exploded every organ? Yes, without a doubt. So why was Hywl not a quadriplegic oozing kidneys out his eye sockets right now? Sure, Berserkers had recovery clauses in their modified mortality contracts. While the contracts varied soldier to soldier, Hywl had been screwed in his. As long as he kept his head, he'd heal, eventually, but he'd bleed and break like any otherwise healthy human. He *should've* been a wet noodle in her grip, worse off than his fearless leader. Instead, he was understandably exhausted, yet in better condition than the demigod who'd hit the water with him. Maybe it was the benevolent ley line. Maybe it was something more.

"Bix, Drew's with the other drained gods at the bottom of the lake." Ashtad groaned and lolled his head on her darkness. "Which of us wants to go diving for them?"

Feng laughed, an unexpectedly cheerful sound amid the doom and gloom. His tail spun a circle in the lake. The ribbons of magic whirled like fan blades, pushing aside water until three overlarge animal bodies slumped one atop the other came into view.

"Well, that makes it easier." Ashtad chuckled wearily. "Bix, I suggest a contained environment nowhere near base. Wherever they go, I should go with them. Secure the witnesses and smooth over pantheonic panic, yeah?"

Gods who'd been prisoners of Devourers needed special handling. Bix didn't know the pantheons' details for in-processing, but she knew someone who did, someone who might not insist on Drew's destruction for defiling a divine vessel. Someone who'd probably find a briefing on the whole sitch quite useful. Someone who could tell her what sort of trouble was going on in the main cavern.

"I'll do it," she dismissed gently. "You're needed to back up Cian on Resen with whatever fallout is on its way from this mission. Hywl, you and the guys are still on point for protecting the samples, the scientists, and the kid."

"It's our honor, my lady." Hywl saluted.

"Where *are* the samples?" she asked, praying the mission hadn't been a total bust, between the skirmish and the water pit.

Hywl fished in the pockets of his tactical pants. In one hand, he presented a clear palm-sized disk filled with mud. In his other hand, an opaque indigo cylinder. "Pockets laden, my lady, every Berserker, when we swam out of the line. We collected core samples right up till the enemy got the drop on us."

"Well done, Hywl," she admitted, feeling a wee knot of tension loosen within her darkness.

"Whenever you're ready to send Chief back to us, my lady, we'll take him with open arms." Hywl stuffed the samples back in his pockets. "We understand his, uh, quirks and the danger that sometimes comes with them."

"Being surrounded by his men might be the best thing for him right now," Feng suggested. "I'll stay with him, just in case. You chase the Devourer inquiry, Bix. There's nothing more you can do while the scientists work on the samples."

She resisted the urge to snatch Tobek from Feng, to bundle her Berserker in her darkness and whisk him to some private sanctuary, someplace only he and she knew about, someplace he could get well without harming anyone. She wanted to cosset and coddle him, her brave Berserker who consistently gave everything for the betterment of those he loved.

"He'll be fine," Feng assured. "Go. We don't want the ley line to suffer any longer than absolutely necessary."

Before she could give in to temptation, Bix returned the boys to base, collected the unconscious gods, and took off for a distant World, leaving the camp of Devourers intact in the core of Ariel's home World.

May the ley line forgive her.

CHAPTER 10

On a World far from the Mids, where perpetually sullen midnight skies thundered and disembodied cackles overrode baleful moaning, Phobos, the Greek god of fear, stood on an onyx terrace overlooking a gore-slicked ravine containing a raging battle of demons versus golems. An arm across his chest bracing an elbow, Phobos puckered his lips against his fist. The blackish-burgundy of his bespoke three-piece suit shimmered in the warm glow of bronze braziers spread among columns carved with red-eyed figures that tracked every flit of movement on the terrace. Tall, with a dancer's build, Phobos exuded old-World elegance even when preternaturally still, from the choppy layers of his dark collar-length hair to his polished wingtip ankle boots.

"If you're going to invade my home, do me the courtesy of being corporeal." He remained focused on the conflict below, his words the only acknowledgment of Bix's arrival with her divine packages in tow.

Bix gave texture to darkness, shape to shadows, and malleability to mist. A flush of tingling, a surging of pulse, and a judder of resistance to containing herself in a corporeal state confirmed the replication of a functional humanoid body. Perspective adjusted, flexibility returned, and limitations settled.

"Clothes?" she prompted. Of Phobos's many responsibilities, being her caretaker probably annoyed him the most; however, it also gave him opportunities unimagined by his peers, which, for bored immortals, made those experiences priceless.

Phobos flicked two fingers. Underpinnings and a black bandage dress snugged around her, the length of the latter hitting below the knees, naturally. His magic tamed her mane, painted her nails, and provided new shoes with a bestial pattern. The pattern mimicked the three animal gods she'd brought with her: a bat, a boar, and a bull.

Bix ambled forward to watch the skirmish. Alas, it wasn't meant to last. The army of demons scrabbled futilely for purchase on the slopes before being trampled by gleeful golems who then melted into the mud.

"Training them?" she asked.

"We need all hands in this conflict with the old foes." He unfolded his arms, finally looking at her. "Why are you bringing me your dinner?"

"Those guys?" Bix pointed to the gods. "Not it. Devourers got to them first. Then Drew got to one of them, but she hasn't roused yet."

"Kind of hard to move when Ferdinand has you pinned," wheezed the boar, desperately trying to slither out from under the catatonic bull.

Bix slapped a hand over her mouth, but not before a laugh escaped. "What's with you and the pigs lately?"

"Girl, you take a Devourer blast to the face, you jump into the nearest suit. Not really the time to be picky." Drew gasped, freeing a cloven hoof before giving up. "Come on, a little help here?"

Surprise managed to crack Phobos's usual expression of mild irritation. "Is your pet draugr defiling a god?"

"She's my friend, not my pet," Bix corrected. "But, yes, yes she is."

"He, Bixie, he at the moment." Drew puffed the tail of the

bull from her—erm, his—snout. "And so help me, if Ferdi doesn't get off my nuts, he's going to get a tusk in his."

Phobos coughed and waved a hand. Carved pillars split into bulky arms with shovel hands that unstacked the gods and granted each their own breathing room before zippering back into the structural supports of a thousand carvings.

"Oh, praise Jebus," Drew groaned, crossing his back legs. "How that didn't rouse Moccus… Do you know how painful it has to be for *me* to feel it?"

"Moccus?" Bix echoed, trying to place the name. It seemed familiar, but she couldn't quite remember why.

"Moccus the boar of the Celtic pantheon," Phobos said by way of introduction. "Hadhayans the Zoroastrian bull, and Tjinimin the Aboriginal bat. All Mid World guardians."

"All on your list, Bixie." Drew stretched one hind leg, then the other, wincing. "The one you had Sparky and me review before the op. How'd you know they were prisoners of the Devourers?"

"I didn't." Bix pulled a blank on the list. Three heartbeats passed, then it hit her. "The list of memory keepers? These three hold my missing memories?"

Phobos cursed under his breath.

"Memories? Naw, ain't no Bixie bits floating around in here. I'll step out if you want to verify, though." Drew slid the side of his snout along the floor, scratching an itch. "You had ten names on that page. You knew some were bogus, right? Tell me I didn't just poop in the party pen."

"Oh, for… What is it you require to vacate that body?" Phobos demanded.

"I'm in a god of sex and shopping, a *male* god of sex and shopping. Do you know how rare they are?" Drew snarked.

"Fertility, hunters, and shopkeepers," Phobos corrected. "Agrarian product life cycles, if we are to split hairs."

"I ain't leaving until he evicts me, and that is going to be well after I remind him how to have a good time." Drew flipped his tail as if batting away flies. "Based on what little is left of his mind, I could be here awhile."

"The issue, creature, isn't Moccus's public humiliation. It is the fact Devourers husk gods of lesser power. Mid World guardians are upper-middle caste gods. It means the leadership of Devourers inside the Mids exceeds captains and colonels. It means we have generals in our midst. Do you comprehend the number of troops a general commands?" Phobos crouched in front of Hadhayans and laid a hand on the bull's head. The skin on Phobos's fingers rippled. Crimson millipedes marched from under his cuticles and into the ears of the unconscious bull.

Drew squealed and bolted to his hooves, scampering behind Bix. "The hell, man?"

"Quiet," Phobos demanded. His red pupils, universal to all gods, clouded and deepened in hue. "Husked. Repeatedly. Bled frequently. Hadhayans is conscious but defeated. He has no concept of who or what he is. He exists in a state of constant fear and only fear."

Bix clenched her fists and stared up at the bleak sky. She'd lived in that state for an eternity after she'd forfeited her mind. The memory remained so raw thirty years later that she could still taste the acrid terror. "He's like an infant ten seconds into the World, where everything is overwhelming and petrifying."

"Only because he possesses a god's ability to heal do we not see his wounds. His fear is well justified." Phobos turned his palm up. The millipedes departed the bull through tear ducts and returned to Phobos's hand. "However, as the draugr said, there is no evidence of your influence cushioning his mind."

"Will we be zero for three, do you think?" Bix knelt beside Tjinimin. Like all animal deities, he was exponentially larger than the common beast. With his furry walnut-gray body twice her size and his leathery black wings tangled around him, she had to summon tentacles of darkness to gently straighten him out. The moment her darkness reached beyond his flesh into his essence to check his mental welfare, she felt them, the pieces of herself stored within his divine shell for safekeeping. Parts of her memories rushed toward her, eager to return home.

The bat screeched, a brain-bleeding sound that existed on a frequency beyond audible norms. The surprise and pain drove Bix out of his body, her darkness wrapping protectively around her. Tjinimin's red eyes snapped open. In a poof of instant night, he vanished.

"Shit," Bix sighed. "He's a memory keeper."

"It's okay, Bixie." Drew nudged her with his snout. "We'll find him. We'll get you your marbles. Hunting people is our thang."

Bix pushed to her feet and folded her darkness within her body. "The problem is that my marbles are the only ones he has. He thinks he's me. Original me. Boogeyman me."

"The Devourer general couldn't steal your memories from him. Even those tiny little flecks of yourself are too powerful." Phobos hung his head and chuckled wryly. "I worry for the day you are whole again, Chimera. The vengeance you will reap from those who've wronged you in this lesser existence will change collectives, not just Worlds."

Bix worried about that too. The jungle of malice alive and breeding within her was the only emotion she'd kept for herself after she'd given everything else away. There was a reason for it, but she didn't remember it yet. It was out there in those three remaining segments, and when she got those back, she'd finally know the truth of why she'd gutted herself. Whoever was behind that reason—confronting whoever it was—yeah, probably the stuff that smote galaxies. She wasn't sure the she of this moment would be able to stop her fully intact self. She liked to believe she'd at least try to save the Worlds she was fighting so hard to save now.

"Bright spot, Batty's only got a seventh of your marbles, so…" Drew playfully hip-checked Bix. "It's probably the best game of Mad Libs ever."

"Tjinimin is a night god, which makes it easier for him to believe he is a she who is *the* Chimera. Unlike the real Chimera, however, he is a creationist god, capable of making whole armies.

He was still a prisoner of the Devourers despite this ability." Phobos dusted his hands on his suit jacket as he stood. "Believing he is the all-powerful Chimera, Tjinimin will look upon his liberators not with gratitude, but with suspicion. Hostility, even."

"Chief," Drew groaned. "Chief freed us from Devourer jail. If Batty thinks Chief is in cahoots with the Devourers as part of some elaborate scheme, then the battalion is his next target."

"I'm still missing the bulk of my Tobek memories. Tjinimin may have them." Bix pinched the bridge of her nose. "In which case, I'd want Tobek to answer a slew of questions. But before that, I'd want revenge. I'd start by blowing up Ariel's World, which we can't allow."

"Destroyer of Worlds is not among his skills," Phobos hastened to assure.

"If Batty can't get revenge, it leaves him with getting answers, which brings us back to Chief and the battalion," Drew said. "Chief can be bait. We head to base, set the trap, and wham blam, you get your memories back."

"Then I disappear for weeks, months, maybe a year as I try to make sense of everything?" Bix shook her head. "No, not yet. We've got Devourers abducting Mid World guardians and living in a root World growing clones of themselves. All that has to stop before I can play catch a bat."

"Show me," Phobos commanded. "This place you say is inhabited by Devourers and their clones. Show me. Now."

"Ha, no," Bix countered. "The magic of the ley line is so powerful it will whiteout viewing gates, which means the only way you get to see it is in person. That requires me to expose you to *hundreds* of Devourers in a fully functional military base. No. It's too dangerous for you."

"Is your plan to leave them there, unmolested, slowly destroying a World with their presence? Or were you expecting me to march an army in there, sight unseen?" He tsked and snapped his fingers. Chitters and hisses flowed up the engravings in the pillars and carried into the ceilings, the molding, and the wainscoting of the main house. Moments later, a parade of minions arrived carrying his god-forged armor and weapons.

"Phobos, no," Bix insisted. "I haven't figured out how the Devourers got there yet or if more are en route. I don't know if the general is the one commanding the base or if he's using the World as a dining hall for his greater forces. I don't know if the bulk of his forces were out on maneuvers while I was there. They may have returned in my absence."

"We are spies, Chimera. Gathering information is what we do. I can only imagine what your crew of misfits was doing on a root World when you may have stumbled upon something for which the war contingents of *all* pantheons have been searching ever since we learned the old foes had set foot in the Mids: their base of operations within the collective." The god of fear stripped out of his jacket and vest, passing them to a dutifully waiting valet. The filigreed fob containing a still-beating heart, he placed on a velvet navy-blue cushion. The minion in charge of the heart took two steps to the side, but not so far as to be out of Phobos's reach. The god had a thing about that heart and kept it with or near him always. The cuff links and dress shirt came off next.

Drew tippy-tapped the floor with his hooves. "I do loves me some hunksome god striptease."

Dropping his pants, commando Phobos didn't pause, didn't blanch, didn't seem inclined to acknowledge Drew's leering in any way. Firstly, Phobos was a god accustomed to being worshipped. Secondly, half his family were nudists. Thirdly, being naked in front of a gathering was probably such a common fear that he found the whole concept of modesty quite tedious. His exquisite sartorial choices were expressions of character, not a balm for shame.

"What about Hadhayans? We can't leave him to suffer like this. I need you to do the POW processing," Bix reminded, watching the procession of minions, not the naked god. "If I knew where to take him, I would."

"We could slap a sticky note on his forehead that reads, 'Devourers did this,' then you wouldn't have to take the blame,

Bixie." Drew wrinkled his snout. "Dude needs all kinds of proper mental health services."

"So does Moccus." Bix stroked the boar's tusk. "Keep that in mind while you're running around in his suit."

"Cease your clucking like old yia yias." Phobos dressed in matte-black long johns shot through with threads of silver and gold. The fob containing the heart slid into a discreet chest pocket. "My brother will take Hadhayans to a rehabilitation resort where other survivors of Devourer imprisonment are receiving the care they need."

"The god of terror is probably not the right guy for the job." Drew harrumphed.

Phobos raked Drew with flagrant disdain as minions buckled the god of fear into his armor. "I have many siblings, some of whom represent love. Not every aspect of that involves a rod and a moist, warm hole."

Bix bit her lip to stop from laughing, but a snigger escaped anyway.

"Point to the grumpy god," Drew admitted, rolling his eyes. "I'll stay here until lover boy shows, then head home to intercept Batty should he go looking for Chief. It's going to take me a few to tap into Moccus's transportation ability anyway."

"Your home is heavily warded now. You might not be able to get in wearing him," Bix reminded. "Odds are, you'll need a human suit."

"Did you hear that?" Drew tipped his head and perked an ear. "It's the sound of fun being sucked out of this World. Both of you. Joy killers."

"My brother is willing to assist you in procuring an acceptable replacement, if you agree to leave Moccus upon receiving such replacement." Phobos flexed his hands in his gauntlets, then strapped on his xiphoi.

"But I'm in a *god,*" Drew whined. "I can use his magic to do good things."

"And we're in the throes of a mission to heal a ley line, evict a warren of Devourers, and get Resen launched." Bix tapped the end of Drew's snout. "If you can use Moccus to advance the mission, then do so, but when you're done, you still own the fallout for this portion of his development as a reborn god. He's like a baby. Do you really want to be a nanny again?"

"I'll think about it." Drew sniffed the air. "You two should go. Pretty sure his brother is here but waiting for you to leave, Bixie, and the ley line ain't getting any healthier while we bicker."

Phobos put on his helmet and extended his hand to Bix.

"For the health of the ley line." Bix sighed and opened gates.

CHAPTER 11

Devourers marched to and from the pit Tobek had created, carrying strange metallic implements. The original passage had collapsed, but three new tunnels had been dug to allow the anti-gods easy access. Torrents of water no longer gushed from walls nor crashed over the ledge into the silent abyss. Indeed, centered like a large eye over the pit, the Devourers had installed some sort of curious technology.

Their scientific division. That's a resonance scanner. They're trying to identify which gods were here and who created the hole. Phobos spoke into Bix's mind, maintaining outward silence as he and she stood on a threshold of many staggered gates constructed to mask their presence from the anti-gods. *Take me to the growing field of the things you called clones.*

Bix layered more gates in front of the threshold, effectively relocating to the main cavern with one step. She chose a recess in the ceiling framed by stalactites and chrysalises. The lakes and roots of the ley line pulsed brighter for three beats, then returned to normal. The fine threadlike roots around her location dimmed.

The line knew she was there. Apparently, no number of stacked gates could fool it. Good to know. Would the Devourers detect her? Without Feng leveraging the power of the ley line to hide her, it was possible.

The hive, Phobos hissed in her head as he reached beyond the frame of the gate to stroke a chrysalis. *You found the damned hive.*

Bix didn't dare speak. She lacked a real understanding of the unique skills of Devourers. Sure, she knew the obvious: their toxic magic blasts, their proficiency with weapons, their perfect columnar invasions of foreign terrain. She even knew how consuming their essence numbed her senses and suppressed her superego. However, none of that told her what made Devourers worthy opponents of gods, capable of capturing or routing divine armies. Now wasn't exactly the time to find out. Instead, she twirled her hand, encouraging Phobos to elaborate.

These pods aren't clones. They are how Devourers come into existence. This military base began as their nursery. Unlike gods, who come from their parents in one way or another, then undertake a cycle of growth and development, Devourers are born fully adult and mostly educated. They're born knowing their purpose, how they fit into society, who their enemies are, etcetera. The only thing a hatchling lacks is experience.

Bix gestured to the hundreds of Devourers training below them, then made like she was cradling a baby in her arms.

Likely, most but not all are hatchlings. Some are training officers; some are senior specialists who would've brought the scientific equipment. Phobos lingered on the edge of the threshold, scratching the soil of the core and funneling it into a vial that manifested in his hand. *Because the hive is here, this World will become their main base throughout the occupation, and it will be the last to fall when they have robbed the collective of all magics. A general being here means we are running out of time to stand up* Resen *before the full Devourer army charges the Mids.*

Bix pointed to the nearest chrysalis and drew her finger across her throat, followed by a question mark.

Absolutely not. Phobos peered around a stalactite. *Kill them, and new ones grow in their place. Now that the hive has been established, every Devourer who dies in the Mids will be replaced by a pod grown here. The*

Devourers born in this World, suckling on the teat of purest Mids' magic, are the next evolution in their race.

Fuck. There really was no better term to express how flabbergasted she was. How was she supposed to heal the ley line when the tumors would grow back? How could Resen defend the Mids when the enemy was part of the infrastructure?

If we had found this when one or two pods had affixed themselves to the core, we could've exterminated them and secured the World. This infestation has gone on far too long for that to work now. Our only recourse is to destroy this World—obliterate it—so nothing, not even a micron of infected soil is left.

Bix crossed her hands repeatedly, making the universal sign for "hell no."

Chimera—

The tremor of a programmable gate opening within the core snatched their attention, stopping whatever argument he thought he'd win. Brilliant ice-blue light streamed into the cavern as the gate stabilized. The Devourers paused their work.

Consortium guards marched through the gate. Logos shimmered on the matte black of their uniforms. Three dozen Chweds of the Mids crossed into the core without a second glance at the ley line, the pods, or the Devourers. The troop parted, and through the gate stepped a muscular, broad-shouldered woman with bark-brown hair in a loose chignon. A floral chiffon blouse and wide-legged pants were nothing compared to the lush brown wings tipped in cream arching above her head to frame her all the way down to the floor.

Archangel Ariel, Chair of the Consortium.

The ley line pulsed brightly in greeting. Ariel's throaty chuckle carried around the core, echoed by the line as Ariel brushed her wings against a lattice of roots growing along the floor.

A particularly towering Devourer waded through the others gathering around the gate. Gathering, not fleeing. No one had weapons in hand, even those who'd been training with them set them aside before joining the gawkers.

Ariel smiled a perfectly soulless smile at the looming Devourer. Ariel's lips moved, but Bix couldn't make out what the archangel was saying. She had the same problem with the Devourer, who seemed to be the base commander. Possibly the hungry general? The embroidery down the side of his bronze uniform was far more elaborate than any of the other anti-gods', and the collar of his jacket stood higher than others with more stitching, as if it'd been copied from Dracula's cape. Ariel's brittle laugh was piercingly clear as she motioned to the gate.

More Consortium guards came through, only they didn't come empty-handed. They came bearing prisoners, shackled and stumbling, covered by magic-nullifying quilts Bix recognized all too well from her tenure with Ariel.

Bix's gut sank and her pulse raced. She tugged Phobos away from the edge of the threshold into the more protective stacks of gates as his voice, brutally cold, circled in her mind.

What am I witnessing?

Bix didn't release him. On the contrary, she let a few little tendrils of night hook the back of his armor. Goose bumps dotted her skin as a dozen Consortium guards shed their disguises. The others of the Consortium's elite, the actual Mids-grown mortals, retreated toward the gate, subtly regrouping as eyes widened and hands went to weapons belts.

You aren't surprised, Phobos accused. *How long have you known about this?*

No way was she going to pantomime that discussion. Instead, she held tightly to Phobos's arm as Ariel whipped the quilts off the prisoners. Bix didn't recognize their faces, but she knew their resonances.

Gods.

Screaming and pleading, the gods tried to flee but couldn't. Their Devourer escorts grabbed the shackles and jangled them, expressions mocking. Jeering and laughter erupted from the gathering. The Devourer general snatched a goddess by her raven-black hair and dragged a talon down her cheek. Ichor pooled in the cut and dribbled down her neck. The general spun the goddess toward the gathering.

From the back lines, Devourers pushed other Devourers forward, some placing weapons in the advancers' hands as they neared the inner circle.

Ariel beat her wings, stirring the air. A flick of her wrist flung the gods across the cavern, pinning them to stalagmites. Devourers stamped their feet, a drumbeat. The general raised his hand. A singular united low note from the gathering accompanied the stamping.

By the Chaos and the Cosmos, Phobos swore. *Surely, they aren't…*

The general dropped his arm. The gathering chirred and closed around the armed Devourers. At first, it was a mosh pit of encouragement, but it quickly turned. Weapons swung, jabbed, and pierced as those Devourers in the center of the gathering fought to get free.

The fight was the point.

The first hatchling to the food gets the food. Phobos pressed his palms together as if resisting the urge to grab his short swords. *It's disturbing how many traditions our races share.*

Bix debated whisking the gods away from their impending nightmare, but to do so would alert Ariel to her presence, glue bull's-eyes on her teams, and jeopardize any progress Cian's scientists were hopefully making.

Leave them. Phobos pushed aside Bix's grip on his arm. *In this moment, we must be spies, not soldiers. Evidence is what we need. Evidence and leverage over the treasonous Chair of the Consortium. Proof that who we're seeing is, in fact, she and not some other Devourer in disguise.*

Bix pointed to the ley line, then the roots, hoping he'd notice how they responded to Ariel's movements like a pack of puppies hoping for attention.

I must be certain, beyond all doubt. Feathers from her wings will suffice, preferably one dipped in the ichor of her captives and another dredged in the blood of a Devourer to prove her actions to my higher-ups and the other pantheons.

Bix took his hand and folded his fingers into a gun. She aimed it at the ley line lakes, then at his temple and pulled the trigger. The line was the biggest power in the core, and it would protect Ariel at all costs. Alas, Bix had a feeling the god of fear was scowling at her beneath his Corinthian-style helmet as if she were a raving loon.

A ball of darkness burst into existence in the middle of the core, between the northern and southern lakes of the ley lines. It struggled to grow, a jut here, a ripple there, but grow it did, like a black star of a dozen points.

The Devourers leading the race to the gods abruptly diverted around the expanding penumbra. Chirring at high pitch brought their peers away from the gate and the ogling of the actual Consortium guards. The Devourer general grabbed Ariel by her arm and pointed at the visitor. Ariel snatched her arm back and lifted her pointy chin. With far too much confidence, she strode through the Devourers toward the dark star.

"Chimera, you've got balls coming here. I thought I'd made myself clear in the messages I left with your little friends." Ariel clasped her hands in front of her, ever so pious. "Now they'll have to die, and it's all your fault."

Bix raised her shoulders to her ears as the urge to rip Ariel into motes prickled every nerve. Nothing she could do would correct Ariel's misbelief. Whoever the newcomer was, it wasn't Bix, despite the archangel's assumption that anything dark and unexpected had to be the infamous Chimera. Bix and Phobos were still safely ensconced in gates that no one but the ley line had noticed. Still, the damage was done.

Shit. Shit. Shit.

If Resen didn't need Ariel alive and well in order to keep her ley line alive and functioning as part of the foundational magics on which the defense system was built, Bix would exterminate the very real threat to her friends this instant. Alas, no matter how badly Bix wished it true, there was no automated defense against traitorous archangels. Resen was designed to deter, detain, or detect Other World entities like gods and anti-gods; not beings created by Mid World magic. Mids' native races were supposed to be policed by the Consortium, which was of zero help when the leader of the Consortium was the problem.

She looked to Phobos for suggestions.

Wait, he urged. *There are many ways this could still go.*

The ley line lakes brightened as the archangel drew closer. The dark star grew, as if drawing power from the line—a thing Bix could never do. Ariel was too arrogant to see her mistake. No, the archangel flared her wings and raised her hands to her chest. Angel fire crackled around her fingers. She kneaded the air between her hands, building a ball of fire larger than a prize-winning pumpkin.

The supersonic scream came first. Devourers went to their knees, clasping their ears. Consortium guards blacked out, dropping in front of the gate. Ariel stood her ground. Ears bleeding. Lip curling.

Darkness faded from the star, revealing Tjinimin in his true form, with wings wide and claws aimed at the Chair of the Consortium.

"You," Ariel shrieked in an equally horrific pitch. "How did you escape?"

Tjinimin screamed again. Waves of Mid World magic carried on the ripples of his tone. Stalagmites undulated, spawning arms and heads. Stout legs of mud walked the new army free of its tethers and into the Devourers slowly gaining their feet. Golems stood no chance against the Devourers, but Tjinimin wasn't the only god in the mix. Phobos curled his fingers, and the golems developed purpose and strategy. Theirs wasn't to survive but to delay.

The bat god was a Mid World guardian, his magic rooted in the collective. But this was Ariel's home World. Tjinimin didn't stand a chance. Ariel unleashed her angel fire. Tjinimin's fur ignited. The bat god screamed again, vanishing in a flare of shadows.

"Idiot." Ariel smoothed her hair from her face and brushed aside the tendrils of gooseberry vines growing from her blood.

She turned back toward the gate and rubbed her temple. "How did he get loose? Where are the others?"

Shadows appeared behind Ariel, solidifying rapidly. Tjinimin raked his claws down her wings, shredding feathers and membrane. Crimson angel blood spurted everywhere. Ariel keened in agony. The ley line flared. The World audibly inhaled, constricting the core.

Bix watched the concussive waves from the lakes spread in slow motion. Alarm raced through her on the rush of adrenaline. A passing thought placed tiny gates to break the shackles holding the prisoners helpless and muting their magics. Re-empowered, gods sprung free of the stalagmites as Bix reached for Phobos. Her hand slid through vacant air. In the next breath, his strong hand on her abdomen shoved her backward through the layers of stacked gates as the blasts of pure native magic licked down the opening.

CHAPTER 12

Theirs was not a graceful landing as Bix and Phobos tumbled across the terrace of Phobos's home World, safe from Ariel and her ley line. For the moment, at least. Minions helped Bix and Phobos to their feet. A chaise was placed behind Bix, allowing her to collapse into its cool burgundy silk. There was no sign of Drew or Hadhayans.

"The Chair of the Consortium is beyond guilty of high treason against the Mids." Phobos's voice was straight-up spooky coming from under a helmet that covered his whole head except for his eyes. "What surprises me more is that you knew."

"I suspected, but I didn't have proof, and I still don't have motive." Bix draped her arm over the armrest.

Phobos reached inside his breastplate and held up two fistfuls of saturated brown feathers. They disintegrated the moment they touched the air of his Other World, unable to exist so far from the Mids whose magic made them.

"It was a valiant effort." Bix laid her head on her arm. "At least you know I'm not full of shit when I say the Chair of the Consortium is aiding and abetting Devourers."

"Do I strike you as a nincompoop who has never dealt with the limitation of Mids' magic in the greater existence?" Phobos removed his helmet and handed it to a minion. "Samples were delivered to the pantheon offices inside Consortium chambers, plus a few extra locales."

That should've thrilled her wrathful heart. Alas.

"Tell me you didn't," she groaned.

He arched an indignant dark brow as he widened his stance and extended his arms, allowing his minions to unbuckle his armor.

"She can't be allowed to die, Phobos. Every archangel alive and well is necessary for the success of Resen. Same for her poor ley line and root World. That's why I can't annihilate the place and expunge the Devourers."

His brows furrowed. His lips pursed. It was long moments before he slowly nodded. "Then you need to visit your brother."

She lifted her head. "Excuse me?"

Phobos had met her eldest brother, and by "met," she meant he'd been carved up and experimented on for many months by her brother. Other than Tobek, Phobos was the only one who'd knowingly met any of her siblings. Unlike Tobek, Phobos had an idea as to her complicated relationships with her family and was willing to discuss them with her. Dude had his own messy family stuff, so he empathized.

"Our collective knowledge and needs place us at an impasse. Frankly, you can't have it both ways with Ariel. You now have a time limit to provide an alternate solution that keeps her alive—though not anywhere near a position of power—and purifies her World without harming it. Otherwise, the pantheons will have her assassinated and her World destroyed. Resen be damned."

"They'll have to get in line behind the Phoenix and the Angelic Host. She's blasphemed against pure Mids' magic, which carries a death penalty for any angel. I'm sure the Dragon Horde will also be in the murder queue once word gets out." Bix rolled to her back and studied the carvings in the molding, who, in turn, studied her. Normal people would be freaked out by them, but they looked after her as much as they looked at her. She wiggled her fingers in greeting; they lashed their cerise tongues in return.

"If you want to be her savior, you have to consult your brother. He's the best lead you've got." Phobos ambled to her side dressed in nothing more than gauze pajama pants. He stared down at her, a trace of sympathy softening his harsh features. "Tjinimin attacking Ariel buys you some grace, but not much. As long as she has to defend herself against him and the rising revolt, your mortals have a bit of breathing room. However, the moment my brother delivered Hadhayans to rehab, rumors of the hive's location spread. I will do what I can to redirect ire and focus, but…"

She folded her arms behind her head. "I asked my brother for help recently, and he betrayed me. I'm not sure how I'm supposed to consult him on anything without expecting it to blow up in my face."

"Figure out *why* your brother acted against your interests, and in so doing acted against his own. He is, after all, depending on you to free him from prison." Phobos offered her a hand. "You don't choose family, Chimera, and you don't get to walk away from them either, certainly not when they construct the very universe in which you exist."

He was right, of course. Didn't make the impending visit any more palatable, though. She placed her hand in his and sat up. "While I'm gone, see what you can learn about how the Devourers got an army in the core of that World without anyone noticing, would you, please? They've only recently mastered portal technology, yet the hive seems to have been there much longer. Even with Ariel's help, the timeline is wrong."

"Agreed." He pointed to a minion holding the vial in which he'd collected a soil sample from Ariel's World. "I suspect the answer lies with who created the core. Gods maintain access to their creations, even when it seems we've forgotten about them. Ariel is unlikely to be the only one complicit in this scheme."

"Great, just what we need, another rogue god collaborating with the enemy, and a planetary god to boot."

"Planetary gods are a malignant lot, more so than the rest of us." Phobos smirked, exposing a long canine. "But let's be sure with whom we're dealing before you husk an entire class of gods, eh?"

"Fair." Smiling wearily, she squeezed his hand. "Thank you for working on this and more."

He inclined his head. She opened gates.

CHAPTER 13

In a long hallway with thick black baseboards and blacker gabled ceilings, arched windows in sets of threes looked out to nebulas growing and dying. Ambient sounds and scents didn't exist, as though intentionally stripped from this isolated environment. Triangles of garnet tiles turned their points in silent guidance as Bix strode through the cosmic prison tethering her eldest brother for crimes she had yet to discern.

She pondered Phobos's question about why her eldest brother would've betrayed her by inviting their other siblings to desecrate Tobek. The simplest answer was…he wouldn't. He was the origin of instinct, and there was no greater instinct than personal survival. That left her eldest sisters holding the blame bag. They knew Tobek. They'd chosen him as a guardian of the Mids, of the collective they'd created and subsequently refused to help. They'd come to her asking to "fix" Tobek. She'd wanted to believe in their benevolence so badly that she'd stupidly agreed. When the time of reckoning came, she'd have it out with her sisters, not her brother. Not the guy who was depending on her to spring him from this place, a place in which their other siblings had trapped him. No, he was as much at a disadvantage in their sisters' scheming as she was.

"Three?" she called.

"Why do you infantilize him with such a moniker?"

Bix drew up and cocked her head. Memories, loose and incomplete, rattled in her brain, the censure in the tone a trigger. Emotions entrenched in her childhood pulled taut. Fear. Recalcitrance. A broad but not deep dislike. Her tutor, her *other* tutor. They'd worked as a pair, schooling her. Knowledge Innate and Knowledge Amassed. Instinct and Experience. Her brothers, twins. Not identical. One greatly favored their mother, the other their father.

"Do you ask because you lack the insight or because you disdain the intimacy?" She pivoted on the balls of her feet, then clacked down on her heels loudly enough that it echoed in halls built to accommodate a cosmic entity whose preferred form was bigger than a McMansion.

In a sparsely furnished solarium, lying on a golden floor cushion the size of an Olympic pool, was a similarly massive white fox. The sunflower yellow of his socks matched the tufts of his ears and the tips of his four tails. It even painted a starburst across his shoulders that reflected the lights of surrounding galaxies. He studied her with eyes of changing stars. The fourth child of seven First Children born to the Chaos and the Cosmos. The second son, closely aligned to their father. A defiler of her bond with Tobek.

Darkness unthreaded from her spine as she remained in the hall. Tendrils of shadow danced around her, malice ready to strike.

"What I *know* is that you cannot recall his name is Eko nor that mine is Esiw." A soft indulgent chuckle, and the fox pushed himself to a sitting pose, ever so regal. "What perplexes me is your choice of delaying the recollection of all the sublime knowledge you once possessed."

"Ah, and you are keen to chastise me for my choices, is that it?"

"So defensive, little sister," Esiw tutted. "Put away your tantrums. I've no desire to pick a fight with you in your current condition. When you are hale, we will resume our lively debates over ethics and morality, free will versus destiny, innovation over tradition. We shall include your recent spate of decisions as well."

"Recent" to someone older than time was awfully vague, but Bix had enough common sense to not go toe-to-toe with a brother who believed in the School of Cataclysmic Knocks. Even with half her wits, she knew the difference between dumb and stupid.

"Where is Three or Eko or whatever it pleases you to call him?" she asked instead.

"Playing with the toys you sent him." Esiw arched his back as he stood, flicking his tails. "I wonder at your interpretation of incarceration. How is he to learn his lesson if he is distracted?"

"Incarceration should involve rehabilitation. Otherwise, what's the point?" She leaned against a wall, not tucking away her shadows as her brother had requested. "What's he in for anyway?"

Esiw stilled. One ear twitched, the other lay flat. He seemed to ponder the questions, his tongue flashing against his teeth as his lip curled. At length, he deigned to answer, "When you remember, you will know."

Yeah, she didn't think it'd be that easy. Eko was equally reluctant to discuss it, which complicated her release deal with him. She really ought to know what horrible, awful thing her eldest brother had done that'd made five out of six siblings turn on him before she freed him from this prison. She had until the Devourers were expunged from the Mids to figure it out. Before that, however, she needed to be able to rout the Devourers from a root World.

"All right, then, let's try a different tack. What's the point of visitation when he's not hanging out with you?" She pushed off the wall and ambled away from the solarium, curious if Esiw would follow.

"My presence here was necessitated by the most recent gifts you gave our brother." Esiw moseyed beside her, his stride accommodating the vast difference in their sizes since she didn't even reach his belly.

"The last presents?" Bix had to think for a moment to

remember what she'd recently sent Eko. When it hit her, she snickered. "The Devourers from the Crimson Market? Why would you care about the microspawns of the Chaos? Shouldn't they be beneath your concern?"

"Little sister," bellowed her blacker-than-Vantablack, overgrown-minotaur-ish eldest brother as he charged down a perpendicular hall, smile broad, marbled fangs gleaming, three tails tipped in cherry-red tufts whipping behind him. He scooped her up in his three-fingered hands and twirled her around like a doll. "Thank you for my toys. They are most entertaining."

Bix held a finger to her lips and waited for the room to stop spinning. "The party pooper doesn't approve."

"Esiw?" Eko laughed and set her on his naked shoulder where she had a close-up view of his black horns veined in garnet that caged his wild array of cherry hair. "Of course he disapproves. Contrary to their appearance, Devourers are creations of order. They are entities of light just as he is."

"Oh, you're messing with me." She thumped her heel against the meaty round of Eko's shoulder. She wanted to be mad at him because of what he'd allowed the others to do to Tobek, but damn if she could stay mad in the presence of his abundant joy at seeing her. "I've consumed their essence and made them burst in tarry spatters. There is nothing light or bright about them."

"Come now, sister, think." Esiw sighed. "There are gods of fire, of suns, and of auroras, yet they are all derivatives of the eternal darkness."

She opened her mouth to argue but shut it again. When she searched for her memories inside a god, her memories shone like stars amid the god's darkness. When she culled a god's memories, they didn't emit light like hers. She actually hadn't gone after a Devourer's memories, because their mortal bodies tended to explode first. Yes, their emotions came along with their essence when she fed, so she was abundantly clear on how they felt about things, but she normally didn't care. Yes, she had dinner issues.

"It is your broken mind that equates the gods as light and the anti-gods as darkness," Eko said. "Think instead of the contrasts as facets of wildness and structure. You feed on the wildness of the gods just as you feed on the structure of the Devourers."

"Since when does structure act like morphine?" she countered. "Devourer essence numbs me and, if anything, suppresses my rational mind letting my instincts run without—"

"Censure?" Esiw finished for her. "You are the two-in-one, equal parts Chaos and Cosmos. Devourer essence is regulation, process, A then B then C. When you consume it, you satisfy your body's need for it. It is the overabundance of control that prods your instinctual side to rise up and demand your attention until it too is equally satisfied."

"When you feast on gods, your instinct assumes dominance and you crave order. Functioning in this mode since you broke yourself into pieces is how you've survived. However, this is not healthy for you, this unbalanced gluttony." Eko patted her head with his fingertip. "When you consume Devourers, you have salt. When you consume gods, you have sugar. You need maple bacon for balance."

Esiw looked at his brother like the eldest had lost all sense. Bix laughed.

"You've been learning allegories from the gods, haven't you?" She tugged her brother's earlobe. Tobek had been on her ass often enough about consuming a balanced diet. He hadn't wanted her to husk the Devourers at the Crimson Market because she'd then have to husk an equal number of gods. In the throes of a war between gods and anti-gods, she had to pay attention to how many of each she consumed. Portion control. Not even cosmic entities were exempt from it, dang it. "But I get it, sort of. Mostly. That's the personal reason I don't erase the Devourers from existence. I need them to maintain my balance and the balance of the cosmos."

"Exactly," her brothers said together.

Devourers were a militaristic race, so the whole structure, order, and compliance was believable.

"Okay then, help me riddle this problem: a Devourer hive has taken root on a Mid World that must be purified of their presence. How do I do that without exterminating the Devourers or the World?"

Esiw scowled and shook his head. "That collective was created by our sisters Music and Movement. If they deem the collective worth saving, let them save it. Did they petition for your interference?"

"No," she bit out as anger flashed from the reminder of her sisters' treachery. "Music and Movement have given the native races the tools they need to survive. Unfortunately, those races procrastinated until the nuisance became a real problem. The superpowers allowed their private quests for personal gain to overshadow the security of their collective. Now, they're screwed. Since I care about people living in those Worlds, I vowed to help them. Plus, I'm pretty sure their leadership petitioned me for aid before I gave up my mind."

"Hence the existence of the ether," Eko supplied for his skeptical twin.

"Ah." Esiw nodded slowly. "The shortest answer is you must drain the World of order, thus depriving the Devourers of the nutrition within the magic on which they feed. The hive will not exist where it cannot thrive."

Ariel's root World was already out of whack due to the death of the dragon queen, who would've provided an influx of order to counter Ariel's natural chaos. Dragons were the offspring of Music, who took after the Cosmos. Angels were creations of Movement, who took after the Chaos. However, making anything too off-kilter would break it; so after Bix robbed the World of its last bits of order, she'd have a small window in which to restore balance. Restore too soon and the Devourers would come back. Restore too late and the World and its ley line would die. Gah.

"Assuming I don't screw things up, there's a chance the archangel can live, her root World be saved, and the ley line made healthy?" Bix asked, still unsure of the plan. When her brothers nodded, she grimaced. "I don't know how to begin draining the World."

"To be crass, you feed off the World, taking on its gross inequity," Esiw cautioned.

"You must be able to hunt, then extract order from a complex state," Eko clarified. "Although it is a part of you, it is in the part you reject. You should practice on me, yes? See if you can find the parts of our father within me. I am mostly of our mother, so the challenge should be sufficient."

"Perhaps she should begin with me," Esiw interjected. "I am mostly order; therefore, she will learn its many facets before she hunts within you."

"Yes, yes." Eko slapped his twin's back. "That is a wise plan. Yes, start with him, little sister. Learn the basics, then we will test you."

Bix stared at her two nutter brothers. "Are you both crazy? I'm not going to dissect you. You're my family."

"You've been brimming with ill will toward me since you arrived. Why not get it out of your system? Lash out? Be angry? Rail against me?" Esiw chuckled as fur faded and starlight blossomed until he resembled a bright constellation. The barest hint of a fox lay within the dots waiting to be connected. "Come, little sister. It will be like the days of your youth, eh? When you were more our mother's feral child with so much yet to learn about being our father's discerning daughter."

She began to argue, but her high chair surrendered solidity to become amorphous night with infrequent twinkles of red starlight. The contrast between brothers made it hard to believe they were twins.

"Native state, little sister," Eko encouraged. "Reach out to Esiw not with your darkness, but with your light."

That was easier said than…understood. Oh, she could revert to her native state easily enough, but reaching out with her light? Uhm. Uh. Huh?

"Your light, little sister," Esiw urged. "Reach for me."

"I-I don't know what part of me you're talking about," she confessed. "The only light within me are my memories."

"Oh, I see." Esiw sighed. "Then this will be an extremely remedial lesson, but we will get you to where you need to be to save your precious toys, never fear."

It wasn't fear rolling through her, it was conflict. On the one hand, she was still angry with these two for the parts they played in defiling Tobek. On the other hand, she blamed her sisters more than her brothers. Music and Movement knew better than the others what Tobek meant to her, so their betrayal cut way deeper. Plus, she couldn't ignore that she'd come here asking her brothers for help, and neither had hesitated to offer it. What...what was she supposed to do with that? Be less angry and more grateful? Like a godsdamned adult? To save the Mids, she didn't have the luxury of being a sullen brat. Oh, she wanted to be. Definitely wanted to be. But, she wasn't twelve. She should shut it, take the help they offered, and stow the ire about Tobek until the ley line was healthy again and Resen launched. *Then* she could demand an accounting from all her siblings...starting with her sisters. The thing about timelines and true immortals was that emo shit could wait. Right? Gods, she hoped so.

"Okay, okay. Light within me. What does it look like again?" she asked, surrendering herself to the tutelage of Instinct and Experience.

CHAPTER 14

Socks in a front-loading washer on an endless sudsing cycle; one sock happily battered while the other desperately searched for an escape. That was what Bix felt like by the time her exhausted brothers had voted her minimally competent. She now knew how to locate the light inside her, but her jungle of malice didn't want to let it out. Malice didn't want any strictures limiting her darkness: self-preservation at its most basic. Eko had been delighted at its tenacity; Esiw had been coldly surgical in the battle he'd waged against it. Accessing her light had required both brothers' concerted and united efforts. Directing that light had overwhelmed her and her brothers repeatedly. She'd left Esiw demonstrably worse for wear and Eko downright gleeful to play nursemaid to his twin. Did surviving their brutal instruction mean she was ready to drain a root World of order? Hell no. It just meant she'd survived one lesson with her brothers. And to think she'd had a robust childhood filled with lessons more advanced than this one. Holy shit.

She needed succor and a long, sound sleep before she had to do something that could totally derail the mission and leave the Mids defenseless against the Devourers. One hand over her twitching Eternal Knot, she stepped through gates to Cian's renovated apartment. Her heart caught in her throat.

In the silence of hard night under the light of the harvest moon, eight Berserkers lay in sleeping bags arranged like petals around their fearless leader. Layers of ice built up a dense shell around Tobek, then melted only to rebuild. The cycle repeated in slow beats of eight that were echoed in the currents of the thin rivers of dark green magic linking Tobek to the men surrounding him. His magic, connecting them like multiple IVs, was feeding his men, enabling them to change along with him.

Bix steepled her hands against her lips and drew a measured breath, a teensy bit smug and a whole lot of wary. She'd wondered if Tobek's recent upgrade had impacted the Berserkers. After the great pit fiasco, she'd wondered if Hywl's good health had been an anomaly or proof of hypothesis. The proof lay before her. Now the question was: how, in what ways?

"Safe to say we know why Ariel targeted the battalion in a smear campaign." Feng's barely audible greeting came from the shadows blanketing the kitchen. He sat on a swiveling barstool at the long counter, elbows on the quartz countertop, idly spinning a bottle top between his fingers. "They're no longer human. They're not Chweds either. They're evolving into a new class of Other World entity, a derivative of whatever Chief is becoming."

She toed off her shoes and tiptoed to the stool beside the Phoenix, noting that the sectional and coffee table had been stacked against a wall to make room for the guys. "Do they still have souls?"

Feng nodded. "Something is infusing their souls, voiding the claim the gods who'd provided them once had. Their bodies, created by dragons and angels, are no longer solely under the purview of native magic. The ley line couldn't tell the status of their threads of Fate. Though, I suspect they've gone much the route of his. In short, the contracts that made them Berserkers are blown to hell."

"The Consortium no longer has a means of forcing them to heel, thus, Ariel's creating the evidence trail to permanently retire them before they lead the Chweds and humans in a rebellion against the superpowers." Bix set her pumps on the counter. "Tobek won an impossible war before when he led the Fates against the pantheons."

"Ariel has closed herself in her offices, fired her personal guards, and called her choir to attend her. I don't suppose you know anything about that?" He bumped her with his elbow.

"Ariel is delivering Mid World guardians to the Devourers for food and entertainment. Unfortunately for her, the pantheons have coherent witnesses and unassailable proof." Bix laid her head on Feng's shoulder, letting her eyes drift shut as a yawn overtook her. "She, her ley line, and her World are on borrowed time."

"Resen needs all three alive and well. Let's hope someone in the political arena can convince the pantheons to show mercy." He leaned toward her so she wouldn't have to stretch to balance her cheek on his knit vest. "You get anywhere with the Devourer problem?"

"I've got a half-baked plan to save her World and her ley line. Saving *her* might be beyond us," Bix garbled, feeling the pull of sweet slumber.

"Your half-baked plans lead to the most interesting missions." He wrapped one arm around her shoulders and scooped the other under her knees. "Gurp made up the guest room for you. Get some sleep. We'll brief the teams in the morning."

"How are the scientists doing? Any hope there?" she mumbled as her head hit the fluffiest of pillows. Man, she loved that goblin.

"Lots. Cian's been itching for your return to update you. Timeline's getting tight on that front." Feng tucked her in and closed the shades. "Tonight, though, rest. I'll keep watch."

"Cian's alive? Good. Good. Ariel hasn't killed him yet." She couldn't keep her eyes open anymore. "Thank you, Feng, for all you're doing."

"We're a team, Bix. Looking after each other is how we roll." He started to tug the door closed.

"Hey, one thing?" She snuggled deeper under the comforter smelling of lavender and bergamot. "Drew's in a boar god trying to stop a bat god who thinks he's me. Batty is probably going to make a move on Tobek sooner than later. Don't smite the pig or the bat."

"No smoking the bacon. Got it," Feng chuckled.

If the door snicked, she didn't hear it.

CHAPTER 15

Boom. Shudder. Shake. Boom. The fifth time, it pierced her consciousness, Bix finally woke. Superglued to a half-naked body. Erratic magic batted at her, surging in time to the clamor outside the walls. A warm, musky blend of nutmeg, cedar, and sandalwood with top notes of coffee filled her lungs. Tobek. Hale and not glacial. Feeling her body lock into its corporeal form, she stretched along his side. Her head cushioned on the bicep of his amputated arm, one of his denim-clad legs trapped between hers, her arm flung across his chest, her nails digging into the frame of his Eternal Knot, his knot scalding her palm… Wait, that last part wasn't supposed to happen. Mixing a whimper and a groan, she struggled to sit up.

"Easy, sweetheart," Tobek soothed as ceramic clunked on wood. "It's just the wards holding uninvited company at bay."

She gracelessly separated their tangled hair and flipped it out of her face. They were not in the guest bedroom. They were in the great room. On the couch. That'd been put back in front of the TV. The clunk had been his coffee cup on the coffee table. Wiping the crusties from her eyes, she looked around for the indulgent smirks of his men. She always found Tobek in her sleep, regardless of where he was, even if they were Worlds apart. She didn't always stay, but she always showed up. Thankfully, his men accommodated her weird. Did they resent it? Never that they let on. As for Tobek, he got annoyed on the nights she didn't find him because it meant she wasn't getting enough sleep. This from the same man who got on her about her diet too. Mister Health and Fitness, he was.

Speaking of health…

"Where is everyone?" She used his bulk to lever herself out of the wedge formed by the seat and back cushions.

"With the scientists. Think they wanted to give us some alone time." He smiled wickedly and waggled his brows as she straddled him, her dress hiking immodestly high. He had his usual dark jeans on, and she wore sturdy garments made to survive cosmic travel. Definitely no accidental shenanigans happening.

"They're okay? All of them? Even the guys who were bobbing like dead bodies beside you?"

Tobek's playfulness ebbed. "We lost one. Marcus. Been with us since Rome was founded. His absence is keenly felt."

She traced a finger over the light of order breaking through the lines in her palm. "Cause of death?"

"Devourer blast liquified his organs. We can't repair what's not there." He lifted her chin on the edge of his finger. "The stars are back in your eyes. I wondered at the emotions you were sending me. Been to see your brother?"

"Plural." She showed him her hand. "Esiw was there too. You remember him, I'm sure. One of the uninvited three who saw to your upgrade."

He kissed the palm of her hand and laid it over his knot, seemingly oblivious to the way the light from her palm caused the threads of order in his modified knot to glow and spider across his ink. "Restlessness and conflict with a curiously high dose of dread. Tell me why I'm feeling this from you. What can I do to support you?"

She was a cosmic newb who had to do the equivalent of atomic-level surgery on a godsdamned planet? Oh, and the brothers who could've helped her do the actual job wouldn't? They'd given her the lesson. Saving Ariel's World was the test. If there was an option to retire from adulting…

"Hey." Tobek bent his knees behind her, jostling her gently. "Talk to me."

Normally, she'd pounce on Tobek's offer to help, but the odds of him turning into a paperweight in the middle of the mission were way too high, which was its own special problem. She couldn't risk him near the Devourers. First, he'd been unable to control his temper in the Crimson Market, then he'd been unable to control his magic in the hive. He was a risk to everyone around him, and she wasn't sure he was aware of just how big a risk.

"Look, I know we are disquieted in each other's presence right now." He winced slightly as he adjusted their clasped hands, breaking her contact with his knot. "These changes brought on by my evolution have ruined the normal ways we found comfort. New beginnings are like that, though, right? We work through it. We find our new normal. We've done it thousands of times before, and we'll do it thousands of times again. That's part and parcel of being a committed couple."

"That's a wonderful answer to a question that hadn't crossed my mind, but has apparently been on yours." She leaned back against his legs, flummoxed. He'd never let on that he was miffed with her. With the circumstances, with himself, with lots of other things, but never with her, or so she'd thought. She'd been blithely blundering ahead, trying to be as supportive of him in his time of need as he always was of her. If she was screwing that up, then…well, then she wasn't sure how to be better, since he remained tight-lipped about the whole upgrade thing. He wasn't leaving her a lot of options beyond handling him like an asset, one who happened to turn into a clump of ice after being deep-fried. "This isn't about us. This is about you. Are you conscious in the moments, sometimes hours, after you're injured?"

"What?" He shifted his hips under her. "Is that what's causing your dread? Me? There are many ways I can take your mind off that."

"You're normally way better at evading questions and redirecting conversation." She poked his belly button. "Your 'hiccups' are a risk to the team, Tobek. Do you know what's triggering them?"

"It's the new layout of the ley lines, I told you. Nothing to worry about." He grinned with a hint of playfulness.

"When you sell me a lie, you always smile like that." She crossed her arms. "Stop it. I need to know if you're mission capable or if there's going to be another pit problem."

"Down to business, are we?" He released her and folded his arm behind his head, fluffing his pillow. "The pit wasn't a problem. It was a solution."

"That nearly killed your men. You couldn't control the flood once you lost consciousness." She happily let ire replace self-doubt, something he'd probably intended. "Never once did you signal me, which you should've done the instant you spotted the first Devourer. I know you get off on being the mission martyr, Colonel Extra Crispy, but this time, you went too far. Your men aren't immortal."

"All right, that's fair criticism." He looked up and away. "Yes. I lose a minute here and there. Yes, I lost more than that creating the pit. No, I don't know what's triggering the blackouts."

She had a suspicion, but one issue at a time. "Are you aware that your hiccups now involve encasing yourself in something that feels like ice and looks like Snow White's coffin?"

He scoffed a chuckle, then sobered. "You're serious."

"You've done it four times since we've been back in the Mids, that I've observed. Whatever's happening when you're in that state also removes your prosthesis." She flapped her hand against his amputation. "Did Runjit not tell you any of this? Gurp?"

"They've been with the scientists since we lost Marcus." Tobek stared at his amputation scars and frowned.

"Okay, last one. Are you aware that your guys are evolving with you?" She tipped her head at the floor. "Last night, the connection was visible while you all slept. You were like an octopus with your tentacles of green magic."

That question shot his brows to his tangles.

"She's not wrong," Ashtad added, leaning on his cane at the corner of the hallway. "The connection was noticeable the moment you showed for demo day. It became tangible when we exited the ley line on Ariel's World. Didn't touch me, didn't affect me, and didn't seem bothered by me either. Appears to be limited to Berserkers only."

"Ashtad, good to see you're up and mobile." Bix dismounted Tobek and tugged her dress down, earning an eye roll from her dear friend.

"When a ley line takes it upon itself to speed one's recovery, it doesn't matter that one happens to be an Other World demigod. Or so I've discovered." He wagged his cane at the windows still trembling with the wards repelling whoever was trying to get in. "That is the twelfth visit by the Consortium's goons since we entered Ariel's domain. Feng usually zaps them. I guess he's with the scientists?"

Bix ambled to the window. Sure enough, a team of four in Consortium op gear tried to step off the sidewalk to advance on the town house's corners and steep steps. Two more teams tried to advance via the neighboring buildings. Late morning's sun gave away the teams trying to take the roof access by playing their shadowy failures on the front of the building across the street. Resonances of the would-be infiltrators confirmed they were Mids' mortals, not Devourers in disguise. Not bearing a murderous grudge like Feng did, Bix dispatched the guards via gates to a World on the far side of the collective. They didn't need to die; they were just following the orders of a wholly corrupt Chair.

"As long as we keep repelling them, Ariel knows where we are. It's passive monitoring." Bix turned from the window and motioned to the otherwise empty apartment. "It sounds like Cian outed his secret assets. Was that crisis necessitated?"

"Scientist demanded." Ashtad limped to the kitchen and fixed himself a travel mug of tea. "Everyone involved in the mission had to give samples of all kinds of parts and fluids. Whenever you're ready, the kid is dying to brief you. Apparently, we did something that's shortened our window of opportunity."

"Pretty sure Ariel's the one who did that," Bix muttered, heading for Cian's room.

"He's not there. He's with the scientists. Chief and I will take you." Ashtad pointed his cane at the front door. "Don't worry, it's a short walk."

"Due to the intense scrutiny they've had me under, Cian's scientists can probably answer my mission fitness questions better than I." Tobek got to his feet and grinned. "However, when we get there, you're going to have to answer one question for me."

"Could just ask me now, you know." Bix found her shoes next to Tobek's biker boots on the tray by the door. He took the lead down the tiny interior stairwell separating the apartments while she used gates to move Ashtad and herself down the landings to a basement she didn't remember existing before.

"When we get there." Tobek held up his hand, and the illusion of a wall vanished, revealing a warded iron door. Hand on the knob that looked more like a demon's maw, Tobek paused. "Remember that you like surprises, sweetheart. The kid is full of them."

The door opened to a pair of overgrown, red-eyed, slavering hounds of Hel.

CHAPTER 16

"A programmable gate would've been too easily tracked. A pair of hounds, courtesy of the Norse pantheon, covers the distance in an acceptable time, wouldn't you say, Chimera?" Samael, archangel of the disavowed, greeted in his natural form of bull-necked bodybuilder standing cross-armed in the glow of a pair of simplistic torches burning with unnatural fire. Behind him, a massive, plain, earthen door hinted at something other than dirt filling the winding tunnel. The whole area pulsed with magic native and Other, running the gamut from lesser Chwed to the heavy hitters of the Consortium.

"I'm surprised to see you here," Bix said as Hel's hounds slowed their approach.

"After that bit of unpleasantness at the market, word about the Devourers mixing among us is everywhere. Hysteria is rising and the Consortium is staying mum." He turned a cheek as one of the hounds sniffed him. "So, I'm doing my damn job investigating why those things are after me. That's when the kid tells me you guys found Devourers in Ariel's home World. No way was I letting you proceed without me."

"Is this the part where you tell me I wasn't totally off base thinking your sister was involved?" Bix scratched her hound behind the ear, and it sat before the archangel.

"I really wish you had been." Samael licked his teeth. "You may as well know, I've spoken to Michael, seeing as how he's leading the Host's military response to the invaders."

"Tell me he's not barging into Ariel's office to demand an accounting. That'll only inflame an already bad situation." Bix slid down the furry back of her ride. As much as she adored the beasts of the various Under Worlds, the fact they were in the Mids and the Primary Mid World to boot filled her with so many questions. Almost as many as the winding maze through which they'd traveled.

"He's agreed to let you handle the Devourer part of this equation." Samael inspected the sole of his black jump boot and glowered at the beast. "The pantheons haven't shown themselves to be reliable when it comes to serving the greater interest, leaving you as the lesser evil. Michael recognizes how hard you've pushed for Resen, thus he is willing to grant you a bit of room with this complicated mess."

Tobek muttered something behind her, the gist of which was not flattering to the Angelic Host.

"He's trusting me with the life of your sister, the significance of which is noted and appreciated." She knew Ariel's actions cut the other archangels the deepest. Family betrayals were the absolute worst. "Enough about her. Care to tell me where we are?"

"This?" Samael spread his arms wide. "This is the reason I bought the whole damn neighborhood instead of just the kid's building."

"This is the reason you let the Consortium raid Cian's apartment?" She surveyed the small, compact-dirt courtyard. "This doesn't feel like a pop-up shop."

"As long as Ariel's idiots got what they wanted, they didn't look for the obvious under their noses." Samael bowed as he rapped on the door. "The entrance is newish, but the work site has been here longer than humans have existed."

There was only one place in the Primary Mid World that fit that description.

"We're about to enter Consortium Chambers?" Bix moved to the cold fire of the nearest torch, causing Ashtad to lurch around her with a curse. His tea audibly sloshed against the lid of his mug.

Samael laughed his best Vincent Price laugh and wiggled his fingers at her. "Hiding in plain sight. Why investigate a hot spot of various magics when it looks like political staffers at work? There are many, many sections of chambers that have been lost to time or conveniently erased from the records. Not that an upstanding archangel like myself would have anything to do with that last bit, eh?"

The torches flared, and a monstrous golem took shape within the door. Eyes of loam scanned their small gathering. With a voice like Wellies slogging through muck, it addressed them. "Archangel. Berserker. Demigod. Chimera. Presence expected. Welcome."

The golem retreated into the door, and the door retracted into the wall with a shudder and clank. A narrow tunnel seemingly of soil but brimming with hidden life extended another twenty feet before opening to a sprawling, brightly lit limestone chamber the size of a pro-football stadium. Races of all types collaborated in organized pandemonium. Technologies native and Other anchored workstations. Under World demons engaged in lively arguments with gnomes. Nymphs wearing jumpsuits of contained flowing water bent over microscopes displaying results on large monitors, while sprites carried trays of beakers and flasks from autoclaves. Beeps, whirrs, and chugging rode on the white noise of cooperative research.

"See what you started?" Tobek offered Bix his arm.

"Not it," she breathed, awed by the unity of individuals from oppositional races. She blindly grabbed Tobek's hand.

"Totally it." Ashtad hobbled around her, raising his travel mug as Feng hailed them from a far station.

Tobek led her deeper into the laboratory. Researchers—she assumed everyone down here was either scientist or specimen—glanced up as she strolled by. A flash of a smile, a lift of a chin, and back to work. There was an air of excitement, as if the next breakthrough was one eureka moment away.

This was how the Consortium should've worked. Together. For a greater cause.

"How did Cian assemble all these folks? Where did he even know to look for them?" Bix kept close to Tobek lest she knock over someone or something amid the flurry of activity.

"Your cluelessness brings me untold joy," Samael taunted, drawing up as a knocker—not of the door sort, rather of the mining race of Chweds variety—separated from a gaggle caught up in a heated debate and planted himself in front of Bix.

The crisp white lab coat in place of the perpetually grimy overalls favored by knockers was as unexpected on the diminutive man as the man himself. Bix knew exactly to whom his resonance belonged…and it wasn't a dude, much less a Chwed. It wasn't a Devourer either, thankfully. Beneath the lab coat and wiry body was a dragon, one Bix had saved months ago from execution by the Consortium, one who would be executed for real if she—yes, she—was discovered. She also happened to have the most brilliant scientific mind in all the Mids when it came to cooties.

"David, my *man*." Tobek waved his amputated arm in subtle greeting. "I believe you two know each other."

"Chimera, it is good to see you again." David bowed. "Your many questions are irrelevant to the current research. We should stick to the ones pertinent to the immediate crisis, in which your young Sage plays a significant role. He is with the Berserkers. This way."

Yep. The body could change, but that personality was rather distinct.

"Um, David?" Bix had a few pertinent questions, but she didn't want to shout them. Who'd vetted all these researchers? How secure was this facility? Who here secretly worked for Ariel, and when could they expect the Consortium to sabotage the work?

"You gave me two tasks." David held up two fingers. "We are close to solving both. Please do not waste time. We have so little of it."

Bix shut her piehole and let the dragon—no, knocker—lead the way.

"I think I do a better imp than she does a knocker. Then again, she's cheating by using *my* pilfered feathers in her antidetection spell," Samael whispered on a tickle at Bix's ear as he fell into step behind "David."

Tobek leaned over so his lips brushed the top of her head. "WITSEC from the Consortium? For that particular enemy of the Mids? Well done."

She poked the ink curling over his hip. "Is that your special question that had to wait till we got here? Because those are two questions."

He laughed against her hair. "Are you aware of her ties to the ley lines?"

Bix shook her head, the activity around them more fascinating than his naked chest for a change. "I know who her cousin is."

"Then take a beat to think about how one gets to be the cousin of her cousin." Swinging their hands, he resumed their stroll, eventually catching up to David and Samael as they approached the workstation commandeered by Cian, Feng, and the Berserkers.

Bix pondered Tobek's cryptic question. David's cousin was the reigning queen of the Dragon Horde. Dragon queens were created from pure native magic, but they had kits, or hatchlings, or whatever baby dragons were called. Technically, a dragon queen's siblings were the ley line and archangel with whom they were born. However, within the dragon matriarchy, to be a first cousin to a dragon queen meant…

"Her mother's a—" Bix shut her mouth before blurting out the answer in front of anyone who might be listening.

Tobek inclined his head. "Deceased, but yes."

"Is it you-know-who's birth mate?" she mumbled as they joined the group sitting on and around an octagonal tempered-glass conference table. His only answer was a brow waggle as Hywl jumped out of his chair next to Cian and waved Bix into it.

"My lady," Hywl greeted as she took his seat, confusion flashing across his features. "You're looking…brighter."

"Hard work makes a girl glow." She winked, then gave Cian her undivided attention. "How's the mission going, team leader?"

"Bix, Bix." Cian pressed his fingertips into the table. His green eyes were bright with enthusiasm above big purple bags of exhaustion. "So, so much has happened. David, man, he's *on it*."

Cian held out his fist for a bump to the knocker. David grimaced but met the gesture. The kid's enthusiasm was as infectious as any of David's designer diseases.

"We've run a battery of tests across all samples. As suspected, the samples from the core are replete with Devourer toxins. Much like a slow explosion, those toxins are seeping outward into the World." David typed something on a wireless keyboard, and the monitors around the conference table displayed all kinds of charts, numbers, and chemical composition images. Bix didn't strain her brain trying to decipher it, but Tobek's jaw went slack as he studied the results.

"Less than a quarter of a percent World saturation." Tobek bobbed his head from side to side. "Not great, but nowhere near as bad as it looked from the surface."

"It hasn't reached the surface. It's maybe a hundred miles beyond the core, with thousands of miles to go." Cian tapped his tablet, and one of the monitors brought up an image of the World. "What you guys saw on the surface is straight-up decay."

"Completely natural in origin, just at an accelerated rate," David elaborated. "Likely a result of the ley line's mourning the passing of its dragon queen."

"It damaged its own World?" Runjit asked.

"It didn't want to be alone in its pain, so it inflicted it on the only thing that couldn't escape it." Feng sighed. "If Ariel wasn't there to help it through its grief, it could've become self-destructive."

"Put a brave face toward the other lines while it raged and grieved." Samael nodded. "Lines have intense feelings. There is no greater loss to them than a birth mate. Lines have died because they couldn't handle the sorrow. We've lost archangels and dragon queens because they couldn't stop the downward spiraling of their line. It's rare, very rare, but not unheard of."

"Damn. Makes you want to get it a poppet to cuddle, eh?" Hywl cooed. "The wee *bwlyn*."

"How badly infected is the line?" Bix asked.

"Samples from the roots here in the core are tainted, but below the levels we were expecting based on the soil saturation." David hit more keys, and a rendering of the ley lines coming out of the core appeared. Colors depicted the infusion levels. "The taint carries right up to the edge of the glitter."

"But it's not in the glitter," Cian crowed. "The glitter is acting like a stopper."

"The line is stopping the spread? It knows how to arrest the dispersion of Devourer toxins?" Bix couldn't help the tickle of pride watching the kid in his element. She wasn't his mom, but she'd known his mom. That hard-hearted woman would've been pleased as hell seeing her boy excel amid all this.

"All the best discoveries are accidents, right?" Cian wriggled out of his jacket, revealing he'd skipped laundry day. Then again, none of the Berserkers had their shirts on, so maybe it was a dude-bonding thing.

Feng pushed a large tray of test tubes and petri dishes across the table. David lined up a row of dishes in front of Cian.

"These are the surface and core samples." David tapped each lid. "We've explained our findings so far. Nothing visually unexpected."

"Okay," Bix said slowly.

"These are the samples from the line." David slid two dishes and three tubes in individual stands toward Cian. Glitter in the samples shimmered.

Cian's crystallized shoulders glowed.

CHAPTER 17

"What the…?" Bix gasped. "May I?"

"You can touch me." Cian leaned toward her. "We already know you don't affect what's happened to me, where you might still affect the line samples. I feel the movement in my skin, or what used to be my skin."

"The effect does not carry out in his blood, where we would expect to see it, nor in any of his other samples." David placed a vial of blood with Cian's name on it next to the line samples. No reaction.

"Best we can guess, whatever is keeping my crystallization localized is also what the line is using to block the Devourer toxins." Cian dipped his shoulder at the line sample, then stepped away from the table. The glow of his crystals faded the farther he got from the sample, then brightened when he returned to his seat. "I'm thinking the illuminations are like recognizing like."

"Yeah, well, your body is made from Mids' magic, so it's plausible. This is huge. Right? If we can figure out how to stop the spread of Devourer toxins, then we can figure out how to contain it, which maybe leads to us being able to contain them, which bolsters Resen." Bix looked to Ashtad as she laid a hand on Cian's shoulder. It was still hard crystal. No vibrations or heat variances. It was the Devourer blood in his system interacting with Mids' magic that caused his condition. How he'd been afflicted was a whole other story, and finding a cure was one of two reasons she'd saved David.

"With a reliable containment system, the Mids wouldn't be sitting ducks anymore." Hywl scratched his black muttonchops. "The Mid World Army could corral the trash, and the Consortium could pay the pantheons to dispose of it."

"Arresting the spread of Devourer poison would prevent their blood from being used as a biological weapon as well." Tobek nodded. "This is a great breakthrough."

"Not great, not until we identify what elements are blocking the spread. At the moment, we are no further than recognizing the possibilities. I'm afraid time is what we need and what we most lack." David motioned to Runjit. "Cian is not the only one affected by what's happening on Ariel's World."

The Berserker medic took a vial of blood with Cian's name on it, removed the stopper, and held it out to Tobek. Hywl took a knife from his boot and grabbed Tobek's hand. Tobek didn't question his men; instead, he watched Bix, lips twitching as Hywl nicked his finger. Hywl dribbled Tobek's blood into Cian's vial, then into the petri dishes of all the samples.

Nothing happened with Cian's blood nor with the samples from the surface of Ariel's World. Toxins swirling in the polluted samples from the line and the core…vanished.

"A cure?" Bix bolted up from her chair. "You're kidding me."

"We've had Chief's blood on file since files were kept. The Sage, we've monitored since his infection. Every test we performed at the start of this mission, we've done a hundred times before. This time, the results were different." David narrowed his eyes at Tobek. "Chief was recently exposed to Devourer viscera and magic, which changed something in his makeup that now causes this."

"Causes a lot of other things too." Runjit handed Tobek a Band-Aid. "Wait for it."

Fractals spawned over the samples. Within moments, samples and containers were covered in ice. Bix gave Tobek a flat stare. He pointed to the samples, then to himself, eyes wide and brows raised.

"Did this happen to all the samples you've collected from him since we've been back in the Mids?" she asked Runjit. "Including the ones after the Crimson Market but before Ariel's World?"

"Took longer for the samples from the market to freeze." The medic ran his thumbnail along the edge of his turban. "It seems the more exposure to Devourers Chief gets, the faster it happens."

That was probably…not good. Tobek's evolution was supposed to make him level up, not ice over.

"How long does the deep freeze of the samples last?" Bix pressed.

"They have yet to melt." David gestured to a clear-door freezer in a nearby workstation. "We've tried all the usual suspects: heat, chemicals, magic."

"Double dose of his blood," Runjit added.

"I took a few frozen samples to Ariel's ley line for a consult. It couldn't get past the ice to help." Feng braced his hands on the back of Runjit's chair.

"Ditto. I took a few to my ley line. It's as stumped as we are." Samael crossed his beefy arms.

Was Feng purposely not mentioning Tobek himself freezing over? Bix waited for Ashtad to say it, but he was studiously avoiding her gaze. She looked to Hywl next, but he was fixated on sterilizing his knife. She knew they'd seen it happen on Ariel's World. Feng and Ashtad had seen it in Cian's apartment, more than once, presumably. They'd been there when he'd melted too. Maybe. She'd been asleep one of those times, so she couldn't be sure who'd witnessed his last defrosting. They all knew Tobek turned into an ice cube. Why not mention it to the researchers?

"Where's Gurp?" She scanned the lab for her favorite goblin, who knew Tobek better than anyone.

"Getting some hard-to-find supplies," Tobek answered.

"Anyone ask him about the ice problem?" She directed the question at David. Goblins got zero respect. Sidewalk gum had higher standing than they did, but Gurp was beyond a genius. If the scientists were playing with any part of Tobek, Gurp should've been their primary consultant.

"Yeah, I did." Cian propped his head on his palm. "He said a lot of things, but two words were the only ones he'd repeat in English. 'He change.'"

The trifecta of silence across the table snorted.

If Gurp wasn't freaked out, then Bix would endeavor to be chill about Tobek's affliction. Sort of. For now, at least.

"Anyone apply Tobek's blood directly to Cian's crystals?" She helped the kid pull his jacket over his shoulders. Cian couldn't raise his hands over his head, so getting dressed had to be a bitch.

"No," cried a chorus of medics, researchers, and even Tobek.

Bix staggered back and held up her hands in peace. "Sorry I asked."

"They're worried what'll happen if his blood does affect my crystals," Cian explained, zipping his jacket. "How much of me freezes? Just my shoulders, or does it reach my brain and heart too? If it stays at my shoulders, will it cause necrotizing fasciitis? Does it actually clear the Devourer blood from my system, or will it speed its spread into the parts of me that are currently unaffected? There are a billion more questions like those."

"A cure that causes another problem isn't a cure. Chief's blood is, however, a launching point." David scribbled the time on long stickers and set the frozen samples atop them. "What you see happening around you is the exploration of the many paths diverging from this critical discovery."

"Human trials would be way, way down the line," Tobek said. "We need a certain level of confidence in how the cure would behave inside a mortal body before we'd test it on a living being."

"Okay. I get it. Can we all agree that Tobek doesn't generate enough blood to drown Ariel's World and purify it? That is a logical statement, right? Thus, under no circumstance will he be strung up and bled as a sacrifice. We *are* all on that same page, right?" Bix shot Tobek a look daring him to volunteer. He scratched his Eternal Knot and kept his lips zipped. Wise man.

"Don't think anyone wants to turn the archangel's World into planet Hoth," Hywl joked. The Berserkers around the table guffawed quietly. The researchers remained notably silent.

Bix took note. David had a history of ignoring processes and protocols for assorted reasons. The exsanguination of Tobek would not end well for anyone involved in the matter. Bix's reaction would be the least of their worries.

"Okay, we've identified more problems that require more time to yield solutions." Bix sat down and turned to Cian. "Cian, is time still a mitigating factor?"

"It is, and we have less of it than we thought." Cian pointed to the large monitors on the nearest wall. "I've been taking daily data grabs from Resen. Ariel hasn't killed me yet, so why not keep pushing my luck? After your, uh, visit, the glitter moved farther up the line. We have three days max before it reaches the intersection. Its effectiveness as a stopper will likely fail when it splits, thus allowing Devourer toxin to spread into the foundation of Resen."

"If we purge the Devourers from the core, can we slow it?" Bix asked.

"Possibly. Without knowing the exact date they arrived in the core, the camp's growth rates, what technologies and magics they're using, etcetera, we can't give a firm answer." David stared at the screen. "If we at least knew how they'd gotten past the ley line initially to infect the core, then we could extrapolate and run models."

Feng slid his hands in his pockets. "Think it's safe to say Ariel showed them the way in."

"No. No way would she volunteer her World," Samael argued, a vein in his temple twitched. "Somehow, they got past her and her line, then they used that sneak attack to force her compliance."

"But how, eh?" Feng pressed. "How does *anything* get past a ley line on its root World?"

"Used a traitor within the Consortium to coopt a gate? They did it at the market, right?" Samael looked to Bix, brows raised as if he were expecting her support. "Something like that. Surely. An archangel would never, ever sacrifice their ley line. Ever."

Despite Samael's confidence in his sister, his faith was horribly misplaced. Alas, he and the rest of his kind would never believe what Bix and Phobos had witnessed without experiencing it firsthand. Archangels were a family, and family could cough up a litany of excuses on a whim. Ariel was exploiting their blind faith to continue her crimes.

Wait. Phobos. The obvious hit Bix like a brick in the face. Phobos had said as much.

"It's not something. It's Other. The core is made from Other World magic. It's the creation of a planetary god. Gods are like computer hackers. They maintain backdoor access to all their creations." Bix rapped her knuckles on the table as the Devourer sourcing started to make sense. "That's how they got there. The hive. The Devourers. They've only just mastered portals, but the hive has been there long enough to become an infestation. The exposure to the line would've made them sick—did, in fact, make them sick when the ley line blew out of its banks. They had to bypass it completely."

"A *planetary god* put the Devourers there?" Feng breathed. "Hand-delivered? Despite them being enemies?"

"Gods aren't the most cohesive bunch, so it's entirely possible. Remember, deities are known to literally eat their children. Sacrificing another god as a means to an end is completely in character." Ashtad sipped his tea. "Strategically, a root World is the last place the pantheons would look for the hive."

"The least protected too." Samael rubbed his neck and stared at the ceiling. "Ariel's been Chair for two hundred fifty years, rarely been home since taking the job. The dragon queen's been dead for—"

"Six hundred and five years," David interjected flatly. "This great heart of Mids' magic was left without its defenses."

"Mourning," Feng added with sympathy. "When its populations died off, it probably rejoiced at the initial arrival of the Devourers. Company at last. The Mids have never faced Devourers before. The line didn't know they were the enemy until—"

"Until the line connected to the foundation of Resen." Cian sat back, his crystals scraping against the high-back chair. "The newest ley line in the Mids had firsthand experience with the Devourers. It told the others when it joined the network of lines. They talk to each other more than we do."

"Then you started tests on the system, pushing our code, educating the lines with the defense plan that includes the pantheons' history with the old foes." Ashtad massaged his scalp. "The history was part of the build code the line took from me."

"Ah-ha!" David smacked his hands together. "That's it. That's why Ariel hasn't offed the Sage and the demigod. The ley lines aren't letting her."

"That's a possibility." Samael stopped rubbing his neck. "She doesn't respect the Chimera enough to let Bix's retribution stop her, that's for sure."

Bix shot the archangel a droll look.

"Samael, does your line know about Ariel's?" Tobek asked. "Specifically, that it's ill?"

"It knows something is amiss, but all the lines are still adapting to the new weave and the infusion of the Fates' magic." The archangel shook his head, paused, then pointed to Cian and Ashtad. "But it knows you two. It knows you're the architects."

Hywl pounded his chest and hooted. "Not one damn line, but all of them. That's who's got your backs, mates. Oh, your futures are fucked."

A round of affirmative commiserating grunts came from the rest of the Berserkers. Cian glowered and pointed at his deformed shoulder.

"Bah, all these smarties on it? They'll get you your cure." Hywl wagged the hilt of his knife at the kid. "Besides, how many Sages grow up besties with the Chimera, eh? Eh? Kid, you're not lucky enough to die from petrification. Not a single Fate is going to allow that."

"For sure, kid, you'll be a living rock. The kind tourists rub when they visit you on vacation." Samael slapped Cian's back.

Cian rolled his eyes, but his fair skin couldn't hide his bright blush.

"Our scenario suggests Ariel might not have known about the Devourer infestation in the beginning," Tobek ventured. "Infecting her World would force her compliance. Promising to cure her line keeps her hooked."

"That's plausible motive if they caught her unawares initially," Feng reluctantly conceded. "But it doesn't explain why she's allowed it to continue. All she had to do was bring it to the floor of the Consortium to alert her peers. She has no excuse."

Unless the Devourer toxin poisoning her World and her line had poisoned her too, but Bix kept that to herself for Samael's sake. He was smart enough to make that connection on his own, and so were the other archangels. Once they could turn the glitter containment into a cure for anyone infected with Devourer ick, then Bix and Samael could discreetly discuss Ariel's possible ailment.

A glance at the mulish set of Samael's jaw confirmed he wasn't as sold on his sister's innocence as he wanted everyone to believe. That, and he'd stopped arguing her defense.

"Which brings us back to the mission, right?" Bix asked with artificial cheer. "To purify the line so we can launch Resen and have it work as designed?"

"Realistically, we're not going to discover how to leverage the line's containment ability by then or know how to extract Devourer toxins once we do get the taint contained." Cian sighed miserably. "We're on a doomsday path to that stopper failing and the toxins spreading to the entire collective."

"That's why there's always a Plan B." Tobek leaned on the arm of his chair. "This is your mission, so tell us what your fallback is."

Cian started many sentences. Finished none. His floundering

was cute, painful, but cute in that hard-lessons-always-involve-humiliation way. After being schooled by her brothers, Bix empathized.

"May I make a suggestion?" she whispered to the kid.

"God, please take charge. This team leader stuff is hard." Cian folded his arms on the table and planted his face in the crook of his elbow.

Everyone at the table nodded and quietly laughed. They'd all been in a leadership role at some point or another.

"We have three different issues. The first, Devourer taint in the ley line. Whether it's containment, an antidote, or both, Cian, you and David should stay on that. Going to be needed regardless. We will not give up Resen without a fight, got it?" Bix paused for the nod from David and a thumbs-up from Cian. "Second, the Devourers in the core. Feng will calm the line while I remove the Devourers."

"Happily." Feng bowed from the shoulders.

"Third, Ariel's imminent demise." Bix paused at the gasps of surprise. "If the pantheons' assassins don't get her for treason or the Devourers for exposing their base, there's a Mid World guardian who nearly took her wings in their last meeting and is eager to finish the job. We need her alive for the sake of Resen."

Samael cupped his ear and leaned forward. "What was that? Especially the part about her wings?"

"In front of a camp of Devourers, no less." Bix wrinkled her nose as he swore. An archangel's wings contained untold power, and if the Devourers ever figured out how to use that power... "Team, we need to keep her alive and away from her World while Feng and I do our thing."

"That's a big ask," Samael harrumphed. "The coup d'état hasn't happened yet. She's still Chair of the Consortium with enough allies to keep her there. *We* may know, understand, and act on all the evidence before us, but the Consortium will not. Remember, anything you're involved in, Chimera, the Consortium thinks *you* caused. When it comes to Devourers, you're automatically implicated. For better or worse."

"Guarantee that's the story she's peddling to her peers right now," Feng grumbled. "The pantheons might have all the proof they need that *Ariel* is the one behind the downfall, but the other three races? Much harder sell. Those inclined to believe the gods? They don't favor a leadership change during crises. The smart ones know the vacuum will destabilize any defensive response to the invasion. They think they know how to work around her."

"The devil you know," Hywl muttered.

"Her crimes are so extreme that no one *wants* to believe her guilt because then they have to admit they were fooled by her bullshit." Samael widened his stance. "We're dealing with the arrogance of superpowers here. Their faces have to be rubbed in the excrement of her mess before they'll concede they might've been wrong and the Chimera was right."

"If a shitstorm will accelerate a coup, think I can help with that." Ashtad grinned and glanced at the Berserkers on either side of him. "The Berserkers are still under investigation for raiding local governments and stealing stuff, right?"

Hywl opened his mouth, but Runjit beat him to it with a succinct "Yes."

"I'll round up some demis, some spooks, and some illusionists from the Crimson Market. If we can borrow some of your choir, Samael, we could do unto the Chair's personal guards as the Devourers have done unto our fearless soldiers. We'll glamour ourselves as the Consortium's elite and stage a slew of raids." Ashtad thumped his cane. "There are high-profile places anyone wanting to hold on to political power simply can't ignore, especially when they're implicated in the destruction."

The Berserkers agreed a little too eagerly.

Feng sucked air through his teeth. "She fired her personal guards. That's Consortium speak for executed them."

"Did she, though?" Ashtad put a finger to his lips and cocked his head. "Did she? Or did she task them to nefarious deeds and only *told* the gossips she'd fired them? After all, who would question the Chair of the Consortium?"

"One way or the other, gods ended up with the souls—thus the knowledge—of those she executed. If they don't out your scheme, we'll know for sure the pantheons are rallying against Ariel," Feng reluctantly admitted.

"You're a devious bastard, Ba'al," Samael declared approvingly. "Can't guarantee it'll keep her out of her World, but she'll effectively surrender her authority if she doesn't respond personally to the upset. I've got a few surprises I can add to encourage her participation. Consider my whole choir in."

Tobek chuckled and nodded. "I like it. Count me in too."

Bix looked to Ashtad, wondering if he'd take the risk of the Great White Paperweight. Her old boss gave her a wink and a nod.

"Okay, then, Feng, you're stuck with me." Bix raked her nails over her palms. "Once we get confirmation from the guys that Ariel's tangled in their traps, we're going to purge the Devourers from her World. If we're successful, it'll buy these scientists some time."

"If you're not, the collective will be infected in less than seventy-two hours," Cian cautioned. "Good luck, everyone."

CHAPTER 18

"We didn't want to expose Chief's weakness in case it turns out to be permanent. None of us wanted that data on file anywhere to be used against him at some point in the future."

Bix eyeballed Feng in his preppy professor ensemble as they loitered in the outer atmosphere of Ariel's World, waiting for the comm chirp that would confirm the archangel's location. "I respect that. He wouldn't, though. If understanding any of his weird could save the Mids, he'd slap the details on billboards. That's just the guy he is."

"That's why none of us told *him* he was blacking out and turning into a block of ice." Feng huffed through a smirk. "It's more than respect his men have for him. It's something kings and creators of all stripes covet. Beyond unshakable loyalty, but never so blind as zealotry. It's a remarkable feat, an enviable one."

"He's had a long time to perfect how he leads. Long time. Long, long, long time." She knocked Feng's elbow. "Pretty sure there are some dumpster fires in his past that keep him humble."

"That's what makes it even more extraordinary. They know he messes up. They know he's not always right, that he's fallible, and still they follow without quibble or resentment." Feng raked his hand through his hair; the strands fell in perfect feathered layers. "Runjit was the first to voice it, withholding the truth from him for a short while. That Berserker must be Chief's fiercest protector, yet he didn't have to sell his case to his brethren. Everyone instantly agreed. Cian included."

"I'm surprised Gurp went along with it." Bix refrained from mentioning she'd already let the ice cat out of the bag. Firstly, she hadn't known they were trying to keep it a secret. Secondly, she wouldn't have agreed to do so. Tobek needed to be clued into every detail of his evolution so he could decide what was important and what wasn't. It sucked when folks around you knew your weird, but you didn't. Personal experience speaking there.

"Everyone but the goblin agreed, I should say. Unified effort to keep the two separated." Feng laughed. "I get why you like being around that fraternity. We're greater entities, you and I. Our place is on the outside. We look up and see the shitstorms. We look down and see the struggle. But if we look to them, we see the value."

"Ariel's left her chambers, full fury," Samael's voice cut across the comm clipped to Bix's ear. "Coming your way, Ba'al, in five, four, three—"

"Got her," Ashtad whispered. "Delousing's a go."

"Delousing's a go," Bix confirmed. She removed her comm and tossed it through a tiny gate to the stash she kept at home. "To reiterate, Feng, your sole purpose is to reassure the line. It'll no doubt feel like I'm trying to kill it and its World. At the very least, it'll feel like extreme torture. I will have to leave it in that state of dangerous and complete imbalance to ensure the Devourers are truly gone. I'll fix it though. But if the line attacks me, I'll instinctively respond, and not in its favor. Mentally, I can only focus on the one task. Even then, success will be dicey."

"I will stay in and with the line until balance is restored," he vowed. "What about the Devourer blood you're going to spill? Can you keep it from the roots?"

"If this works as I plan, no blood will be spilled."

"Famous last words." Feng expanded into his native state of the Phoenix sans flames. "If you need me at all, touch a root or call my name. I'll come running."

"Thanks."

"Wish there was more I could do to help." He mocked a salute. "See you on the other side."

Bix dissolved into her native state and reached from one atom of darkness to one cavern of diffused light. The line's earlier defense of Ariel had left notable damage to the core. Large chrysalises were scant, yet the buds of new pupae abounded. Stalactites and stalagmites had fallen, shattered, or been turned to golems that had collapsed to form hills that blocked lines of sight. Ill and injured Devourers had been herded into one section of the core, while their healthy counterparts hustled to and fro, carrying weapons and gear as if prepping for a mission. Scorch marks where Ariel's gate had been told of the demise of the true Consortium guards. The archangel hadn't bothered to save her own troops. Ariel had probably never intended to bring them back across the gate. More sacrifices for the amusements of the enemy and no witnesses to her perfidy. Why, though? Why align with the enemy? Sure, being tricked in the beginning, before witnessing the devastation Devourers brought to the Mids and to angels specifically, was totally understandable for a myopic power-hungry poohbah. But after? Even if they had her over a barrel, Ariel could've made the problem go away. She had the capital to pay any price.

Motive. The only motive Bix could imagine was that Ariel wasn't right in the head. That the sickness of her World and line was eating at the archangel's brain. It was way out there as far as motives went, but it was the only one that fit.

A group of Devourers hauling technology of some sort stopped below Bix, looking up and around. A sharp trill erupted from the one staring bug-eyed at her slowly spreading amorphous form. One trill became a hundred, and if it ever made it to a thousand, she didn't know. Gates worked in tandem with tentacles, sweeping the anti-gods and their technology from the core. They hacked at her with weapons and blasted her with magic, but she was as insubstantial as she was effective. In deference to her meal plan, she dumped the Devourers in the ether, where their greater army was exploiting the vast nothingness as a staging area. Admittedly, the ether was immeasurable. If she got them close to their army was anyone's guess, but they had built-in trackers. They'd find each other…maybe. Regardless, if they died in the ether, they died outside the Mids, which should mean they wouldn't regrow in this hive.

Next, she expanded her footprint until she filled every divot, dome, and pit, every crack and crevasse of the core. Careful to keep a hair's distance from the line and its network of roots, she let the line adjust to her greater presence. She didn't know if it would thank her or fight her at this point, but if it was at all possible for it to brace itself, she owed it the chance.

Roots flashed in asynchronous patterns much like the crystals of Cian's shoulders. Wouldn't it be a riot if the line was trying to talk to her? Her? Its cosmic boogeyman? Then again, the line had used the brightness of the roots to acknowledge her before. Oh hell. Could it be? No. Not her. It would've told Feng if it had something to share. Right? Sure. Focus. No distractions allowed for what she was about to do. Try to do. Do. Confidence. Yep. She could do this.

"Be brave, line," she whispered. "I need you to be brave for both our sakes. I'll do my best not to hurt you, but I can't avoid scaring you. I'm sorry about that."

The fluttering of the lights flashed seven times in unison.

"For the love of my sisters' creations, we can do this. We can. We can and we will."

Verifying one last time that no one beyond the budding pupae and the ley line was in the core with her, Bix set her mind to draining order. It started with her barriers of malice, with the thorns and brambles, the twists and knots, the complex weave caging that which aligned her with the ultimate entity of order, structure, and exclusion. Her father, the Cosmos.

She didn't need her instinct to fight for her survival. It had to stand ever ready, but not fight. Not her, not now. She needed the clarity of order. The surety of structure. The precision of exclusion. She needed the nascent, the frightened, the stunted light within her to grow beyond her. To seek out its likeness in the World. Unnecessary senses went dormant to give all her attention to the task at hand. Parking her emotions and forsaking all notions of time, she exhaled from lungs that didn't exist, causing a ripple along her darkness that peeled back the first layer of malice. Again, she inhaled focus and breathed out distraction. Ripple by shudder, the thorns protecting her loosened. A tendril of instinct unraveled here, a vine of hate uncurled there, until slowly, ever so slowly, the petals of fragile order opened. Light spilled forth on rays finer than spiders' silk to pierce soil and pupae.

The order born of Devourers was the easiest to locate and cull, as it was the most familiar. Then she went after the order of the planetary god who'd created the core. That was harder, much harder, but not impossible. Hunting it was akin to hunting the parts of her father within Eko. She could do it. She could. She had and so she would. As she sorted and siphoned, surrounded by the ancient fabrication of the planetary god, the identity of the creator made itself known. She tucked away that information for later, when her focus could afford to be divided. For now, concentrating on the elusive and rare within the core was paramount.

Eventually, she finished with the creation of the divine and pressed outward from the core, into the sacred soil of the root World, ever mindful of the ley line and its bountiful presence. Oh, how order abounded on the World. It thrived in the echo of the dragon queen long dead, in the ground she'd terraformed and the rivers she'd carved. It was in the plants that'd drunk the nutrients of soil and water. It was in the structures mined from the minerals she'd made. Absorbing them was like drinking clarity, and Bix had a desperate thirst. Consuming the order of the World forced the flowers of Bix's order to propagate, to grow along the shoots of malice, to blossom between the protections of thorny instinct.

To find balance.

Alas, resources were limited even in a root World. The glut waned to scarcity, upping the complexity of the challenges. Still, Bix persisted. Her light pushed clear of the soil and scoured the air, the territory of chaos and welcome. It examined spores caught on breezes and grains churned by the line. It explored particles microscopes couldn't detect while expanding to the farthest arcs of the atmosphere.

There was an echo in her chest. No, a tempo. A song. Songs belonged to Music. Music was order. Music was the daughter aligned with the Cosmos. Music was a creator of the Mids who also lived in the magic that pushed Tobek through evolutions. It took precious moments to sort that it was Tobek's song playing through the piece of him Bix kept near her heart when she was corporeal and protected by darkness while she was less than ethereal. It wasn't a symptom of excess or a message from her sister. It was Tobek, pulling on their connection. He banged quite the rambunctious beat, a distracting rhythm, to be honest. A distraction she…could afford now that the soil and skies were clear. She'd double-check her work, of course, but the proof of success would be in the Devourer pupae dying off now that they had nothing on which to feed.

The lights of her order bent and bowed on their way back to her. They paused above the surface of the World. The damage she'd wrought upon the ley line by starving its roots of necessary nutrients showed in the sputtering of power and in the myriad ropes of magic peeling from the main line to flail madly and tangle in great mats. Chaos dominated. Feng, in fully fiery form, soared up and down the line like a firefly in a bendy straw, trying his damnedest to soothe and comfort.

Her heart panged. Tobek's song turned erratic in response. Odd.

Without a concept of time, Bix had no idea how long the ley line had acquiesced to her thievery nor how long Feng had been burning. Her lights continued their journey home, retracing paths through the World, verifying the purity of chaos. When they folded back into her greater state, they did not hide within the malice of instinct. They wove the finest sheaths around the brambles and thickets, protecting them as their thorns protected the flowers.

Cosmic balance.

She shrank her form, pulling shadows and light from the farthest recesses of the core while marveling at the sensations awakened within her newly balanced state. As she passed, shriveled pupae broke from the roots of the ley line, tumbling and bouncing like little acorns into gates that scattered them across the ether. Sighing wearily with the sweet, sweet satisfaction of success, she assumed a form half feminine but not of flesh. Her full suite of senses reengaged. Her emotions rose from quarantine. A long indulgent stretch and all parts light and dark slid into proper alignment for a body infinitely more compact.

"Behold, my esteemed peers of the Consortium, the Chimera herself," a smug feminine voice announced, "destabilizing *my* home World in yet another sickening ploy to paint me the villain of her actions."

CHAPTER 19

Fates, dragons, angels, and gods assembled in the core of Ariel's home World, taking humanoid form and size. Curved mahogany stands with elaborate carvings manifested in a massive ring surrounding the tainted ley line lakes. The representatives took their seats in the mimicry of the Consortium's courtroom. At the center, Archangel Ariel levitated between the lakes, wings tucked away.

Had Bix been corporeal, her unexpected audience might have seen her guts clench and knees weaken. Vivid, cloying memories of her farcical trial a decade ago clogged her mind and scattered all sense of accomplishment and confidence. The chill of nausea rippled through her as Ariel's self-satisfied chuckle echoed through the core.

"I believe it was a human who famously said to accuse your enemy of that of which you are guilty. The Chimera has done quite the job of that lately." Ariel raked her cold black eyes over Bix, contempt arching her brow and disgust curling her thin lips.

Bix hung her head, fighting panic, and beheld her own body, a body she recognized only from Tobek's drawings. Teeny pinpricks of light made moving patterns in her darkness. Shades of bronze and gold, of pewter and platinum, flowed through her, revealing the presence of order no longer starved and repressed. Tobek. Her rock no matter what may come. Thinking of him calmed her, steadying her thoughts. She placed a hand over the erratic thumping of her Eternal Knot.

It wasn't a song. It was a summons. Something was wrong.

Fuck. She had no idea how long she'd been playing World surgeon, so she had no idea if Tobek was still antagonizing political hot spots or if he was at Cian's…or with the scientists, or with his battalion, or at any number of other places a grown-ass man might go. Ariel being here instead of at one of Ashtad's raids was a sign either the guys had failed or that shit had already hit the fan and this was the fallout.

Damn it.

She couldn't leave, not now. Not with the entire freaking Consortium staring her down in this…this impromptu trial. Probably all part of Ariel's plan to keep Bix tied up while the guys faced off against the Devourers.

Damn it, again.

"We exiled the Chimera for treason," the Chair of the Consortium continued, pivoting slowly as she addressed her vaunted audience. "She wormed her way back by fooling those desperate to believe she would save us from an enemy who had yet to appear. An enemy who didn't set one foot in our Worlds until *she* was back in the Mids. Curious timing, isn't it?"

Bix's instinct wanted to rip the archangel's pernicious tongue out of her head. Bix's sheaths of order bid her to wait, to watch, to remember who held the true authority here. The Chair of the Consortium was an elected position. If a three-quarter majority lost confidence in Ariel's leadership, they could vote her out. A bloody coup wouldn't be necessary, which would minimize the damage to domestic defenses a typical change in leadership caused.

"Since her return, she has led disinformation campaigns targeted at each of our races that have cost the lives of respected peers." Ariel folded her hands in front of her, a pious stance for such inflammatory lies. "And now, as we teeter on the brink of launching our own Mids-made defense system, she is here actively trying to destabilize it, to break it, to leave us utterly dependent on her mercy."

Just how gullible, how willfully stupid, did Ariel think her peers were? Yes, the best lies threaded close to the truth. Yes, Bix and her team had exposed traitors, which sometimes had led to their execution, but her highest body count had been in support of Resen. Ariel was guilty of the crimes she spewed, and the archangel was so blinded by arrogance, she chose to hold this trial right in the middle of a ley line so tainted by Devourer ick, it lingered on the surfaces like oil spills. The Fates and gods might not get the relevance, but the dragon queens and the other archangels sure as hell should. The gods didn't need to spot the slicks to know Ariel's guilt. They had multiple witnesses—living and dead—along with tangible proof of Ariel's involvement with the Devourers. Of course, the pantheons could do as they'd done in the last trial and get their petty revenge on the cosmic entity they viewed as a bogeyman. Gods were capricious and vindictive, but they also liked to eat and be worshipped. For that last part, they needed the Mids. If they thought they could save the Mids without Bix, the evidence wouldn't matter. Which way would they go? Coin toss.

As for the Fates, they'd seen shit coming before half the Consortium was born. They arranged for evidence to be discovered as often as they arranged for bad guys to have their heyday. Again, coin toss. The archangels likely sided with their sister for the sake of face and family, which left the dragons. The majority disliked Bix; then again, the majority despised Ariel. The queens and their courts had seen Devourers in action, and they'd ruthlessly exterminated traitors from their inner circles. On the other hand, they'd gone along with Ariel's circus before. No certainties there.

Bix really didn't have the time for any of their chest puffing and pontificating. Whatever had Tobek calling to her was more important. Locating Tobek simply required her to ping the displaced piece of herself he kept above his heart, yet as his summons continued to thunder within her, the blossoms of order held her in place.

Not yet. He had to wait. For the sake of the mortals for whom they cared and who were trying to step up where the Consortium had failed to step in, he had to wait and she had to endure. The Consortium could end the mortals as quickly as she could end Ariel. No one would gain anything, the Mids would still be in jeopardy, and this World and its ley line wouldn't heal.

Man, she really hated being an adult sometimes.

"Even now, she holds her silence. No rebuttal, no denial, no regard for the republic that *we* built. Look at her." Ariel pointed one long finger at Bix. "She disdains us. To her, we are nothing of consequence. We are puppets to be manipulated, then discarded. When she is at last amused, *she* will end our Worlds. Our kingdoms. Our homes. Reach out with your magics, right now, and touch my World. Feel what her hunger has done to it."

Ariel's opening gambit at the last trial had been to shatter Bix's knees to demonstrate that Bix couldn't retaliate. Waterboarding had come next. When Bix hadn't used gates to escape, Ariel had taken it as a green light to level up the public persecution and humiliation. Ariel hadn't grokked the reason Bix had stayed was to endure the agonies she'd believed she'd deserved. Bix had led her team of covert agents on a mission, and they'd all died. All but her. She was the immortal one. So at that last trial, Bix hadn't spoken up in her own defense because she'd *wanted* to be punished. It'd taken her years starving in exile to reason out her why and wherefore, but that was then.

Now, with experience balancing instinct, Bix could extract herself from Ariel's machinations and see them for what they were. Fear. Ariel had dragged the entire voting membership of the Consortium to this confrontation not as witnesses or judges, but as backup. Ariel knew Bix could end her in a blink, so this inevitable altercation was never going to be about magics, brute strength, or any kind of physical set-to. Ariel's power lay in her influence over others. Political power. Ariel would be a fool not to use it.

Bix could respect that. She didn't like it, but she respected it.

"I call on you, my friends, my allies, my fellows in serving and protecting these our Worlds, to banish once and for all this enemy of our very existence," Ariel cried with an orator's best emulation of fire and brimstone, magic churning a breeze to amplify the echo. "Condemn this entity of hate, this divider of loyalties, this traitor who brought anti-gods to destroy our Worlds. I call on, no, I *demand*, she be exiled for eternity and all her associates executed forthwith. Cast your votes now."

That crazy ultimatum was the reason Bix had stayed instead of answering Tobek's urgent call. If she'd left, it would've looked like she was fleeing the Consortium's judgment. Any allies she might've earned over the past year of busting her ass for the greater good would've been outnumbered and overruled. Cowardice was easy when there was no one to call you on it.

Scanning the members of the Consortium, Bix gauged their responses. Yes, she could fight back, refute Ariel's insinuations, and leverage the ingrained trepidation everyone here had for her now that she appeared as they expected the Chimera to appear. However, as Cian and Ashtad had warned at the start of this mission, if she took down the elected leader of the Mids, she would be asserting herself as the new leadership. Not it. No. That never was her goal. That never played to her desires. The Mids were her sisters' creation. The Consortium the caretakers. Bix didn't want to rule, but she wouldn't be a junkyard dog either.

Meat Loaf sang it best: she would do anything for love, but she wouldn't do that.

The Consortium had not only made this mess, they'd prolonged and compounded it. It was theirs to clean up. Bix had repeatedly given them opportunities to fix their shit. She'd empowered them in every way conceivable to fight the foreign invasion, from the ether that served as a cosmic moat to the Resen defense system. This domestic problem was wholly theirs. Ariel had kicked the ball into the court of her peers, confident their fears aligned with hers under the banner of cross-World security and independence. They knew full well what had to be done. How would they play?

Muttering. Mumbling. All indecipherable.

"The Houses of Fate wish to address the Consortium."

Ariel swung around to the collective of erstwhile humans missing an arm, a leg, a foot, or an eye—all a price for controlling destiny. The archangel's black eyes narrowed. "It is your right. Do you wish to enter your vote?"

"We do."

Every Fate in the Consortium left their seats and marched down the risers to crouch along the veins of the ley line. The Fates set two fingers to the line and two fingers on the soil. Green eyes of every shade glowed. Threads in the colors of rainbows grew from their palms to weave a massive tapestry in front of Ariel. Its edges extended to the lakes, where tiny curls of unstable magic made the weaving spin. An image built within the movement of threads. A picture of Ariel in front of a programmable gate. Her personal guards at her flanks. The delivery of three Mid World Guardians. The acceptance by the Devourer general. The scene played out in full damning sound. The captured gods fighting to get free of the shackles forged by the anti-gods. Ariel pinning them to the stalagmites, the struggle of the Devourers to reach their prey.

"Lies," Ariel keened, releasing a bolt of angel fire at the weave. It caused the image to change, but not burn. This time, the image displayed her chambers inside the Consortium. She was surrounded by Devourers in their pristine uniforms, directing them to attack Samael at the Crimson Market. The Devourers shifted shapes to appear as Consortium guards, and off they went through Ariel's official gate.

"The Houses of Fate vote nay," the Fates announced as one.

Stunned, Bix inclined her head at the Fates as they reclaimed their seats. One or two deigned to respond in kind.

"The pantheons wish to address the Consortium." It was an indolent drawl underscored by steel that came from an eternally handsome river god who was not among Bix's fan club.

Ariel's features lit. The gods and the Fates were adversaries of old. Then again, the gods had always been their own worst enemies, so a unified vote was unlikely.

"The Chair will hear your vote," Ariel sniped with all the haughtiness of her position.

Gods, to a one, stood. Bursts of Mid World magic preceded the arrival of four Mid World guardians, all of whom had escaped the Devourers. Each of the former prisoners raised their left hands, fists closed.

"What sort of statement is this?" Ariel demanded. "Who are these nonmembers?"

Ariel's victims opened their hands. Brown feathers painted in the ichor of the gods or the blood of the anti-gods fell to the subtle drafts rising from the angelic representatives. The breezes carried the evidence through the stands for the scrutiny of the voting members.

"How *dare* you," Ariel hissed, unfurling her wings and lurching at her victims before recalling her audience.

"The pantheons vote nay," the river god proclaimed.

In unison, the gods sat. Not a one stepped out of line. Bix choked back a gurgle of disbelief. Instead, she inclined her head at the gods just as she had done with the Fates. Gods aplenty returned the gesture. Well, hell, this trial was just full of surprises.

"The Dragon Horde wishes to address the Consortium." The reigning queen of the dragons stood, her sister queens and their enforcers stoic in their protective stances around her.

"No, denied," Ariel sniped. "I will have my rebuttal to these spurious accusations."

The intricate swirls of plums, grapes, and lavenders brightened in the ebony skin of every dragon in attendance. Oh, this could get ugly. Nemeses by nature and enflamed by circumstances, the dragons and the angels could obliterate the core without much effort. This poor World couldn't survive their clashing, not as out of whack as it currently was. Bix readied to toss them all out on their keisters.

"A point of order."

That sharp outburst came from the least expected contingent. Archangel Michael, leader of the Angelic Host's army and actively on the front lines in the war against the Devourers. He'd lost numerous members of his choir to the appetites of the Devourers; he was second only to Samael in understanding precisely the dangers of the anti-gods.

"The Chair has called for a vote. The time for prosecution and defense is over. *All* votes must be heard and counted before moving on to the next issue." Michael stared pointedly at his sister.

Ariel countered her brother's stare, but he didn't bother to blink, much less look remotely flummoxed. At length, Ariel straightened and folded her wings back. "The Chair will hear the Dragon Horde's vote."

The six queens extended their hands, palms up. Smoky wisps of purple magic streamed from their hands and connected with the lakes. The lakes flashed brilliant blues as currents formed lavender whitecaps amid the stains of Devourer gunk. Guttural hisses and growls reverberated from bodies much too small for the sounds as the queens disengaged from the ley line.

"The Horde votes nay," the reigning queen said with a distinct chill in her tone.

Ariel mouthed the queen's words, nostrils flaring and jaw jutting as she turned her ire on Bix. Bix was enthralled watching the mighty Chair being dethroned before her, so no way was she going to open her yap. Apparently, Ariel's political rivals had been busy setting all this up. Sure, put the Chimera on trial again. Sure, that'd end well...for luring Ariel to her downfall. It was brilliant, and Bix didn't mind one iota being bait in this maneuver. Let the glare of a thousand daggers proceed. Ariel had already been overruled by simple majority. Would her family back her? Would they stand with her even though she was the guilty party? Inquiring minds really wanted to know.

"How does the Angelic Host vote?" Ariel asked through clenched teeth, her rage still focused on Bix.

"We vote nay," Michael said flatly. No dramatic shows of evidence. No countering demonstrations of innocence. Just one succinct statement. A statement that visibly infuriated their sister.

"Unanimous, is it?" Ariel dug her nails into her palms until blood welled. "Let the record show these feckless cowards, blind to the true enemy of our collective, have voted unanimously to keep the Chimera and her little friends alive and well in the Mids."

"I put a motion to the floor." Michael sighed, waiting until Ariel flapped a hand in his general direction. "I motion for Archangel Ariel, Chair of the Consortium, to be removed immediately from her position and remanded to the custody of the Angelic Host on the grounds of insanity."

"What?" Ariel shrieked, ripping her attention from Bix as representatives of every race surged to their feet, shouting, "Seconded."

Bix curled a finger of darkness over lips that didn't exist, sending gales of laughter through her connection to Tobek as beautiful chaos erupted within the Consortium. Members yelled over one another, insisting on an immediate vote to remove the Chair. Some argued for the execution of Ariel in addition to removal from power. Some voiced that Bix should be the one to execute the soon-to-be-former Chair. Some…

Tobek. Shit.

Bix reached for him but didn't have to reach far.

A Devourer portal opened in the core. Covered in blood both tarry and crimson, Tobek stood on the threshold as the sounds of a brutal skirmish tumbled around him. He raised his arm and took aim at the cluster of archangels furiously trying to contain their treasonous sister. Gray magic built around his arm.

Gray, not green.

"We have been betrayed," Tobek yelled in a voice that was a dissonant mockery of his bass-baritone gravel. "Traitors must d—"

Tobek gagged on his last word. Black liquid tumbled from his parted lips, staining his beard and combat uniform. His blue eyes widened and looked down at his chest.

A fist of bright green magic protruded from his abdomen, clutching organs gray and foreign. Hair once blond turned black, revealing a crown of pewter horns. Flesh, once pale, darkened. His black-and-brown fatigues brightened to metallic bronze as the Devourer shed his disguise. A surge of deep green magic illuminated the Devourer inside and out. Two beats later, the anti-god exploded.

Tobek, the true and actual, wiped spatter from his blistering cheek. The floodlights of his Berserker's rage tinted his green magic teal. He held up his glowing hand and waved it forward. Berserkers in worse states of blisters and bleeding advanced around him into the core.

"Cover Ariel," Tobek barked, "Tjinimin is coming for her."

On the surface of a ley line lake, a cloud of shadows took form.

The sonic cry of the bat god silenced the Consortium.

CHAPTER 20

Half man, half bat, Tjinimin strode around the heart of the core, eyeing every dragon, god, and Fate as they drifted back to their seats, faces alight with astonishment and curiosity. Experiencing the unexpected for the long-lived and immortal was priceless, possibly the only thing more valuable than power. This session of the Consortium had just deviated sharply from the plan, even the future-seeing Fates seemed surprised. Only the archangels remained at the center to shield Ariel from the bat god, while also preventing their sister's escape.

The butt of Tjinimin's spear slammed into the mud with each of his heavy steps, dripping tarry black blood that caused blisters to rise and ooze over his hand. Tjinimin bore the same physical evidence of having battled Devourers as Tobek and the Berserkers. From the looks of things, Tobek had found the anti-gods who'd been impersonating his men, but how Tjinimin fit into that was…probably important, but not as important as the Consortium taking the final vote to oust Ariel from her seat.

Alas, a motion was not a vote. It was the step *before* the official vote that would end Ariel's political career. The Consortium was so close to closing the deal that Tjinimin's timing couldn't have been worse. Even a monofilament of wiggle room in procedure would be enough for Ariel to keep her seat, because every member of the Consortium was a hawk about details and loopholes. They'd been fucking over people with the fine print for millions of years. The vote *had* to be taken, now.

Bix could remove Tjinimin and let things proceed. Yet if she did, would that be the crack through which Ariel kept her position? Would trying to keep the meeting on track backfire? If Bix were anyone but the Consortium's favorite punching bag, maybe not. Bix looked to Tobek and his men, pondering the risk of doing what instinct demanded but order cautioned against. The Berserkers stood at attention in the breaks between the risers, ready to act, but holding fast, deferential to the greater powers to whom they officially reported.

Tobek caught her eye and gave a slight shake of his head. As much as he hated politics, he was better at the game than she was, so she followed his lead and waited, hoping Ariel's sickly ley line would abide too.

"Where are they?" the bat god demanded of Ariel. The long scar curving over his flattened, crooked nose made his congested demand nigh on unintelligible.

"Get away from me, vermin," Ariel spat, pumping her wings in a vain attempt to break free of her kin.

Tjinimin flicked his wrist, and shadows backhanded the not yet fully overthrown Chair of the Consortium. The lakes rippled, but the ley line didn't defend its archangel.

Archangel Michael inserted himself between Ariel and Tjinimin. "Friend, I don't know your issue, but you are interrupting an official meeting of the Consortium."

Tjinimin's leathery wings flared. Michael's feathered arches burst from his back. The bat god's wing claws clutched at the air. Michael's wing claws peeked out from his amber-and-black feathers. Tjinimin's diaphragm visibly tightened and his chin went up. The bat's mouth opened wide.

An iron arrow pierced Tjinimin's throat, silencing the dawning sonic scream.

"Damn it, Batty," boomed a buzz-cut, auburn-haired god in the combat uniform of the Berserkers. He stood in the mirrored surface of the Devourer portal, nocking another arrow in his longbow. The moment he stepped through, the portal winked shut, stranding Tobek and his men in the core. Unfazed, the Berserkers parted to allow the archer into the center of the Consortium's traveling courtroom. "How many times do I have to tell you, mate? You are not the Chimera. You think you are because some cockwomble put it in your head after they stole your marbles."

Whispers and murmurs ricocheted through the representatives unwilling to miss a moment of the drama.

"Moccus," Ariel seethed. "She husked you. I saw it. She took everything from you."

"Not everything, Ariel. Not enough to wipe my memories of what you did to me, to us, to every Mid World guardian you arrested under false pretenses, then fed to the Devourers." Moccus the Celtic boar in his human form, or rather the draugr occupying Moccus, stopped behind Tjinimin and popped his knees into the bat god's, forcing Tjinimin to kneel.

Bix had to give Drew credit. Drew had said he'd keep an eye on Tobek in case Tjinimin went after her Berserker. Clearly, her bestie had been right about Tjinimin's plans. Whether it'd been Drew or Tobek who'd decided to leverage Tjinimin's Chimera delusion to take down the Devourers impersonating the Berserkers, Bix couldn't say. Either way, adding two armed gods with a need to right some wrongs into the mix had been brilliant on many levels.

At the moment, however, Tjinimin struggled to pull the arrow from his throat while choking on ichor. His wings prevented him from reaching behind himself to yank out the shaft. Only the tip of the arrowhead had punctured the front of his neck, not enough to grab. Drew's shot had been impeccable in aim and velocity. Drew was adept at many things, but that level of skill meant the draugr had tapped in to more than Moccus's divine ability to travel and shapeshift.

"How many?" Michael turned toward his sister. "How many guardians did you hand over to the enemy, Ariel?"

Ariel sneered a victorious smile but said nothing.

"Enough to destroy the last defenses of the Mids if Resen fails to launch." Drew planted a boot on Tjinimin's back and jerked the arrow from the bat god's throat. "My buddy here is understandably distraught, so if Ariel will give us the location of the other prisoners, we'll get the hell out of your official business."

Rumbles of support drifted from the section of gods bearing rapt witness to the exposure of Ariel's compounded sins.

"You're too late," Ariel hissed. "The secret network of the Mid World guardians? She's infiltrated. Your security? She knows. You'll never stop her or them."

Intrigued, Bix drifted closer to the confrontation. Who *was* this "she" to whom they were referring? Not the Devourer general. The planetary goddess? The one who'd created this World? "Them" had to be the Devourers, didn't it? Was this confirmation that her team's speculations about Ariel's fall into treason had been spot on?

Did it matter?

No, not for Ariel's future nor the goddess's. Complicity by choice or force didn't change the fact that Ariel and the goddess had paved the way for a Devourer general to enter the Mids, which meant they had access to the leadership of the Devourers. Bix wanted the names, the faces, the locations. She wanted every detail about the highest echelon who could call off the invasion of the Mids. She couldn't rip that intel from Ariel without killing the archangel, but she could take what she needed from a goddess.

To confirm the planetary goddess who'd made this World and Ariel's divine partner were one and the same without fear of lies or prevarications, Bix would have to pluck the identity from one of the goddess's divine victims. Drew was using Moccus to great effect, so that left the one god who'd retained enough wherewithal throughout his tortures to recognize the goddess. The same god who also stored Bix's memories.

Bix had to husk Tjinimin. Fully. Completely. She couldn't leave him with the disjointed memories of the original Chimera's extremely long life. He'd already suffered their agonies and was now fixated on Ariel and the goddess. It wasn't about revenge, contrary to what it might seem. Tjinimin was functioning as the Chimera, High Executioner for All Worlds. Ariel had committed irredeemable trespasses. In the eyes of the Chimera, Ariel had to die. The Chimera pretender couldn't rest until he completed his self-proclaimed order of execution. Bix had enough of her marbles to know that was among the pitfalls of her cosmic duty. Downside of husking Tjinimin? Doing so would lay her low for an indeterminate time while her memories sorted themselves. She still had a vote to witness, a team to return to base, a World to heal, and a ley line to restore.

Alas, the vote wouldn't happen as long as Tjinimin was conscious and therefore capable of attacking Ariel. Not even Drew in his borrowed body could stop the Chimera pretender forever. Tjinimin would keep coming back until the execution was successful. Gods didn't die, and no one but Bix could take the marbles that kept Tjinimin going.

Damn it.

"I thank you for confessing your additional guilt, Ariel." Drew didn't break eye contact with Michael as the draugr nocked the used arrow beside the first on the bow, aiming at the ground…for the moment. "Still need the location, though."

"Take your friend to rehabilitation," Michael murmured. "We'll get that answer and more for you."

Drew inhaled deeply, his weathered face wrinkling as he tipped his head. "Eh, you'll forgive our lack of tr—"

Tjinimin vanished in a plume of shadows.

"Cover Ariel," Tobek bellowed, leading his men into the center. "He's not gone."

Tjinimin reappeared, all monstrous bat, claws dragging down the torso of an archangel shielding Ariel with his body. The archangel screamed, and Tjinimin vanished again. Over and over, the bat god repeated the attacks, lingering no longer than a heartbeat to inflict maximum damage to anyone guarding Ariel—that included Michael and Drew.

Tobek and his men charged the skirmish, full Berserker rage glowing brightly in their eyes as they flanked left and right. Green-and-silver magic built around Tobek and connected with his men, forming a magical barrier around the circle of archangels. Tobek stepped squarely on the roots of the ley line, visibly drawing its tainted blues into his body and converting them to opaque deep greens that strengthened the defense.

Not a Consortium member beyond the Angelic Host moved from their seat. Some manifested bowls of popcorn and trays of hors d'oeuvres to be shared along their rows while others supplied drinks. They wouldn't have to vote out the treasonous Chair if she happened to die, ripped to shreds by a god she'd tormented. If the other archangels should be egregiously injured, there would be a power vacuum every bystander was eager to fill; the greater well-being of the Mids be damned in the name of short-term glory. Besides, who didn't love to see the mighty fall?

Tjinimin landed blows from above, shredding scalps and the feathered arches of archangels trying their damnedest to protect a sibling who in no way deserved it yet couldn't be allowed to die. Relentless attacks ensued before the bat finally drew Ariel's blood, two deep gashes from breast to temple. Ariel caterwauled. Her blood sprayed over her siblings and spattered on the ground.

The ley line absorbed the blood of its birth mate.

Pressure in the core built. Roots lining the walls, ceiling, and ground dimmed. The lakes darkened.

Bix's instinct threw open gates a blink before the full might of the furious ley line ripped through the core. Her particles of night and light blasted apart as unbalanced Mids' magic threw her out of the collective. Panic echoed in her thousands of displaced bits exploding like fireworks.

Bix had no breath to scream as her awareness fractured to follow her pieces scattering across the galaxy.

CHAPTER 21

Focus. Bix had to focus to stop the cloying panic. Allocating one piece of herself to function as a ground allowed her to form semicogent thoughts. The largest intact fragment was naturally the pocket of herself in which she kept the piece of Tobek. She fed her stalwart Berserker the emotions that overwhelmed her, yet received no response.

That couldn't be good.

Think. Think. Think.

She'd never forfeited pieces of herself before...except she had. Original her, that is. She'd done it with the piece of herself that Tobek carried, and she'd done it with the packets of her memories she'd embedded in select Mid World guardians. She would survive this cosmic mincing. It wasn't painful. It was discomfiting and incredibly perplexing, but not calamitous. The disorientation of too much information coming from her individual pieces was familiar. She experienced the same jarring deluge when she cast her many shadows to search vast spaces and cramped crevasses. There was no reason for worry. There was only cause for order. Organization. Process. A then B then C. Rebuild. Energy to essence to atom. Consciousness into starlight into midnight, fragments of herself reassembled until she was mostly whole.

Mostly.

Numerous parts of her were stuck in their disparate locales, repeating their confounding sensory experiences like vinyl hiccupping on a turntable. How was she supposed to get those bits unstuck? She tried yanking, commanding, cajoling, but nothing made those recalcitrant parts return to her. Damn it.

As much as she ought to figure out this newest personal issue, she had a far more pressing problem that demanded her return to Ariel's World. The continued existence of that World, that line, and all the lives tethered to them depended on her not giving in to the fear fluttering at the edges of her mind. She was immortal. This discombobulation wouldn't kill her, no matter how unpleasant it was.

She reached out to a mote of darkness in the core of Ariel's World, shedding pieces of herself as she traveled. Terror spiked. Again, she forced herself to focus and to rebuild her mass. Again, her pieces returned to her. Again, fewer than before. The lost pieces were stuck like the others in assorted locations and in loops of perceptions.

What the hell was wrong with her?

Better question, what the hell was wrong with Ariel's World?

Hundreds of strands of deep indigo from the splintered ley line draped complex tangles from lakes to walls, piercing anything that dared to linger. Air pressure remained too consistent. The aromas of mud, blood, and scorching power lay thick without cleansing breezes. A singular note, like the low pitch of a warbling handsaw, droned, an eerie hum of trapped magic.

In the place she had occupied during the trial, stood a void free of chaos. Contact with her cosmic essence had burned a perfect outline of her shape amid the line's splices.

"Oh, you poor frightened thing," she cooed softly to the line, mindful of the distance between them as concern for it erased the anxiety about her own condition. "You're not supposed to touch me, for *your* sake. This is why. Even the strongest bark will break when colliding against a stronger force. When the forces are equal, we both get hurt."

She'd never wanted to harm the line, but she'd been too focused on removing the Consortium and her team from its attack to spare a thought that she was as much a threat to the line as the line was to the lives of the mortals who'd been here.

Speaking of those mortals…

She searched the web of ley line strands for signs of life or death and found shimmering seams of partially closed gates gaping in the spaces where the Consortium's court had been. Wholly disturbing was Feng's fiery head and wings emerging from one of the lakes, flames frozen midflare. Good to know he'd sensed the disastrophy, even though he'd been too late.

Above a partially closed gate not far from Feng, impaled by no fewer than five threads of the line, hung Tjinimin. Red eyes wide, wings wider, and claws coated in Ariel's flowering blood, the bat god remained poised for the death blow.

Neither the bat nor the bird so much as blinked, much less breathed.

"You've got to be kidding me," Bix groaned as the obvious dawned.

Time. Everything around her was frozen in time.

Whatever had happened during the ley line's attack must have stopped time in the core. That was a logical supposition, right? After all, the four superpowers comprising the Consortium dictated the flow of time in the Mids. Something in the line's defense of Ariel in the presence of the Consortium must've arrested the flow of time. Bix and Feng could monkey with that flow when working together, but it required spilled blood or potent spells. The only thing more potent than the broken Chimera and the broken Phoenix collaborating was a broken ancient ley line. The ley line *had* booted her squarely out of the Mids, no question there. Perhaps it'd kicked her out of the Mids' timeline too?

Plausible. All she had to do was get back into the flow so she could fix the World and thereby fix the line. How? That was the great big gotcha. She knew full well time moved differently depending on where she was. Time in the Under Worlds moved differently from that of Phobos's World, which moved differently from that of the Mids, which moved differently from that of the Upper Worlds. Tracking those differences was second nature. Hopping from one timeline to the next was effortless.

Praying her gatekeeper magic hadn't been affected by her cosmic shedding, she opened viewing gates to various Worlds in assorted timelines. Nothing moved on those Worlds. Not the lightning on Phobos's World, not the river in the Greek Under World, not the blossoms in the Norse Upper World.

"I hope you're proud of yourself," she drawled to the ley line. "You kicked me out of all timelines, didn't you? Is that why my missing bits keep replaying the same moments? Because the bulk of me is out of time?"

What was she supposed to do when she didn't exist in any timeline? What was she supposed to do to get her recalcitrant bits and pieces to come back to her? And what, oh what, was she supposed to do to stop the ley line from repeating its attack once time restarted? She couldn't very well heal it if it kept kicking her out of the flow of progress.

Her attention drifted back to Tjinimin, keeper of her memories, possibly the memories that could help her unsticky herself and the memories of Ariel's divine accomplice in treason. She needed everything Tjinimin could offer for the sake of the Mids and more. Assimilating her lost marbles was never convenient for her, for her team, or for the mission, but if time in the Mids was frozen, maybe she had all the time in the Worlds.

Deploying carefully crafted gates, she removed the bat god from the broken ley line and opened a pair of gates to a place far from the Mids and hopefully far from any flow of time. If something went wrong while reclaiming her mind, only a greater power could help her while protecting the Mids from her.

All hail Instinct and Experience.

Who would've guessed one entity's prison would be another's sanctuary?

CHAPTER 22

"Eko?" Bix called, lugging her discombobulated self through the empty halls of her eldest brother's prison. The garnet tiles didn't direct her to him as they usually did, which didn't bode well for her whole existing-outside-of-time problem. "Esiw? Anyone home?"

Keeping Tjinimin in a box of gates that followed wherever she went, Bix peeked in doorways and peered down oubliettes. For a place that was a prison, Eko's home was awfully big. Not just tall and wide, but seemingly endless.

"Three?" she shouted this time, using the endearment. "It's me. I need your help."

Something wriggled on the wall. She took a closer look and gasped. The whole wall seemed like a bazillion magnified amoebas linked together by gossamer strands. She skimmed her fingers over the surface. The amoebas squished under her touch like gelatin and sent tiny shocks that made her inner starlight brighten.

Weird. She'd poked and prodded a lot of stuff in this place during her numerous visits, walls included. None of them had squished or shocked. Nope. If anything, the solid surfaces were super-duper solid and wholly inert. Was this something to do with being kicked out of time? Even here? If a cosmic prison existed outside of time, shouldn't she be in sync with it? Or was this some side effect of having bits that wouldn't come back to her? Or none of the above?

Something else to ask her brothers once she found them.

She continued her haphazard search, skirting laboratories and workshops filled with projects she didn't want to investigate too closely. Some of the things looked totally sketch and probably alive.

A winding passage opened to a jet rotunda. At its center, suspended by absolutely nothing, dangled a disturbingly huge hourglass. Gods and anti-gods as still as statues had been arranged like plastic soldiers atop and within black sands. Grains that should've tumbled, instead hovered midair. Bix tapped the glass with her fingertip, only to have her finger slide through. She jerked her hand back. The glass bore no evidence of her meddling. Because she was a glutton for punishment, she tried again. This time, her whole hand went through. She grabbed a fistful of sand and retreated. The glass remained unmarred and intact. The teeny divot of missing grains near the middle of the hourglass also remained. Sand didn't trickle to fix the displacement.

Definitely still outside time. Damn it. Upshot, she hadn't left a piece of herself in the hourglass. Whatever the rules of shedding like a Bernese mountain dog, it seemed to have limitations. Screwed level? Moderate.

"Eko?" She drifted away from the rotunda toward a place that whispered to her darkness. At first glance, it was a big black void stretching as far as she could see, but the closer she got, flecks of cherry red emerged. "Three? Three, it's me. I'm sorry to barge in on you."

The void spun in a great tornado at half shutter speed. Hope sparked within Bix. She gaped in awe, watching her brother compress his form in excruciating slow-mo. The massive minotaur opened his eyes. Red flames looked…right through her.

"Ugh. No. Are you kidding me?" She waved her empty hand in front of his face. Nothing. No reaction. At least he was capable of movement in whichever time he occupied but she didn't. Muttering nothing kind about time and its fucked-up fluidity, she used her darkness to lift his huge mitt. She dumped the pilfered black sand in his palm and waited. Waited. Waited some more. If this was what animators went through drawing movement frame by frame, it was a wonder they weren't stark raving mad.

There it was. Eko noticing the grit. Finally. She might've fallen asleep in the time it took his maw to open. If sound came out, it didn't touch her. Great. Not even her more powerful brother could join her out of time. Now what? She side-eyed the bat god in his cage of gates. No, she didn't dare extract her memories from Tjinimin. Not now. If he was stuck on Mids' time, what did that mean for the memories he held? And if she couldn't amass the bits of herself that weren't contained, what was to say she could reclaim her marbles from Tjinimin? Plus, the whole taking-back-her-memories thing was not pleasant for either party involved. Not the kind of experience she wanted dragging on and on and on.

Damn it. Think. Think. Think.

Light flashed. Bright netting firmly ensnared her and flung her forward. She slammed into unmovable mass with a squeak. Her lost bits pattered around her like a hailstorm before refitting themselves into her singular state.

"Got her," Eko crowed, cradling her against his chest. "I got her, Esiw. I got her."

Netting softened to starlight that blurred into fur as Esiw reclaimed the form of the white fox. Droll chastisement painted his vulpine features. "I haven't had to do that since Father put you in solitary, and you tried to manipulate time to hasten the end of your punishment. Disastrous then. Pitiful now."

"You can see me?" Bix giggled with relief, patting Eko's chest. "And I can hear you. Both of you. And you, biggest bro, are blessedly solid."

Eko threw back his head and laughed. It was a very loud sound, and she was very grateful to hear it.

"Little sister, you embraced the parts of you that belong to our father." Eko nudged her into his cupped hands. "Good for you."

"Accessing those abilities does not equate to controlling them, clearly." Esiw sniffed.

"Which of those abilities allows me to pass through solid objects without the use of gates? And which one is the one that makes me shed so badly, I can't put myself back together? The first one is useful. The second kind of terrifying." She cataloged her bits and pieces. All the parts with which she'd started her day were snugly home within her. Ah, and there was the warm reassurance from Tobek thrumming through the piece of him she nestled close to her figurative heart.

"Time, sister. The most rudimentary method of order is time." Esiw twitched his ears like semaphores. "When you recklessly removed yourself from the flow of one timeline without anchoring in another, your chaotic half reinserted you in different streams, thus making you stuck among many."

"I didn't kick me out of time. That was the damn ley line," she quibbled. "How do I stop it from doing that to me again?"

"The problem isn't with the ley line, it's with you," Esiw chided. "If you were whole and truly balanced, you could exist concurrently in infinite timelines moving at different speeds without issue. That feat was once second nature to you and your rapacious curiosity. Currently, however, your chaotic half still dominates, thus you are limited to one timeline."

"Wait, are you saying if I was wholly me again, I could travel *through* time? Backward? Forward? Round and round?" Bix asked, perking up. If she could do that, she could go back in time to when Ariel had first colluded with the planetary goddess and stop that from happening. Hell, she could go back to when the goddess had first colluded with the Devourers. Better still, she could go back to when she had doled out her marbles and stop that foolishness from becoming more than a passing thought.

Eko shook his head. "Moving ahead of time requires you to create."

"Lives, locations, events, time itself," Esiw chimed in, irksomely dour.

Bix's hopes were dashed. "And creating is something I cannot do."

"Architecting so others build for you? Yes, but such occurs as part of the flow of time. Creating on your own? No." Eko set her atop a long table covered in maps dotted in assorted colors. Six colors. Each a sibling's sacred hue.

Big bro was up to something, but she couldn't focus on that right now. She had more immediate concerns, like intentionally versus accidentally skipping through time. And healing Ariel's World. And healing Ariel's ley line. And getting Resen launched. And her team. And her marbles. Unless…

"Okay, I can't move ahead of time, but can I go backward?"

"If you want to effect an extinction event." Esiw leaned toward her, his nose a mere millimeter from inhaling her incorporeal state. "It's one of your more effective methods of execution. I say this with admiration and pride. Knocked Father back on his heels the first time you pulled that unexpected option from your arsenal."

"An extinction event?" she echoed, horror prickling through her even as she refused to give ground to brother know-it-all.

"As the two-in-one, the part of you that is Father allows you to move along an established path of order. However, the part of you that is Mother cannot abide the established order and thus destroys the path as you travel." Eko drew a line of red light in the air, then slashed his fingers through it, shredding it into motes of nothingness. "You may go back, but you cannot go forward because—"

"Because I'd have to recreate the future," Bix finished for him as disappointment let go of unobtainable possibility. "I destroy the present the moment I step backward. Each step back is a moment unlived for those in the timeline."

"No matter who is involved or how we may try, we can never recreate the past in perfection." Esiw flicked his four tails and cast a commiserating glance at his twin. "Mother never permits it."

"Chaos must live alongside order. True for me. True for all existence." Bix allowed the tumult of conflict to churn within her as intuition cautioned that her return to the flow of Eko's time meant time in the Mids was moving ahead as well. The fractured ley line's condition was deteriorating, Ariel's World teetering on collapse, and the Consortium… They'd better be taking the critical vote to impeach Ariel.

Bix should return forthwith to fix Ariel's World, but she was still vulnerable to the ley line punting her out of all timelines again. The best hope she had of fixing the line was to fix the World, and to do that, she had to fix herself. That meant reclaiming her lost memories. Oh, she wouldn't be balanced completely, not until she had *all* the remaining segments. Tjinimin had merely one of them; however, he also had firsthand knowledge of the goddess in cahoots with Ariel and the Devourers. A goddess who was breaking down the Mid World guardians' defenses even as Bix scrambled to get an alternate defense system up and running. The traitors' subversion could not, under any circumstance, be allowed to continue.

To finish the mission and get Resen ready for launch, Bix had had to level up in ability and knowledge, even if it meant taking herself offline for a while. Sometimes the cost of success was simply taking longer than convenient to complete the task.

"Eko, I need to reclaim another segment of my memories before things in the Mids worsen. Would you mind if I stayed with you while I recover from it?" Bix held her breath, not sure if she was choosing the right sanctuary. Unfortunately, as Esiw had pointed out, she could destroy Worlds. Plural. In her less-than-lucid state during a memory assimilation, she worried she could destroy the very collective she was trying to save by fumbling backward in time. Eko had his ticket to freedom to lose if the Mids were destroyed before the Devourers were evicted, so he had a vested interest in her getting her shit together sooner rather than later.

"Of course, little sister." Eko threw wide his mammoth arms.

"I am prepared for your needs. Choose where you wish to—"

"This is a prison, not a hotel," Esiw interjected. "Come, I will take you to my home where comfort is assured."

"Esiw, that is incredibly generous." Bix meant what she said, even as she died laughing inside while imagining his home as a pristine altar of order. "But I, uh, I make catastrophic messes. The kind that would ruin any semblance of cleanliness, organization, and sanity you have going on at your place."

"Big, big mess, huge," Eko somberly assured. "Uncontrollable. Destroys her room and herself. There's a toy that comes with it, but you can't play with the toy. She gets angry."

"Really?" Esiw's ears perked. "This I must see for myself."

"It's not a Vaudeville act," Bix opined.

"What if the history you recall grants you more access to the magics of order? What happens if you get trapped in time again, hmm? Maybe you need me to stick around." Esiw manifested a large golden pillow and sat, tails curling around his paws as he stared at her expectantly.

"He's not going to leave," Eko whispered loudly. "He never does when there's something new to learn."

"New?" She snorted. "As if I'm the first one of us to give up her marbles."

"No First Child has ever done what you did." Eko shrugged and tipped a horn at his brother. "He wants to figure out how you did it by watching you undo it."

"I don't recommend repeating my special brand of stupid," she mumbled.

"It might be something only *you* can do as the two-in-one." Esiw walked his front paws forward until he'd stretched himself in a languid sprawl across the cushion. "Either way, this is a topic about which I know so little and desire to understand all its intricacies."

She couldn't begrudge him the info. It wasn't a state secret or anything. He wouldn't be the first to watch her lose total control of her everythings. Yes, she'd be completely vulnerable, but he'd saved her from the time gaffe even though he hadn't had to. Besides, maybe smarty-pants would have tips for making the next two infusions less horrible. She'd created seven memory packages, and taking Tjinimin's would give her five of the seven, so two redos were still in her future.

"Okay. Your weird is your weird." She looked to her eldest brother. "I don't want to befoul your bedroom, so if you'll just point me in the direction of my padded cell..."

"This is not my bedroom, and I was not sleeping." Eko chuckled. "I was planning new games for the toys you sent me. Make a mess of this room. It is fine by me. We are here for you. Always."

Aw, the temptation to hug the lug was up there, right behind the resignation of having to completely husk Tjinimin. Once she took her memories, he'd have only the horrors of what Ariel and her cronies had forced him to live. That was a cruelty she couldn't abide.

She dropped the gates containing Tjinimin, setting him free in the room.

The bat god snapped his wings and readied for flight. His mouth opened, but Esiw caught him between two paws, choking off any sonic defense. Tjinimin might have been large for a god, but he was in the company of First Children, and therefore tchotchke small by comparison. Esiw shook his prey like a twenty-sided die, then parted his claws just enough to get a good look at the frantically struggling bat.

"Ah, so this is how you stored the displaced pieces of yourself, eh? Fascinating." Esiw sniffed the god, poked him, then placed him in a birdcage made of starlight. Tjinimin poofed into shadow and instantly reappeared in the cage. He tried again to vanish, only to be thwarted by Esiw's creation. Tjinimin flapped against the bars and burned himself in the process. His sonic cries came out with all the ferocity of mouse squeaks. Defeated, he flew to the textured perch and tucked his wings tightly around himself, silently hanging upside down to sulk.

"Careful, he thinks he's me. My memories are the bulk of what he has left after a traitor tried to husk him," Bix warned.

"Then he was never a smart toy to begin with." Eko tsked. "Gods should heed their instincts more than their logic. They are creations of the Chaos, after all."

Gods heeding their instincts was what made them raging assholes, but Bix wasn't going to get in an argument about that when she'd come here for Eko's help. Again. Esiw still being here was a bonus since she could now get tangled in time.

"Alrighty, then, Esiw. You want to dissect memory transfers? Watch and learn." She sent filaments of her reassembled being into Tjinimin's cage. The bat god squawked and fluttered, but he couldn't escape the threads of her wended darkness and light. They pierced his body and dove deep into the recesses of the god. She began by scraping his memories of his time with the Devourers, the planetary goddess, and Ariel, culling all intel that could help her in the long run.

There. The infamous "she" of Ariel's trial, the one Ariel had claimed infiltrated the Mid World guardians' network. The face was familiar. It wasn't a mere planetary goddess who'd husked him; it was a greater goddess. One who'd been eluding Bix for months. Bix pushed the intel into the collection of her recent memories before summoning her missing parts to her.

Memories of starlight clustered together like lilies on the pond of her invasive midnight. Leaves of shining metallic order folded around them, bringing them home. Scents came first. A barrage that reeked of an overflowing dumpster until snippets of sound blasted them apart, allowing individual fragrances to blossom. Fragments of tactile facsimiles caught on edges of images spiraling through fractured mirrors in search of pieces that fit their jagged edges. Incomplete stories rose up by the hundreds of thousands, each one demanding her attention. She made it through a dozen or so before her brain shorted out and her body shut down for the hard reboot.

Her final cogent thought sent the hollowed husk of Tjinimin to his pantheon for rehabilitation.

CHAPTER 23

Assimilating memories from a life longer than measurements had existed was akin to an elephant stuffing its migraine into a peahen's skull without anesthesia and doing it twenty thousand leagues under the sea. There was no part of Bix that didn't hurt. Toenails. Eyelashes. Tailbone. Surrendering her preferred form for her native state didn't help. Everything still ached. Corporeal, she could fantasize about ice packs and Devourer-brand painkillers. She'd whine, but that'd require movement, and movement was so no bueno.

"What *is* that getup you've put her in?" Esiw hissed.

"It's clothes," Eko grumbled.

"It's a barbarian fantasy costume and wholly inappropriate for our sister."

"She did not object the last time I dressed her in this."

"She likely viewed it as a gift, thus showed appropriate gratitude. Ask the toy how long she kept it after she departed your unenlightened presence."

"I will *not* ask the toy how to care for our sister," Eko huffed. "We raised her. We know better than any entity what she needs."

"We educated her. We did not raise her."

"Same thing."

"Hardly. Raising her was a family affair. You must not diminish the contributions of the others just because she remains forever a child in your eyes." An imperious sniff. Esiw, definitely. "Toy, dress her appropriately. I believe she is waking."

"Toy, do not, or I will add you to my collection."

Laughter made every nerve twinge and pang, but laugh Bix did. How marvelous and endearing to hear her brothers squabble over her well-being. With each delighted giggle, her aching body pressed into a downy-soft featherbed of cool comfort lightly fragranced with teak and peppercorn. Sitting up was difficult, so she rolled to her side, then tried to lever herself up. Failed. The bed kept sucking her in.

"Wait to see if she holds this form," Eko encouraged softly.

"I wouldn't if I was forced to wear that," Esiw drawled. "Toy, she is fine now. Care for her as is your job."

"My pleasure."

Those two acquiescent words came from Phobos. Poor guy had to show up anytime her pain threshold was exceeded, part of his obligation as her caretaker. Memory jigsaws booted her way past comfort with sensory overloads, so her survival instinct summoned Phobos to attend her. He had no say in the matter. He did, however, have every say in the silk underpinnings and fitted raspberry pinstripe dress manifesting on her.

"Thank you." She held up her hands with a grunt and a wince. "Little help? I'm stuck."

"That's me," Eko blurted.

"Not unless you shrink sixfold. Let the toy do its job."

Two strong tawny hands gripped Bix's wrists and hauled her out of the featherbed. Make that one very large pillow, the one on which Esiw had been lounging when she'd last been lucid.

"Sorry I stole your bed, Esiw." Bix smoothed her hair from her face and tugged down her skirt, giving Phobos a grateful yet apologetic smile. The god of fear inclined his head, exposing some sort of fat silver half-moon implanted behind his ear. He appeared otherwise unmolested in his tailored navy windowpane three-piece suit. Still, the thing behind his ear bugged her. What had her brothers done while she was too out of it to protect Phobos from them? They knew he was off-limits.

Phobos must have noticed her glaring at the thing because he distracted her by coiffing her teal tangles and providing her with holographic black ankle boots whose chunky heels were perfect for helping her maintain her balance while her equilibrium tried to stabilize.

"I can manifest any comforts to suit my whim, little sister." The large white fox scraped a paw over the yellow polka-dot pillow on which he sat. "I have many questions about all you allowed us to witness during your refitting. Whenever you are agreeable, of course."

"About how I travel when I'm asleep or unconscious? How many of you guys did I take with me this round?"

Phobos dropped his chin to his chest but failed to hide the quaking of his shoulders.

"All of you? Oh that, that must've traumatized everyone we encountered on the way." She hobbled to Eko perched upon his plain three-legged stool. She tapped her forehead. "Can you do that thing that makes my head stop hurting, please?"

Her eldest brother laid one massive finger to the side of her head, instantly arresting the throbbing and quieting the sounds looking for the memories to which they belonged. "You did not like it when I sorted your memories the last time, but I could not let you feel so much unnecessary pain again. I did only the minimum required to bring you comfort. Esiw, however, …"

"She and I are aligned with the Cosmos. Order is paramount." Esiw fanned his four tails. "And I had to ensure you didn't place things out of context."

The twins glared at each other as Bix fought down a flash of wrath. She despised third parties messing with her mind. What lay between her ears was her biggest weakness, so others mucking with it really pissed her off. Logically, however, she'd accepted the risk of her brothers' interference when she'd come to them for help. Logically, she shouldn't be cranky when they did what she'd anticipated. Logically. Emotionally, though, it was a good thing Tobek was absorbing the brunt of her temper and pushing calmness to her.

"Thank you for telling me. Either of you remove anything, bury it, or something equally devious?" She massaged her Eternal Knot and took in the room. They were in the solarium; a smattering of nebulas glowed like LED art through the curved panes. She'd probably wrecked the hell out of Eko's plotting room, forcing everyone to retire here after each of the trips dictated by her memories.

"We cannot remove anything from you," Esiw said crisply.

"He tried." Eko wagged one meaty finger at his twin. "You retaliated by rearranging the pieces of Mother within him. He did not find that amusing. I did."

"It was merely a test to see if the initial extraction had created a weakness that would allow them to be extracted again." Esiw's ears flattened, and his lip curled as he hissed at his brother. "Relearning all you once knew at an accelerated pace, little sister. What is that like?"

"Like a train wreck, and you're the cow who chose the worst place to graze." Bix shook her arms and stomped her feet, trying to get her body of flesh to function as designed. Ghosting sensations from the memories clamoring for her attention felt like that song, *The Worms Crawl In.* "Did I get us stuck in time, destroy a World, or euthanize a race?"

Esiw and Eko swapped amused glances. Phobos winced and rubbed the moon behind his ear as he reclaimed his seat in a crimson wingback chair lushly upholstered in a textile more sumptuous than velvet. He had a book and a balloon of elixir set upon a side table, all of which looked ridiculously small in the scale of things. Sure, he was a god, so he could've made himself larger to fit in with her brothers; then again, he was merely a god, so it was probably wise he didn't do anything they could interpret as presumptuous or as a passive challenge. The fact they kept calling him "toy" probably clued him in to that.

"What? What's funny?" she prompted, resisting the urge to rip that thing out of Phobos's skull. Maybe. Probably would do it eventually, but one thing at a time.

"What do you know now that you didn't before?" Esiw flicked one of his four tails. The pillow on which she'd awakened vanished. In its place, a chair similar to Phobos's yet in rich teal appeared.

"Ha," she groaned, using the chair as a balance bar instead of a seat. "I don't wake up suddenly enlightened. I regain consciousness because I've built a mental dam to stop the onslaught. With prior assimilations, I haven't dwelled on the past because the memories are snippets that make no sense. Any magics to which I suddenly have access are as much a surprise to me as the people around me."

"Then you should stay and let us train you until you are clear on your abilities and limitations." Esiw crossed his front paws. "It's the only sensible thing to do."

Bix grinned at Phobos, whose lips twitched as he sipped his drink. He'd been her tutor and tester in the early goings, saying much the same thing as Esiw. Phobos's faithful minions had suffered the consequences, for which she still felt guilty. "Your offer is quite generous, brother, and I'd love to take you up on it. You two seem blessedly immune from my foibles."

"We've done this before," Eko reminded, setting one fat ankle on his knee.

"Yeah, but…" She gestured to Phobos. "I've left my friends in the lurch as it is. Until the Devourers are purged from the Mids, I need to be there to finish what I started. Hopefully, I've got enough new power within me now to resist the ley line's attack as I try to restore order and balance to the World I drained. I assume they're both still there? The World and the line?"

"They continue to exist, yes," Esiw hedged, swapping a bemused glance with his twin.

"Little sister, you *cannot* restore order. It would require you to create, which you cannot do," Eko said gently.

"But I can move things from one place to another," she

argued as dread soured within her. How had they not mentioned this ginormous glitch in the plan before? "I can take the order within me and implant it in the World. Can't I?"

Her brothers shook their heads.

"Your order would be too powerful. It would destroy that which you seek to mend." Esiw drew two lines in the air, one blue, one purple. The lines twisted together like a strip of licorice. "The Worlds of your precious collective aren't made by us. They are made by entities many steps removed from us, their powers vastly diluted. They are like your toy here. Would you try to infuse him with your chaos?"

"No," Bix and Phobos blurted together. Phobos cleared his throat and picked up his book, studiously avoiding eye contact with her siblings.

"Despite these Worlds being amalgams of different magics, they are still fragile things." Eko leaned forward on his stool, big forearms across his thighs. "But do not despair, little sister. You can still succeed. Think of the ether, yes? How did you make that happen?"

"Through collaboration." She exhaled a long clarifying breath. "I was the architect, not the creator. To fix the World, I must convince others to help me, to act to achieve what we all need."

"A thing at which you are very adept." Eko beamed, his marbled teeth gleaming. "A thing for which you do not need all your memories, yes?"

"I need enough to know who can help me infuse purified order of the right potency, and what leverage will convince them to do what I want." Bix studied the stars overhead, wishing an epiphany would show itself in their gleams and glows. "Unless you guys know the answers?"

"You need whoever supplied the element originally," Phobos murmured, turning a page and not looking up.

"The toy is correct." Esiw inclined his head. "But you do not need us to tell you the who or the how."

Bix perked up. "I don't?"

"You may not be able to create, but you are an expert on the processes of creation," Eko reminded.

"That knowledge currently resides within you in great abundance, but you've built barriers around it because there is something related to it that you refuse to examine." Esiw glared at his twin.

Eko hung his head and picked at his pants, saying nothing.

"All memories are relational," she acknowledged, mentally skimming along the dam holding back the deluge of experiences. Oh, yep. There. Big, nasty, angry thing she kept promising herself she'd scrutinize once the Mids were safe. It was larger now, bulging against the walls, threatening to explode if she didn't deal with it soon. The protections around it were heavily reinforced by her thorns of wrath and malice, but even they were showing the effects of being overtaxed.

Best if she pricked that when she was totally isolated from all living things, including her brothers. Whatever was inside that festering pustule definitely involved her family. All kinds of messy emotions oozed from it in copious quantities, many of which fed her thorns.

"Despite me being selectively ignorant, there are other experts in Mids' creations I can consult." Bix rolled her shoulders and lifted her chin. "Thank you for renewing my hope. Now, I really need to get back to the messes I left in devolving states of chaos."

Eko chortled, mischief stoking the fires of his eyes. "They are glorious."

"Go fix your toys, little sister." Esiw ran the tips of two tails along her cheeks and studied her fondly. "When you're done, come back, and let us help you through these confusions and doubts exacerbated by your broken mind."

She tweaked the yellow tip of a tail. "I will. Thank you, both, for helping me through this."

Eko cupped two massive fingers around her while she closed her arms around a third finger in her best facsimile of a hug.

"Whenever you need me, little sister, I am here." Eko patted her on the head with a fingertip and smiled. "It is a prison, after all."

Laughing, she turned to Phobos. "You ready to go?"

The god of fear set aside his book, stood, straightened his jacket, then bowed to her brothers. "It has been an honor."

"Take care of her, toy," Esiw warned, starlight flashing around him. "We are watching."

CHAPTER 24

Pink and white cherry blossoms fluttered from verdant trees that never ran out of blooms. The soft, fragrant rain danced on gentle breezes while petals sailed like tiny ships upon the currents of a babbling brook. Pale gray boulders worn by weather and time offered elevated seating with a view of the pumpkin sky. Wildlife scampered from the grove, leaving Bix and Phobos alone in this patch of quiet idyll on a World far from the Mids.

"Surprise," Bix cheered, throwing wide her arms and spinning through the floral drift.

Phobos cleared his throat and tugged his kerchief from his chest pocket. "Why did you bring me here?"

"I remembered." She stopped spinning in front of a tree with deep lenticels and gestured to the ground. "It's a clear memory. You, stretched upon the ground, laughing. You looked at me, and you smiled. Your laugh deepened. I think it was our first meeting, which *was* a while ago, I know. The toga was your choice of evening wear, but, yeah, see? I remembered. Yay, me, right?"

"In your mind, this was a…happy event?" He shook out his burgundy kerchief and studied it, not sparing a glance at their surroundings.

"Of course. Why else would you be laughing? Why didn't you

ever mention we *knew* knew each other from ye olden times?" She lifted her face to the gentle caress of the falling petals. "You always let me assume I was the shadowy bogeyman to you and yours."

"What happened after I laughed?" he asked cautiously, meticulously refolding the silk square.

She dropped her arms and cocked her head, searching for what had come next. "Uh, there was a party, maybe? A festival, perhaps?"

He coughed, a wryly bitter sound as he replaced his pocket square. "How did you *feel* upon seeing me laugh?"

"Pfft, emo challenged back then, remember? Feelings weren't my métier." She dismissed his question as something bleak scratched against the dam of memories.

He stared down at her, searching her face. His expression turned into one giant pucker. "There was no festival. No party. No celebration. This? This was a trap my siblings and I had laid for you."

"A trap?" She scratched her head and took another look at the environs. "But the memory of you laughing is crystal clear in my head."

"I did laugh." He sighed. "I laughed because I'd tricked you into showing up, then my siblings and I attacked you."

"Ouch," she mumbled, replaying the memory—her version of it, at least. Nothing about his siblings came into the picture. He laughed. She laughed. She left. The harder she thought about it, the more her head hurt. Various people flashed through the scene, people who couldn't possibly have been there, like Cian and his mom. The more logic she tried to apply to the memory, the weaker the dam protecting her from the deluge of her past became. "Why? Why the trick? Why the trap?"

"You'd husked our father." He caught a petal in his hand. "You left us with a man who didn't know us. Didn't care for us. *Couldn't* care for us. A man *we* had to raise, retrain, and reintegrate into our family and our pantheon."

"He didn't have the memories to trigger his paternal instincts."

She nodded, guessing the issue. "He was just a rando who looked like your dad. You heaped all your histories and expectations upon him, and he didn't react the way you expected. Probably ran from you. Hid. And when you wouldn't leave him be, he fought you, hurt you, and showed none of the remorse a father might show children he once loved."

"You do remember." He huffed.

"No, I don't, but it's not hard to fathom." She massaged her temples as the quest for clarity pained her more and more. "Was he my food, or was I doing my duty as High Executioner?"

"The latter." Phobos shredded the petal with his thumbnail. "Didn't matter to us, though."

"You loved him. It wouldn't. Plus, most of your family are emotion gods, so there was no way you guys could escape being collateral damage. If nothing else, your version is logical." She shook her head sharply, as if the physical act could clear the confusion heaping itself upon the memory. "Was I at least a little bit compassionate in my retaliation against you?"

Phobos's laugh echoed with malevolence, every bit the god of fear, but the laugh didn't match the one in her memory…until it did, like it was data being overwritten. When she replayed the memory, his laugh contained its characteristic tones, but it hadn't before. Had it? Shit. She wasn't sure.

"You dispersed us across galaxies, split us up. Those of us who have twins, you ensured we were the farthest apart." He flicked the flower dust from his fingers. "You stranded us in foreign collectives, amid foreign cultures, and facing unimaginable races. Where we landed, no one had heard of us, our family, or our pantheon. Some of us came home quickly. Some didn't."

She eyed him. "You didn't."

"For the first time in my life, I had no legacy, no external burdens inherited from my family. I didn't have the safety net of my family either. I failed spectacularly in ways I'd never conceived of during my demigod trials." He chuckled wryly. "Utterly alone in a strange environment where the only things I understood were the fears of those around me. Ah, the desperation, the panic, the opportunity, the novelty…"

"You stayed and you learned." She knocked on the curve of skull behind her ear. "That's why Esiw took to you. He recognized your hunger for knowledge. He's the one who put that implant behind your ear. Eko would've left you bleeding to test your instincts. What did Esiw give you?"

Phobos lifted his hair, allowing her full view of the metal moon. "It enables me to reach you when you are spread across multiple timelines. A feat tested often during your recovery. I now understand the root of the divine myth of omnipresence."

That gizmo would probably prove useful in ways she had yet to consider. Leave it to brother know-it-all to plan for her screwups. Cheeky fox.

"Does it cause you pain? Do you want me to remove it?"

"No, but I would like you to explain how you have assimilated five of seven memory segments, yet cannot accurately recall our interlude in this grove. Regardless of your age, that can't be possible. How much of your past are you *choosing* to ignore?" His tone denoted genuine concern, not chastisement.

She crouched and gathered fallen flowers in her hands. Something about them tapped upon a different memory, one shared with Tobek, one festering behind her thorns. Shifting the train of thoughts eased the thundering inside her head, but not the persistent panic fluttering through her whole body. "It's not that I'm choosing to ignore great swaths. It's that I can't sort what histories happened in a timeline that still exists from histories I erased when I traveled backward in time. Some things are similar, some things are drastically different, and some things seem ridiculously unlikely yet not impossible."

Phobos blanched. "Your magics of time erased events from history?"

"Not just events. I expunged *everything*. Lives. Families. Nations. Locations. Evolutions. Days. Years. Centuries. Many people, Worlds, and magics were never reborn." She puffed out her cheeks, then exhaled a noisy raspberry. "I am the High Executioner for All Worlds. There are complex histories only I know because I severed the timeline at some point in the past, forcing my siblings to create new growth. Brand-new. No redos."

"And you have a majority of memories, but not enough to discern what is common history versus unwritten." He tugged his cuffs. "This complicates matters."

"Oh, it gets worse." She let loose a pained chortle. "As you say, I have a majority of my memories now, so my brain is actively filling in the blanks. Like any good artificial intelligence system, it's supplying data where there's a gap, data based on—"

"Experiences from divergent histories," he finished for her. "You weren't being obtuse when questioning your brothers about restoring Ariel's World. You weren't certain of your facts."

"As this disastrous reminiscing of our shared past demonstrates, I can't trust my memories to tell me the truth." Bix wagged a thumb at the grove while frustration mounted. "Despite my progress, I've actually regressed by leaps and bounds when it comes to my marbles. For now, it's better to consult with third parties than to rely on me and what I think I know."

"That's why your instincts still dominate." He nodded sympathetically.

"I'm sorry for bringing you here, Phobos, really I am. I didn't mean to pour salt in a wound. I'd intended this as a show of gratitude for how well you live up to your obligations. Most gods wouldn't handle my family with the finesse you have."

"Once upon a time, you endeavored to teach me a lesson, Chimera. It's possible I learned something from it." He finally took a long look around the idyll. "Let us leave this place in the past and return to the urgencies of our shared present, shall we?"

"Fine. Hope you've brushed up on your life cycles of Worlds, because my muddled mind needs your insight." She opened gates and took him to a different place, not of any World. Not anymore.

CHAPTER 25

Bix and Phobos stood in the empty silence of unoccupied space amid the toxic fumes of Worlds destroyed by the Devourers. In the distance, the collective of Upper Worlds shone with the brilliance of the greater gods who ruled autocratic utopias. In the opposite direction, the rich lusters of the Under Worlds bid the weary and restless welcome. Halfway between the heavens and hells, the opaque blackness of the ether resembled a tar pit seeping between Mid Worlds, only to be contained within an unseen circular border. Beyond that perimeter, Other Worlds belonging to midlevel gods scattered like a sprawling suburbia. Through the divine neighborhood, someone had carved a crooked eight-lane highway connecting unclaimed galaxies to the ether.

"Are you uncomfortable out here?" Bix asked, letting go of the cherry blossoms to study how they lingered in a place where her eldest sister Movement had no presence.

"Not at all," Phobos dismissed, but a hint of wonder crept into his tone. "This is the vista of titans and First Children. Gods tend to become casualties of greater entities when wandering alone out here."

"How do you guys choose where to build your Worlds if you can't see the landscape?"

He turned slowly, eyes in constant motion. "Those of us who have our own Worlds usually received them as a gift, be it from our pantheon upon our ascension or in an act of barter. Those of us who are not planetary or greater gods, that is. If we wish to move, we strike deals with entities who can do the deed."

"Which is what you did?" She knew Phobos's home World was not in this galaxy. He might love his family, but he didn't want to live near them. Greeks and their dramas. "I wasn't your World mover, was I?"

He tutted and shook his head. "I moved my home after you punted me out of my comfort zone. I never again wanted to run afoul of you or the weaknesses that had brought me to your attention."

"Yet you helped me when I was starving and no one else would feed me." She bumped his elbow. "Whoever sent you to intercept me that day, do they know what it cost you to show up?"

"No need to rehash our recent past when we should be focusing on the Worlds missing from this landscape." He drifted toward the crooked highway, reaching out and grabbing emptiness, kneading it through his fingers. "The taint is thick. Devourers were here."

"Before Cian called on us to assist with the crisis of Ariel's ley line, Tobek and I had been traveling this road, trying to find its origin." Bix scratched her Eternal Knot, reassured by its steady thrum. "Our working theory is this is the path of the anti-gods' supply chain. Multiple assets report the enemy is staging in the ether."

Phobos rubbed his hands together and nodded. "Our spies report the same thing, but we can't pinpoint where due to the nature of the ether."

"Any army needs to eat. I think they consumed the Worlds formerly in this path. We know they headed our way a long time ago when I was still the original Chimera; hence, the reason the ether exists." She jerked her thumb over her shoulder in the direction of said ether.

"The path gets wider and wider as forward scouts are joined by other branches of the army, which brings higher-ranking officers, who consume more advanced magics." He tapped a finger against his lips. "Disparity of power could account for their zigzags. I'll have to look into whose Worlds are missing."

"And if those gods are also missing," she added. "Mid World guardians were easy prey for Ariel because they reside in the Mids, but we still have her partner out there, the greater goddess who husked the guardians."

"Goddess? You're sure?" Phobos scowled. "What of the Devourer general? We saw him in the core."

"He may have fed on what remained of the guardians, but it was a greater goddess who first stole from Ariel's prisoners. I pulled her image from Tjinimin's mind before I husked him completely." Bix tapped her temple.

Phobos snapped his fingers six times. Six holographic images of women of different features, coloring, statures, etcetera appeared.

"That's Tjinimin's tormentor." Bix pointed to an image of a plump goddess with hair the color of coral and eyes the color of wheat. "Her name is Indraja. She's the political puppet master behind the faction of traitors in the Consortium. The source of dark funding and strident opposition to Resen. I've been hunting her for months. Who are the rest of these women?"

"You may recall I took samples from the core of Ariel's World in hopes of identifying the planetary god who'd made the World." He tipped his head at the images. "These are she in her various forms."

Bix scoffed. "The same goddess? All these women? Impossible. I would've recognized Indraja's resonance in the core. I've destroyed numerous Worlds she's made in an attempt to force her out of hiding. I know her magical signature. The core's goddess was way weaker."

"Because Indraja made Ariel's home World on the day she ascended to full godhood. It was a thank-you to the Mids for the trials and tribulations that had shaped Indraja into the goddess she'd become." Phobos sidled toward the ether, seemingly measuring the highway of death. "We can amass power even after we ascend. Move one level up. For a planetary goddess, the next level is a greater goddess."

"We need her caught, and I need every detail about the enemy swirling in her traitorous head." Bix planted her hands on her hips. She liked to think she was an excellent hunter, but, despite placing numerous spies within Indraja's organization, the goddess remained elusive. "You and I know that a war with the Devourers doesn't end just because we beat back their first wave or their second."

"They'll keep coming. The greater the challenge, the more incentive they have to crush us." Phobos returned to her side. "We need their leaders, the ones who can call off this invasion and any future ones, and we need leverage."

"Indraja is our best lead for both. Think the pantheons are up to the task?"

"Of locating her?"

"Of gaining leverage over her. Of figuring out what she's really after in all this. It's not political power. She's already got it. Status? She's operating behind the scenes, so I don't think fame is her goal either."

"Love, ego, greed, revenge," Phobos mused. "If it's not the middle two, then that leaves love and revenge. I'll see what we can do about getting the intel. Meanwhile, I'll suggest the war contingents take a closer look at this path through the Other Worlds. Monitor it, even."

"Might also want to encourage them to examine all World cores, Unders to Uppers. Convergences too. They're looking for more than Devourer pupae now. They're looking for anything affiliated with Indraja directly or indirectly."

"Agreed." He stared at the highway and grimaced. "How did we let this get away from us so badly?"

"Same way the Consortium allowed the mess with Ariel to bring the Mids to the brink." Bix patted Phobos's back sympathetically. "Yet another reason I need to get my hands on Indraja. She has to know how to restore the balance to Ariel's World. Without the World hale, we lose the ley line. Without the ley line, we lose Ariel. Without all three, we lose Resen."

"You don't need Indraja to save Ariel's World." Phobos arched a censorious brow. "Planetary gods create Worlds all the time. Very few become Mid Worlds. Why is that?"

That…that was a good question. The Mids was one tiny collective amid all existence. What made those Worlds specifically Mid Worlds? Bix thought back to Feng's demonstration before the team's first mission to Ariel's World. Planetary gods made the core. Other gods dressed the glob in terrain and water to sell it as new farmland to the Consortium. But the World didn't enter the collective until the Consortium voted it in, until the archangels and dragon queens asked native magic to welcome it. Who did they ask? Their birth mates, of course.

"Ley lines. They reach out to the World offered up by the gods. The lines pull that World into the collective and infuse it with Mids magic. Over time, it becomes part of their network."

Phobos inclined his head. "Just so."

"To restore balance to Ariel's World, it's the other ley lines I need, not any god, dragon, or angel." Bix pinched her lip as a plan hatched. "The other ley lines don't like me. Less now that they've doubtlessly learned of what transpired between Ariel's line and me."

"Perhaps an emissary would be of use?" Phobos suggested.

"I need someone they trust. Someone they know. Someone they all protect." Bix snapped her fingers and chuckled. "I need an architect…or two."

Phobos harrumphed and tipped his chin toward the Mid Worlds glittering within the frame of the ether. "Then you'd best be on your way. We've been gone a short while in the time of the Mids. A word of caution, though: we visited often during your recovery. None of the observers you dragged with you interfered, but you were not subtle in your actions. Your brothers' debates over your intentions were educational, to say the least."

"Oh my, let's hope whatever mayhem I wreaked didn't lead to Ariel's assassination, her World's obliteration, or the entire ley line network's destruction." Bix slowly dragged her hands down her face, then peered over her fingertips at her caretaker. "Thank you, again, Phobos. If you get anything on Indraja or the Devourer hierarchy…"

"I know how to find you." Phobos swept a grand bow and vanished.

Bix opened gates to the Mids. Time to clean up the messes she'd exacerbated, starting with a pair of architects she'd left in the lurch.

CHAPTER 26

Cian's apartment held the quiet of emptiness. The wards hummed softly in the background, white noise in a cityscape. Late afternoon sun dipped behind the buildings across the street, throwing distorted shadows against the half-drawn blinds. Gone were the rolled-up sleeping bags of the Berserkers. No extra shoes lingered on the boot tray. A half-burned cone of myrrh incense sat on the otherwise empty kitchen counter.

"Cian? You home?" Bix called but already knew the answer. The only humans in the building were his upstairs neighbors. The resonances of angels belonging to Samael's choir filled the rest of the block. Below ground, Hel's hounds paced alone. No hints of Devourers or Consortium guards. No trace of Berserkers, Tobek, Feng, or Gurp.

All seemed…fine? Too soon to know if that was a good thing.

She opened the kitchen trash can. Takeout for two, not twenty. Three different restaurants. The containers stank but weren't fuzzy. The recycling bin was half full of rinsed soda bottles and cans of energy drinks. A small composting tin by the sink held damp weeds and fruit rinds. A whiff of the rot confirmed it was Ashtad's preferred tea blend. So, Cian and Ashtad were living here and had been home within the week.

The most vulnerable members of her team hadn't died during her absence, and they were healthy enough to eat and drink their usual. Fine was looking better and better.

Next, Bix inspected the bedroom adjacent to the kitchen. Six wallets, two handbags, nine sets of keys, and seven cell phones were in the top drawer of the dresser. Drew's collection from assorted suits. The draugr must've vacated Moccus. Hopefully, the newly independent boar god was in rehab with Ariel's other victims. Bix picked up one of the phones and powered it on, checking for the date and time. Late October. She'd been gone forty-five days, more or less, depending on how long it'd taken her to strip Ariel's World of order. Not her longest recovery period by any stretch, but there were always consequences to leaving so many unattended balls in the air.

She put the phone in the drawer before heading for the front door. She needed to let the mission leader know she was back, get a sitrep, and explain how the team was going to save Ariel's World. First, she had to find her team.

The whir of the big TV in the great room warming up stopped her departure.

A beleaguered cognac gaze stared through the screen. "Bix? You're corporeal. Finally. Thank gods you triggered the motion sensors. Are you *here* here or just passing through?"

Bix ambled behind the large couch and waved to the face distancing itself from the camera. "Ashtad, I'm back, cogent and corporeal. It's good to see you. Cian nearby?"

"Cian is one of many reasons you need to get to the lab pronto." Ashtad leaned sideways, giving her a view of his location. "Our situation is…fraught."

Worry scrabbled along her spine.

"Incoming," she said without further ado, opening gates.

CHAPTER 27

In the underground lab operating in a forgotten section of the Consortium compound, tension had put a damper on the conviviality of cooperation that had been so heartwarming during Bix's last visit. It wasn't to say the many races weren't collaborating. No, no. That was still happening, but there was a desperate determination to their constrained focus. Smiles weren't exchanged as freely. Requests and suggestions came in terse tones. Researchers stayed in their workstation clusters, dispatching the occasional harried gofer to communicate with another group. A shattering of a tray of beakers provoked the start of an angry tirade, but it was cut short by the choice of the speaker. A forced smile. A pained grunt. Work resumed.

Any party was fun for the first hour, but when shit got real, it got real unfun too. Considering the impossibility of what these brave folks were trying to accomplish, grumpy was understandable.

"Bix," Ashtad hailed wearily from his seat at a glass conference table in the middle of the lab. He took her hand and rested his cheek against it. "Have to say, I was worried you'd be offline for six months or more. How are you?"

Bix sank into an empty chair and closed her other hand around his. She tipped her head toward the unfamiliar tech spread out before him. "Where does the mission stand? Ariel, her line, her World?"

"Ariel was impeached by a unanimous vote and frog-marched from the chambers by the other archangels. The last sighting was of her being taken to the Angelic Host's stronghold." Ashtad let go of Bix's hand and keyed something into his computer. "Naturally, there's no third-party confirmation, and Samael refuses to speak of anything happening with his sister."

"As long as she's alive and no longer in a position to call the shots, we should take it as a win," Bix suggested as Ashtad's eyes narrowed at his screen and his typing speed doubled. "Since she's alive, is it safe to assume her World and line are too?"

"Do they both continue to exist? Yes, but that's the only good news I've got for you," he answered with distraction as tech peripherals lit, beeped, and chirped. "Sorry. Someone has been trying to break into our systems. They are fast and relentless."

"Hackers?" Bix glanced around the otherwise empty table. Where the hell was Cian? "Our team's private network or the researchers'?"

"Both. Cian and I are fending them off, but it's getting harder and harder to keep whoever it is out." Ashtad pounded keys, then held up his hands like a conductor signaling a rest. Peripherals did their sound-and-light show. Ashtad hummed with satisfaction. "That stumped them for the moment. Sorry, where were we?"

"Cian?" Bix prompted.

Ashtad swiveled his chair toward an opaque sound booth, hexagonal in shape and slightly larger than a handicapped bathroom stall. Its walls rose a good ten feet. Cords and cables of all colors sprouted from its top and connected with a curved bank of Mids and Other World tech that whirred and flashed.

"You put him in timeout?" Bix asked, utterly baffled. If Ashtad was taking down uncommonly skilled hackers, why wasn't Cian attached at his hip? Yes, Ashtad was an elitist with a demigod's ego, but he was also Cian's mentor and advocate.

"Kid's been hard on the eyes and ears lately." Ashtad aimed a TV remote at a nearby monitor.

Bix's heart stopped. Hooked up to myriad sensors like a triple-jointed marionette and radiating more light than a catacomb rave, Cian sat in an extra-wide recliner with a computer in his lap while wearing nothing more than shorts, headphones, and mirrored swim goggles.

"When did his crystals up their wattage?" She visually retraced the path of the cables hooked to the kid, out the top of his isolation chamber, and into a machine displaying heart rate, blood pressure, oxygen levels, and a bunch of other stats she couldn't decipher.

"It's not just lights anymore. Sound comes out of them too, like the mating cries of wounded whales." Ashtad handed her a headset. "Use this to talk to him. We're running sound filters at both ends, so there might be a bit of lag."

She put on the headset and lowered the boom to her mouth. "Cian? You okay in there?"

The kid looked up and around, smiling. "Bix? Hey. Welcome back."

"Got to say I like your other digs better," she teased.

"Good thing I'm not claustrophobic, right?" Cian flipped up the armrest and pulled a perspiring can of soda from it. "This is way nicer than the quarantine pod from back in the day. These walls are blacked out, and I can leave whenever I want."

Bix was about to question whether he really could leave, but recalled the trash in his apartment. "Well, team leader, care to let me in on the latest?"

Cian barked a laugh around the lip of the can. "Team leader. As if."

"Mission's not over, is it? Or is Resen finally ready to go?" She ignored Ashtad's snort. "Team leader can't quit until the objective is achieved."

"Not to say quitting never crossed a team leader's mind," Ashtad murmured, leaning back in his chair, eyes alight with wry mirth. "Especially if you're on their team."

Bix stuck out the tip of her tongue at her old boss, then directed her question to Cian. "You could start by telling me what's with your dialed-up glow."

"Would love to," Cian hedged, "but that requires me to know something about it. The addition of the sounds drove a bunch of researchers from the lab, something about the subsonic frequencies making them super sick. Like, bleeding-from-bad-places sick."

"Dayum, kid." Bix cringed. "What's David have to say about it?"

"Well, there's good news and bad news on that front." Cian swept his brow with the can, leaving a streak of glistening moisture on his light-bright skin. "See, Feng got sick right after you left. Like, skin turned gray, and veins bulged black. He had a bad case of the cold sweats too."

"Shit," Bix breathed. "His health is a reflection of native magic's health. As in the ley lines."

"Yeah," Cian said, drawing out the word. "So Chief and David decided to go to the core of Ariel's World."

Bix's heart stilled, and her skin turned clammy. "Tell me they didn't. Tell me their grand scheme wasn't bleeding Tobek dry in the middle of a ley line."

Ashtad patted her leg. "Might want to remember David's sketchy history with testing protocols and Chief's martyr complex."

"They are trying to cure a ley line, not exactly a field with a lot of precedent." Bix returned his gesture, mimicking his low-key condescension. He had the grace to look abashed. She didn't hold it against him. Exhaustion brought out the worst in folks.

"Feng insisted on going with them. Nothing's been right since. Not with us or the Berserkers." Cian typed with one hand as he drained his soda in a long slurp. Another monitor inside the lab sprang to life. Runjit's image in the ops room at the coal plant came into view. "Knock, knock. Look who's really back. Third screen. Lab. Remember the shortcut keys? Yeah. Yeah. That's right."

Runjit's brow wrinkled as he finger-pecked his keyboard. Odd, the lead medic was more than proficient with technology, not to mention typing. All the Berserkers had to be since their battalion functioned as a collections unit—as in the collection, analysis, and redistribution of intel—for the greater Mid World Army. Runjit gripped the sides of his monitor. Joy quickly replaced consternation. The medic let out a decidedly feminine grunt of triumph.

"Bixie, babe," Runjit cheered, focusing on his screen as he clapped and bounced on the edge of his seat.

"Drew?" Bix gasped over a horrified chuckle. "What the hell are you doing inside the object of your ardor? He's going to kill you for that."

"He has to wake up first. They all do. It's freaking Sleeping Beauty on steroids over here." Runjit, er, Drew laced his hands atop his turban. "Runjit and Hywl were with us in the lab while David and company did their thing with Ariel's line. Suddenly, Xipil's on the horn calling the boys back to the plant pronto. They don't make it to the door of the lab before they're out cold. Next thing, Gurp's calling in, panicking. The base is on lockdown. Every Berserker is catatonic. Our favorite goblin obviously needed help, so I made a command decision."

"Go back." Bix closed her eyes and tilted her head. "*Every* Berserker is down for the count? And this happened how long after David tried to cure the line with Tobek's blood?"

"Close enough to assume it's related." Ashtad sighed. "We haven't seen nor heard from David, Chief, or Feng since."

"And that was how long ago?"

"Two weeks," Cian and Ashtad said in lag-time unison.

"Chief's immortal, so we know he ain't dead. Can't say the same for the other two." Drew tsked. "As for our brawny boys, herb nerd, show her what the cameras over here are recording."

Cian saluted. A dozen monitors surrounding the conference table switched to live feeds from the coal plant. Every building, every hall, every room…oh, eep, even bathrooms.

Unconscious Berserkers lay head to toe atop tables, benches, floors, beds, showers, parking lots, and more. Anywhere a burly body could fit, there be a Berserker. That wasn't the freakiest part. No, that honor went to the streams of dark green magic connecting the soldiers as if the men were living nodes in a private network that flowed up walls, into ceilings, and down through floors.

Tobek's network. It was a larger, more complex version of what she'd witnessed at Cian's apartment after the first op on Ariel's World. There was no mistaking the hue of magic connecting the men. Bix reached through her connection with Tobek and received only calm, consistent, thrumming. Doodling, welding, or sculpting kept him in his Zen place for a few hours, but prolonged calm meant...corporeal resets formerly initiated by his contract with the Fates. He didn't have the contract anymore, but had he kept the ability to rebuild himself much like he'd kept his Berserker attributes? Yes, he had. When he'd taken a direct hit of Devourer magic in the Crimson Market, he'd iced over. It'd happened again after the Devourer conflict in the core. It didn't explain why he'd turned into an ice cube when Feng had rebuilt Cian's apartment, but every time the ice had melted, Tobek had been good as new. Minus his prosthesis. His prosthesis was an aftermarket addition, so of course it was removed whenever he reset. She was an idiot for not piecing that together sooner.

"Where is Gurp?" she asked the team.

"Camera thirty-two," Drew said. "He's on constant patrol around the plant. Think he's checking wards while also checking on the guys."

"I don't remember this many cameras being in the plant." She crossed her arms and pursed her lips. "Did the MWA install them as part of their investigation into the battalion?"

"You sort of told me to do it," Cian cut in. "When you showed up as a big, silent, black cloud? Totally cool and totally creepy, by the way. One night, you took me to the plant, then filled the morgue with camera boxes. Even a lowly mortal like me could figure out the message. I think you wanted me to capture this..."

More key clacks, and the feeds flipped to videos on fast-forward where every now and again, a Berserker would stand up, move to another location, push a buddy out of the way, then stretch out in a new position.

"None of the guys are awake when they do that." Drew spun in his chair. "They don't eat, drink, or shit. It's all sleep and charades. It's been happening since Chief went MIA."

"Replay the last five minutes, please." Bix leaned on the table as a smirk dawned. Phobos had warned her that she'd been active during her recovery. She wished she could remember the where, who, and why of her meddling, but her subconscious was tricksy like that. By all appearances, she'd known something was amiss with the battalion and had known she wouldn't remember it. Thus, she'd used Cian and his tech to record history so she didn't have to muck with the timeline. Fortunately, the deluge of videos was nothing compared to spying with her infinite tentacles of night. She was a champion TMI sorter. "Show only aerial views."

"Bitch is with her brothers," Drew mumbled.

"Not that Ariel," Bix drawled as Cian refreshed the feeds to only those with top shots. "Compile to show maximum area coverage. Drop any results with fewer than four men."

Feeds tumbled into tiles that scrambled, then rearranged themselves as Cian worked his magic from inside his isolation chamber. A slowly building chortle came from the kid as the partnered feeds blended their edges to form bigger pictures of the literal and figurative sense. Patterns. No. Symbols. The men had arranged themselves to form symbols. The sleepwalking men were changing the symbols, making new ones. They were pantomiming a message.

"Holy shit," Cian breathed. "It *is* charades."

"Synchronized swimming," Drew squealed. "Especially for the boys caught in their BVDs."

"Way too much brawn on the field. More like marching bands at halftime," Ashtad argued playfully.

"Competitive cheer," Cian voted, earning a round of questioning grunts from the team. "Don't. Mom was obsessed with cheer formations. I pirated the cheer channel for her on our first adopt-a-versary."

"Ideograms," Bix declared as her mismatched memories sent up flares of recognition. "The shapes are ideograms from many cultures, not all from the Mids. It's a message but from whom and to what end…"

"On it," Cian and Ashtad said together.

"Before you get lost in that," she hastened to say, "I need you two to make a plea to the ley lines. The whole network."

Both guys hemmed and hawed before Cian finally put words to their hesitance.

"Uh, Bix, Resen's not live," Cian said slowly, overenunciating. "Without it, we don't have direct communication with the lines. We can't turn on Resen until there are enough humans at the data centers to ground the influx of magic caused by the system coming online. Without the grounds in place, we'll nuke nations across the Mids. We're talking billions of lives. It's a no can do."

"The Consortium is in total disarray while they fight over who is going to be the new Chair, but we could try to enlist help from individual archangels and dragon queens," Ashtad suggested. "Feng's the best rep to make our case to them, but he hasn't been seen since he left with Chief."

"No, it has to be you two. The architects. The lines know you and trust you," Bix insisted. "You need to convince them to heal Ariel's World. Only they can restore the necessary balance before her line dies."

"Second big problem with that ask." Ashtad jabbed his fingers in his curls, tousling the locks of sable and gold. "The stopper Ariel's ley line had fashioned to prevent the Devourer taint from spreading to the other lines failed. It blew apart at the intersection, just as we'd feared. The entire foundation of Resen is infected. Even if we communicated with the lines, their efforts would poison Ariel's World. Again. We can't fix her World until we fix the lines, and we can't fix the lines until we have a cure for Devourer toxicity."

"That's the source of Feng's illness and David's recklessness rushing a noncure to Ariel's line," Bix guessed, reassessing the lab, feeling the desperation of the researchers, seeing the creep of hopelessness and defeat in their hunched postures and bursts of irritability. "Have you checked Resen since David probably slit Tobek's throat and femoral arteries?"

"That's when the hacking started." Ashtad leaned on one arm of his chair. "Any attempt to do a data grab opens the door for them to exploit. We can't risk another grab until we shut down these guys."

"They're back," Cian cried, lurching over his laptop. Reflections of code streamed up the mirrored lenses of his goggles.

"Damn hackers." Ashtad surged to the table, manning his tech. "They're getting faster. Cian, any luck with the backtrace?"

"Losing them in the ether," Cian shot back. The rapport between experts devolved into their special geek speak.

Bix gave Ashtad space and took off the headset connecting her to Cian.

"Psst, Bixie," Drew whispered through a monitor's embedded speakers. "If those ideograms are a message, Chief is our best bet at translation. Plus, the researchers need their superstar back to light a fire of progress beneath them, and we need the firebird in case we go with Plan C on communicating with the lines. So, be gone with you, yeah? I'll badger our boys to find a way with Plan A in the meantime."

"Bring the knuckleheads home, got it." Bix nodded. "How is Runjit, really?"

"He's changing, Bixie. I've been overly personal with a few of these guys, testing the patients, if you will. I guarantee they're all changing in the same ways, but I couldn't tell you what ways those are." Drew knocked on his chest. "I can tell you their souls ain't like they used to be. They're weaponizing. I can't stay in much longer, so hurry up, yeah? I don't want to leave them unprotected. Gurp activated quarantine protocols when the battalion went down, so MWA higher-ups are staying away for now. Emphasis on those last two words."

"Understood. See you soon, Drew."

With that, Bix reached out to the piece of her Tobek carried within him. If he was still in the core, there was a very frightened ley line lying in wait. She was about to find out if she now possessed the wherewithal to keep her bits together and in this timeline.

Joy.

CHAPTER 28

Fissures abounded in the core of Ariel's World, where once-thriving roots of the ley line had been. The beautiful rich blue illuminations no longer stretched to every curve and crevice, allowing oppressive darkness to creep closer to the tainted lakes. A morose throb droned from the dying World to be mimicked by the dying line. The tangled webbing of the splintered line had been drawn back to the center of the core, back to the heart of the lakes in ropey braids wending around the Phoenix bursting from the northern lake and David rising from the southern lake. Feng in his taint-limned hybrid form and David in her gloriously scarred dragon form reached their wings toward each other, necks stretched, maws wide as if fighting to defy the line and establish a connection.

A long cylinder of thick ice crackling with new growth engulfed the dragon, the firebird, and the braided lines. More ice blanketed the lakes. In the center of it all hung Tobek, so small by comparison, yet powerful enough to arrest the most potent magics the Mids had to offer.

That wasn't wholly unexpected. The reach of the ice, yes. That was worrisome and problematic. But Tobek being frozen? Bleeding out to purge the lines would've initiated his cosmic reset. She'd warned them not to do this, but knowing him and his gleeful embrace of near death, she wasn't surprised. Once Feng had shown signs of native magic's illness, neither David nor Tobek would've sat on their hands.

That said, the minute this mission was over, she was going to have a Come to Jesus with her eldest sisters and demand they cure Tobek of his contagious cold snaps. Being able to reset himself to a whole and healed entity was great, no doubt. The fact his ice was spreading? Not good. That it was including others, especially Feng who was a fire entity? Also not good. If Tobek only turned into an ice cube when mortally wounded, that'd be understandable, but that wasn't the case. He'd turned to ice in the middle of a harmless remodel. So whatever her siblings had done to him would be fixed to Bix's satisfaction, or else she'd walk back the timelines of everything her sisters held dear.

Letting her spikes of wrath and malice grow, Bix moved through the core of Ariel's World in the shelter of layered gates. She didn't want to cause further harm to the line. It wasn't the object of her ire. Never had been, but she wasn't keen to be tested by it either. No, she was drawn to the clarity of the ice and the original Berserker trapped within. Checking her connection to Tobek for the umpteenth time, she still only sensed calm and serenity, so she dug deeper. Even when he was outwardly unruffled, inside, Tobek carried a persistent thrum of pained loneliness. Sustained grief might be more accurate. It existed just above the bedrock of rage that the Fates had exploited to create the Berserkers. She homed in on that persistent rage. It vibrated, very much awake, very active. Very connected…to an influx of magics Mids and Other World. She focused on those connections, trying to identify the sources.

The ley lines and the Fates' weave.

The foundational elements of Resen were imbuing him? No. He was a cosmic sponge; he was absorbing their power. He didn't need a direct physical connection; he was an antenna. That was how his evolution worked. So why was his rage overactive?

She pushed in on the bedrock. Hundreds of holes shimmered.

Not holes. Chutes. The links to his men. Worlds apart from his men and a captive of his own magic, he was still the nucleus of the Berserkers, the hub of their network dictating the men's movements at the coal plant. *He* was the source of the ideograms. An SOS? But why choose an arcane format? Why not have the men spell out HELP in the parking lot? Probably wasn't asking for help. Probably was giving directions. Orders. He wasn't thinking of himself. He was thinking of the mission. The mission came first.

Fortunately for him and the mission, she knew how to make him melt.

"All right, Snow White, your princess is here to wake you from your curse." Bix reached across the threshold of her gates and laid her palms flat against the ice. A cocktail of blended magics surged up her arms, raising goose bumps over her skin. Her scalp tingled and her toes curled. Initially, his magic fought her, like a rabid dog against a snare. It was the reset, the feral response of instinct. She didn't balk or fight back. She welcomed it as she always did, just as he always did for her. That was their symbiosis.

His magic's assault subsided to its customary relaxed push, pull, and clutch as his reset completed its cycle. In the next breath, ice melted. All at once. All in a silent sluice. All evaporating before it hit the muddy ground.

Gates caught Tobek before he splashed in the muck of the core. The twinned fires of the Phoenix and the dragon blasted harmlessly against Bix's shelter of gates, suspended breaths finally allowed to dispel. The ley line frantically grew its braids, grasping at Feng and David as both struggled to get free while roaring their indignations.

"That is enough," Bix murmured as memories of taming discord percolated in her mind, weaving together tales of potential inaccuracies to present methods and risks. She chose the gentlest option. The lights of order within her corporeal form brightened, bestowing freckles of starlight that crossed gates to shine upon the core in symbols of peace and balance.

The fragments of the ley line unwound, scrabbling at the places light hit the core. They dug at the ceiling and walls. They splashed into the puddles and streams of condensation. A few came at Bix directly. Some passed into the layers of gates while thin strands slithered around the frame to undulate in the open doorway. Assessing her. She held out her hands, palms up, recalling how Tobek had first greeted the line when they'd arrived on this World at the start of this impossible mission. The lines flowed over and around her hands, forming gloves that did not touch her skin.

She held her form and maintained her light even as she braced to be drop-kicked out of time again. She wouldn't make the first hostile move. Nope. She was the greater power. Greater powers didn't punch down. That was a cardinal rule of Don't Be a Dick.

Cool breezes swirled between the lines and her skin. Three distinct yet pitiful pulses of once-awesome magic patted her hands, then released her. The fragments recoiled to their lakes with a whisper of a song. Feng and David collided with enough force to shake the core, then thudded to the ground in a tangled heap. Groaning confirmed they were fine.

Tobek, watchful and silent on his platform of gates, scratched his beard with one hand. He didn't have his artificial one. Nary a spatter of mud defaced his jeans or heather-gray Henley. As expected, he appeared unharmed and good as new…post cosmic reset.

"Pretty sure I warned you not to sacrifice Tobek under any circumstance," Bix chided with all the disappointment this triad's futile actions merited.

"The line wouldn't allow us to drain him," David rasped in a voice both feminine and hoarse, forever damaged by the dense scars of betrayal mapping her throat and underbelly.

"He is a guardian of the Mids. Of course it attacked you." Bix eyed the lakes and what remained of the roots. The line's behavior had been noble despite its fear and desperation, and Bix respected it all the more for its selflessness.

"I'd hoped David being a daughter of its birth mate would help it understand that what we were trying to achieve was for its own good." Feng moaned and extinguished his innate fire, shrinking into his humanoid form. Black veins mapped his skin, proof that the collective welfare of the ley lines was worsening.

"It recognized me and our connection, but that made it more agitated." David stretched a damaged wing. "The moment I severed Chief's carotid, the line separated the three of us."

"It was trying to protect you from him and his magic." Bix angled herself toward Tobek. "As for you, are you even aware of how long you've been frozen?"

"A minute? Two?" Tobek leapt from his platform to the core. His eyes narrowed. He surveyed their surroundings as if he wasn't where he expected to be.

"Two weeks," David corrected dubiously. "We've been trapped in ice for two weeks. How can you not be aware of the passage of time?"

Tobek's nostrils flared and his lips pursed as he crouched over a dying root to stroke it.

"Feng, are you aware of the passage of time?" Bix asked, fairly certain Tobek wasn't altogether in this moment. Being invaded by the foundational elements had to leave some sort of disquiet in his person. Hell, she'd been bested by one line, and a sick one at that. He'd hosted all of them plus the Fates' weave.

"Hard not to be aware of every passing moment when you're listening to the line screaming at you." Feng stood and manifested clean clothes of the casual tweed variety. "I thought I had issues stemming from prolonged trauma..."

"We need to get to the lab. Now." Tobek stepped from fading root to fading root as his fingers massaged mud into the pad of his thumb.

"We can't leave the line alone." Feng gestured to the lakes. "Abandoning it now will make it suicidal."

"The other lines are aware of its condition, as is the Fates' weave. They're trying to get a message to us, but they're being blocked." Tobek finally focused on Bix. "The foundational elements of Resen are trying to reach the architects."

"The hackers are the foundational elements? Ashtad and Cian are going to shit themselves." Bix slapped her hand over her mouth, muting an awed guffaw as she realized Tobek hadn't merely been absorbing the magics of the lines and the weave, he'd been *communicating* with them.

"If pure magic is trying to speak to us, we need to listen." David compressed her natural form of the dragon into the diminutive shape of the male knocker. "I'm with the original Berserker. We should get back to the lab. Now."

"I'll stay with the line," Feng insisted.

"Feng, you're not in the best shape, which, frankly, is the only real-time indicator of how screwed we are. We need you at the lab, if for no other reason as the countdown clock." Bix offered an apologetic smile.

"He is too keyed to the pain of this line," Tobek groused. "He hasn't heard the call of the others. They've been trying to reach him since this line splintered."

"Wait, they *told* you that?" Feng asked aghast, then scowled. "Or is this your usual dislike of me rearing its head?"

"They told me many things," Tobek dismissed with a sniff.

"Since when do you have direct communications with the lines?" Feng pressed.

"Since Ariel was ignoring her line and you've been ignoring the others." Tobek finally looked at Feng, his expression cold, colder than usual. "They had no other options."

That was it. No other options.

The timing should've clued her in. This line's glitter. Cian's crystals. The Berserkers' pantomime. Nonstandard communications. The Fates' weave *and* the ley lines. Cian and Ashtad had started a conversation with source magic and didn't realize it. Experience had conditioned Bix not to expect help from the custodians of the Mids, so she too had failed to notice when it was being offered by the foundational elements of Resen. Talk about blind spots. Yeesh.

"Tobek is an entity of all magics, Mids' and Fates' among them," Bix said aloud. "And he is forwarding the elements' messages to his men. The ideograms are coming from Resen."

Tobek, Feng, and David gaped at her as if she'd lost the marbles she'd just acquired.

Laughing softly with incredulity, Bix opened gates and took the defrosted heroes to the lab. Time to decode one message and deliver another.

CHAPTER 29

"It's a message from *Resen*?" Cian squawked from his isolation chamber in the research lab. "The foundational elements are trying to talk to *me*? A lowly Sage? A mostly human kid? Man, I am living my best life."

"They want to chat with Ashtad too," Bix clarified, giving in to the grin as Cian double-pumped his fist in the air.

"Do *not* stop coding, kid," Ashtad barked, pounding on his assorted tech, a headset covering one ear and an earwig in the other. "We cannot allow the foundational elements to gain unfettered access to these networks."

"Isn't that what we want? To have an actual conversation with the powers gearing up to protect the Mids?" Bix leaned against the conference table, confusion throbbing behind one eye. "We still need to get word to them about healing Ariel's World, and soon. It's visibly dying."

"That much raw power is going to fry our networks, not to mention us personally. We can't simply open the door and bid them welcome." Ashtad paused long enough to flag down a cluster of researchers before returning to his furious tech defense. "If anyone has suggestions for alternate ways to establish safe communication paths without bringing the actual defense system online, I'd love to hear them."

"Bix, Resen's security and data network is spread across hundreds of Mid Worlds to cast a wide net of protection *and* to load balance that much magic across technology that mortal races can use without getting smote," Cian explained. "Remember what I said about needing lots of humans at the data centers?"

"Insufficient human population equals nuclear annihilation once Resen comes online," Bix paraphrased.

"Now imagine all the power of Resen concentrated in one spot, this chamber," Ashtad prompted.

"End of this World and probably a lot of the neighboring Worlds." Cian snuffled and hunkered over his keyboard. "Not even the ether would be enough of a buffer."

"Oh." Bix grimaced, eyeballing Tobek. He'd endured the influx as a big old ice cube, but he'd endured. Then again, he'd endured her at her pinnacle for epochs, so... Was it possible? Could he talk to the elements while remaining conscious? That last bit was probably the problem. "Definite no to letting the powers into the researchers' network. Gotcha."

"How long before we think the Consortium starts doing their part to bring Resen online?" Feng read over David's shoulder as David called up data and reports on various computers under the eager guidance of two researchers.

"Too long." Tobek studied the ring of monitors around the conference table, pacing. Half the screens showed the live feeds of the coal plant and his men coming out of their stupor. The other half played the video compilations of the ideograms. "Can someone put me through to the plant?"

"We here," Gurp's voice answered as the camera in the ops room swiveled to show the goblin seated in the middle of a large table with printed screen captures of the men forming ideograms scattered around him. "We here. Read pictures, yes? I know some. Xipil know some. You know rest. Together we know all, yes?"

Xipil joined Gurp at the table, disheveled but clear-eyed. "Chief."

"Xipil, how are the men?" Tobek asked, concern evident in his tone.

"Reporting hale but bemused. Seems we've all lost a fair chunk of time." Xipil rubbed his neck and smirked as Gurp muttered something unintelligible.

Tobek turned to Bix, questions plain within his scowl.

"Check the timestamps on the feeds." Bix ambled to Tobek's side. "They woke when you defrosted. Best we can tell, you took them down when you froze up. Makes sense since they are a part of you."

"I would never have rendered them defenseless," he growled. "Never."

"You didn't have a choice." She held his hand. "Much like Resen's data network, you exposed a vulnerability, and the foundational elements exploited it. Face it, in the most rudimentary terms, your evolutions have configured you to be a receiver and a transmitter of great magics. When your consciousness is taken out of the equation, you get used."

He brought her hand to his Eternal Knot, letting her feel the thundering of his heart. His eyes glowed faintly. "Is this what it's like for you? When you don't know what you've done, to whom, how, for how long?"

"The fear and anger? Yes." She kissed his knuckles. "That dirty feeling of manipulation? No. Third parties aren't dictating what I do. I have only myself to blame. But what we both have are other people who care for us to help us understand what we've done so we can move forward with intention."

"I don't like this part of the evolution," he rumbled. "If I can't control my actions and my direct influences on the troops, I can't lead them. I refuse to be the danger with whom they bed down. They're not mindless puppets of greater powers. They're honorable men of free will."

"Let's finish this mission, then you and I can figure out our options, okay?" She forced a smile while her thorns writhed at the thought of her sisters allowing this abuse of a guardian *they'd* chosen for *their* Worlds.

"Pretty lady? Runjit need gate," Gurp said in a much clearer tone, packing the printouts into a box.

"Did he say to where?" Bix asked, wondering how Drew and Runjit were handling that intimate moment of occupying the same body.

"To you, my lady, if it wouldn't be too much of a bother." Hywl's distinct voice came from off camera, probably from the doorway of the ops room. "Seems he woke up with an epiphany, and he'd like to consult with the researchers."

"I can speak for myself," Runjit groused, his inflections very much his own again, which raised the question: where was Drew?

"Can you, now, eh?" Hywl taunted. Oh yeah, someone's battle buddy was on to the cohabitation issue.

"Bring a mixed unit across," Tobek suggested. "I'd like David to do medical evals on those of us who ran the last mission against those who stayed at base. If you approve, of course, Xipil. This is still your command, after all. David, if it's not too much?"

David glanced up from his reports and grunted an affirmative while pointing to three researchers, who set about gathering a larger team and clearing an exam area.

"Gurp enacted quarantine protocols, so we'll need medical releases anyway for the whole battalion." Xipil nodded. "I, for one, would like to know the finest details of what we're dealing with. Runjit, decide the order for those who stayed behind, then send them over in shifts. Hywl, round up your teams. Bix, a gate from the morgue, if I may be bold?"

"Done. I'll leave it open," Bix said, creating the requested gate and connecting it to an exterior side panel of Cian's isolation chamber. It was one of the few pathways in the lab that wasn't bustling now that David had returned to orchestrate and invigorate the researchers.

Within minutes, shirtless Berserkers sauntered across the gate from the coal plant in a steady parade of twos and threes. If Drew had been there to witness, there would have been prolonged giggling and a running commentary of the not-rated-G variety. Bix was just relieved to see the men alive, awake, alert, and comedically enthusiastic. Those soldiers who'd previously been pricked by David's researchers showed their buddies to the appropriate exam stations. Now and again, a Berserker who hadn't seen Tobek since his evolution had kicked off peeled out of the queue to clasp forearms with their fearless leader. Banter was exchanged amongst all, and the general atmosphere of the lab regained its bonhomie.

Hywl and Runjit crossed the threshold near the tail of their troops and headed for the conference table. Runjit hosted a crow upon his shoulder. Bix started to say something but kept the thought as she caught the resonance of a very familiar Under World entity emanating from the crow. With the coal plant on lockdown, the bodies into which Drew could've jumped were limited. A bird was better than a fish.

"Seems like I just saw you yesterday, Chief," Runjit noted dryly, sweeping Tobek with keen-eyed assessment.

"Yet he manages to look more refreshed than we do." Hywl clapped Tobek on the shoulder.

"You two good? Truly?" Tobek asked his lieutenants.

"Aye, Chief. Loading up on the centuries of grief we're going to give you over this." Hywl rolled out a chair with his half-laced combat boot and tossed Bix a wink. "My lady."

Bix smiled at everyone as she settled in a seat at the conference table, breathing a little more easily now that all the mortals she cared about were here where she could see and touch them and ensure their safety. Yes, they were in crisis mode, but everyone was relatively okay.

The crow flitted from Runjit's shoulder to settle on Bix's with a soft caw.

"He forgive you yet?" she murmured to her best friend within the bird.

"He'll get there. May take a hundred years, but Gurp's making sure he understands the why of it." Drew bobbed her beak in the direction of the goblin bringing up the rear of the soldier train with a box of loose papers in his stubby arms.

Tobek hastened to relieve Gurp of his burden, taking Gurp's vigorous chastisement in stride. "Yes, you were right. Yes, in hindsight, I should have anticipated the line's reaction. Yes, we are fortunate she returned when she did."

Bix hid her grin in her fist while the others at the table guffawed.

"Hey, guys? Guys?" Cian called, juddering in his recliner. "S-s-something's h-h-happening with my c-c-crys…"

"Cian?" Bix shot up from her seat. A cold wave of fear unleashed her darkness and sent tentacles racing for the isolation chamber.

Tobek chucked the paper box at Hywl, then pivoted sharply, bolting for the door to the chamber. He reached the door before Bix's shadows and ripped it off its hinges. His eyes glowed as he hauled Cian out of the recliner. The laptop clattered to the floor. Cian helplessly flailed against Tobek's chest while cables and cords swirled and twirled wildly around them. The bank of monitoring equipment beeped, flashed, and smoked.

Bix yanked back her darkness, unsure how to help the most fragile of her teammates as Tobek shouted for David. His words were lost in the sonic assault of Cian's crystals escaping the isolation chamber.

Clusters of researchers went to their knees cradling their heads. The spines of the soldiers went rigid as their eyes brightened. Feng keened and covered his head with his arms. David slid to the floor with a gurgle. Drew toppled from Bix's shoulder with a feeble flutter of wings.

The pressure of intense magics converged on the lab.

"They're in," Ashtad cried through the din of dissonance, shoving away from the table. "Hit the deck."

Bix's darkness flared like a dozen umbrellas popping open, desperate to shelter her mortals.

Too little. Too late.

Powers infinitely stronger than Ariel's broken line ripped through the lab, flinging Bix out of the chamber, out of the World, and out of time.

CHAPTER 30

The force of eviction threatened to vivisect Bix as she hurtled across galaxies on blast waves, but she was stronger now. Stronger than the foundational elements of Resen that had punted her from the Mids. Every cell of her corporeal state strained against the lattice of mist and midnight holding together her human form. The pain, the blood, they were affectations of being mortal. She wasn't. She was older than every timeline trying to wrench a piece from her. She was the seventh child of the Chaos and the Cosmos. She was the two-in-one. The Chimera. The High Executioner for All Worlds. And she was done with the tantrums of desperate magics.

With a will stronger than gravity, she stopped. Stopped moving. Stopped straining. Stopped yielding to inferior powers. Her hair snapped in front of her face, late to the memo, then settled around her shoulders. She smoothed her dress, lifted her chin, and tapped one finger against a mote of darkness, connecting herself to the darkness inside the laboratory. The ley lines and the Fates' weave wanted an audience with the architects? She was one.

Separated from the timeline of the Mids, living one unchanging moment, Bix stood amid the smoke and flames of the exploding lab. Particles of plastics, metals, and miscellany hovered in suspended animation. Miles of cables sparked. Wires bubbled. Floors buckled. Walls gaped, exposing shattering corridors of the Consortium's compound. Dirt peeked through projectiles made from the ceiling. Slivers of daylight hinted at greater destruction above ground.

Tobek arched above the bursting isolation chamber, arm high, legs kicked. A sheen of ice coated his flesh. He alone survived. Every mortal Bix valued had come apart in horrific clouds of blood, tissue, and bone. Cian and Ashtad. Hywl and Runjit. Feng and David.

Gurp.

Trembling, Bix held up her hands to the vaporizing remains of the dearest creature ever created. Tears spilled down her cheeks. Tentacles of night unraveled from her spine to cradle what remained of her family, the family who'd chosen her. Who'd stood with her no matter how broken they'd been or how messed up she'd been. Who'd never flinched from her presence. Who'd never feared her existence. Who'd trusted her. Who'd loved her.

Bix bayed with horrified disbelief until her throat was raw.

This wasn't real. None of this was real. It couldn't be. She couldn't lose everyone. Not in one instant.

Her sisters couldn't be that stupid.

Her sisters, Music and Movement. Creators of the Mid Worlds. Creators of the ley lines who'd surged upon this fragile place in the company of the Fates' weave. They weren't the only ones culpable. She knew damn well which of her siblings had made the Fates. It didn't take a rocket scientist. Fates ascended when they'd *amassed* enough *knowledge*. Fates, so often viewed as agents of chaos, were, in fact, agents of cosmic order amid the chaos cultivated by the gods. She'd deal with Esiw after she devastated her sisters.

If her siblings believed she was still too emotionally crippled to desire revenge for the murder of her friends, they were the ones who'd lost touch with time. She'd lived the last thirty-odd years as an emotionally functional entity. Collecting her memories didn't change that. If anything, those unburdened years had restored her access to the emotions she'd suppressed for eons. She'd never been incapable of feeling; she'd been trained to not acknowledge those feelings. Trained to prevent shit exactly like this from happening. Trained to prevent the dangerous emotional response of the High Executioner.

Too bad for her family of birth that the one emotion with which she was most intimate was the only one on to which she'd clung when she'd given up everything else.

Malice.

Richer than hate, deeper than rage, and colder than fury, malice writhed within her, dark and sharp. Calculating. It was honed to a fine point of concentration, shutting out the chaos. It seized the clusters of order and willed them to shine light upon the timeline of the Mids.

Starlight brightened from within her, cutting through the smoke and debris, illuminating the wide ethereal line of translucent golds and oranges. Gates set her feet upon the timeline of the Mids, reconnecting her to the moment.

Deafening sounds. Choking scents. Cutting sensations. Acrid flavors. Blurred motions. All of it flooded over and around Bix. She existed fully in the now, committing every experience to memory. She would remember this. No one else would. No one else would believe it was a possibility. Only she would know it had been an actuality.

She took one last look at the horrors that would never, ever be again.

With the unflinching confidence of pure malice, she walked back in time. The darkness of her chaotic half trailed behind her, destroying established order. Each step deleted moments from existence. Moments from the lab, from the District, from the Primary Mid World, from the entire collective of the Mids. She walked and walked until the present was the past.

She walked until those she loved were alive and well.

***

"It's a message from *Resen*?" Cian squawked from his isolation chamber in the research lab. "The foundation magics are trying to talk to *me*? A lowly Sage? A mostly human kid? Man, I am living my best life."

"They want to chat with Ashtad too." Bix breathed a sigh of gratitude as she sank into the moment that was the now. Everything was as it had been. Everyone was where they had been.

"Do *not* stop coding, kid." Ashtad pounded on his assorted tech, a headset covering one ear and an earwig in the other. "We cannot allow the foundational elements to gain unfettered access to these networks."

"Or they'll blow up the lab," Bix preempted. The past was never allowed to be recreated in perfection. It didn't matter how she changed it. It only mattered that her friends survived.

"They'll blow more than the lab. Try the entire Primary Mid World," Cian snarked, attention returning to his tech.

"Sweetheart?" Tobek pressed his fingertips to his Eternal Knot. "Is everything all right?"

"It will be," she assured. "Ashtad, what exactly is keeping the foundational elements out of the lab's system? Is it just code, or are there tangible elements that can be reinforced?"

"Other World upgrades the researchers from the pantheons and I added," Ashtad answered with distraction. "The ley lines are thwarted by them since they're not of Mids magic; however, the Fates' weave is shifting them. The code we're writing instructs those elements where and how to move to counter the weave's manipulations."

"Like chess pieces, then?" Tobek asked.

"Just sooo… Shit," Ashtad cried as potent magics converged on the lab. "They're in. Hit the—"

Bix tumbled through space and out of time. Again. Malice

grew. Yet again she stopped her eviction. Yet again she reached out through darkness to return to the lab.

This time, there was no lab to which to return. There was no city, no state, no nation. There was only the Primary Mid World coming apart in chunks and slivers. Rivers, lakes, oceans, nothing more than drops reaching for outer space. Streets, structures, caverns, terrains of all types, mere clumps separating from the core of the World. Gods, expressions frozen in bemusement and outrage, floated amid the debris. Tiny dots of untethered souls glimmered. Nothing mortal existed.

Bix licked her teeth and chuckled without mirth.

"If you think making the cataclysmic event worse will stop me from undoing your cruelties, you are mistaken," she shouted to her siblings. Were they watching? Maybe. Depended on whether *they* cared.

With that, she lit the path of the Mids' timeline and erased the fatal events. Again.

"It's a message from *Resen*?" Cian squawked from his isolation chamber in the research lab. "The foundation magics are trying to talk to *me*? A lowly Sage? A mostly human kid? Man, I am living—"

Power surged. Again, Bix shot across space and out of time. Again, she returned.

There was no World in this version. No debris. No gods. No souls. There was only Tobek floating in a block of solid ice amid the sparking energies of what had once been the Primary Mid World as wisps of ether wafted into the emptied space.

"You're only making the cost of this game more expensive for you," Bix called to her siblings as she stared at the rage contorting her Berserker's face beneath the layers of ice. She didn't touch him. She didn't want him lucid in this present that wouldn't exist in a moment. "I don't have all my memories, but I have enough to make every single one of you miserable for as long as it takes for me to be content. Don't worry. That's not a threat. It's a mission statement."

Once again, she illuminated the timeline of the Mids and stepped upon it.

This time, someone was waiting for her.

CHAPTER 31

Standing upon the stagnant stream of golds and oranges, vibrant rays of undulating purples bent and flexed in a feminine form. Each quiver of light built upon a continuous song emanating from the entirety of the entity. Music. Second child of the Chaos and the Cosmos. First child aligned to their father. Cocreator of the Mids. Defiler of Tobek.

"Little sister, why do you think so poorly of us?" Music asked. Each syllable was a lilting note, the sentence a lyric.

"Because I gave you my trust, and you abused it," Bix countered, darkness snapping around her, all thorns, malice, and pain.

Music tilted her head. "In what ways?"

"She's talking about him. She thinks we broke the guardian, don't you, little sister?" A husky feminine voice given to bellowing against the currents carried clearly from a massive gyroscope of orbital particles in motion with multiple gimbal rings in assorted hues of blue that shimmered into existence amid the dying energies of the Primary Mid World. Movement, eldest of the First Children, and much more like their mother. Dangerous for certain. After all, violence was chaotic action. Movement was the origin.

"Look at him, Movement," Bix seethed, needing every micron

of control not to assail her sister as Movement's cosmic gimbals swooped over and around Tobek's frozen body. "When the two of you came to me offering to fix him, to help him continue to evolve, you gave no indication that you would invite *all* our siblings to invade his essence and transmute his energies. Now, what is he? Cosmic rime? Your practical joke?"

"You're an idiot," Movement barked with disgust.

"She is broken," Music countered, daring to close the distance to Bix. "Anger is comfortable when one does not understand."

"I understand the six of you exploited the piece of me within him to wreak your havoc, and in so doing, bastardized the bond I have with him. Did Father put you up to it? I refused to execute Tobek, so Father had you do this as punishment? Does he disdain the creation of this type of Other? Does it skew his perfect plans for order and obedience? Does it threaten his hopes of bringing me back under his control?" Bix let her darkness grow and tumble from the timeline into vacated space as inner malice plotted and schemed revenge.

Music, however, remained unfazed. She drew an ethereal finger along Bix's temple and tucked a lock of hair behind Bix's ear. "Poor little sister. The hate you feed is a shield for the pain you are afraid to address. It makes you lash out for the wrong reasons at the wrong targets."

Bix knocked away Music's hand. "Look around, Music. Look at the Mid Worlds dying because of your indifference. Look at your chosen guardian rendered useless for doing his duty. Tell me again why the two of you are the wrong targets?"

"Esiw was right," Movement howled, changing gimbals to appendages as she consolidated her energies into a spark plug of a woman, sinuous strength rippling through every muscle. "You're looking for an excuse to pick a fight with us because you're feeling your way through this petty crisis rather than thinking your way through. Stop blaming us for the shit you've caused."

"I've caused? *I've* caused?" Bix stepped off the timeline, knowing full well her eldest sister was baiting her. Bix didn't care.

Scrapping with her eldest sister felt better than addressing the weeping pustule of bad memories straining against her thorns. "These are *your* Worlds. He is *your* guardian of these Worlds. *You* chose the caretakers of the Mids, then *you* chose him to be the thorn in their side."

"We chose the caretakers, yes; however, you chose the guardian." Music pinned her with a look of reproach and looped her arm around Bix's, marching Bix to Tobek's side. "You chose to spare him. You recognized his rage and knew it could be shaped into a force for balance in this collective. We backed you in that decision, just as we back your decision to save these Worlds instead of allowing us to create new ones to be your sanctuary."

"My…sanctuary?" Bix winced as a dribble from the pustule formed memories rife with crippling emotions that pounded behind her eye, then spilled into the bond she shared with Tobek. There was truth in Music's chastisement. Her sisters, indeed all her siblings, had petitioned Bix at various times to save this or that creation from the reorganizations and decluttering of their father. In the beginning, she'd been her father's means of thinning cosmic excesses; thus, the moniker of High Executioner. But, like any growing child, she'd developed opinions about chaos, order, and balance. Eventually, she'd stopped being her father's obedient drone and had started questioning what was necessary and what were simply his personal preferences. Since she believed the unexpected and inexplicable had every right to exist alongside the planned and allocated, it'd opened the door for her siblings to come to her for help. She was, after all, the two-in-one, equal parts Chaos and Cosmos.

"Yes, your sanctuary." Movement slapped her hands to Bix's cheeks and tilted Bix's head up, forcing their gazes to meet. "You fight for this collective because it's your home. Father wanted you to destroy something dear to me. You refused, so he destroyed something dear to you instead, leaving you adrift. In gratitude for your sacrifice, Music and I made this collective for you."

"Made. For me?" Bix leaned into her sister's hold as memories roiled and boiled, threatening to buckle her knees. There, amid the quixotic deluge, came the birth of the first triad of ley lines, the seeds of the first three Worlds. Three to represent Movement, Music, and Bix.

"We would've made you new ones to play with." Movement touched her brow to Bix's, bringing instant relief from the physical pains of selective recollections. "Yet, you insist on keeping these broken toys. You could have much, much better ones."

"Better how? I'm erasing time to save the lives that matter to me. Mortal lives. Messy lives." Bix covered her sister's hands with hers and leaned away. "In this collective, we make mistakes that affect nothing and everything. Fixing those mistakes demonstrates our emotional investment. Our caring. Sisters, I am once again *capable* of caring. I am capable of so many emotions, despite Father forcing me to bury them for so long. Here, in this oasis you made for me, I feel. Intensely. Finally. I can act on those feelings because you made these Worlds resilient...until you turned your backs on them and on me."

"Never on you. Ever." Music drummed her fingers along the tomb of ice covering Tobek. "We cannot directly change these Worlds. Like you, we are too powerful. He, however, we can affect, especially now."

"Now that the six of you had your way with him." Bix put distance between herself and her sisters as her temper rose once again. Movement had a hell of a left hook and delighted in testing Bix's reflexes. Yes. Many, many memories of that last bit.

"You want him to continue to grow, to continue to evolve, to continue to strive to be your eternal partner. There is no such entity out there. How do we, twins created by intention of balanced energies, foster an oddity capable of balancing *you*?" Music waved a hand, and scales of light manifested. Weights thunked side to side, off-balance. "For him to become what we all hope, it required the efforts of every First Child."

"Which of you hoped for the ice cube?" Bix scoffed.

"That is not our doing." Music sighed and glanced at Movement.

"It's your presence within him that causes it." Movement poked Bix's Eternal Knot. "You are the two-in-one. *Your* contributions to his evolution took him only so far before they started undoing *our* contributions."

"What?" Bix gasped.

"Balance, little sister." Music aligned her scales. "Your instinct is to instill balance in all things. That includes him."

"Each time he encounters great magic, he absorbs it, thus pushing his evolution forward." Movement pushed the space around them, sending a great gust rippling to the edges of the ether. "You undo it."

"I force him back to his newest factory setting, to the state of balance created by all of you?" Bix whimpered as horror dawned in her guts and branched out to every nerve with a billion pinpricks. The piece of her that lived within Tobek provoked his cosmic reset. It was undoing his progress. Despite every step forward he took, she returned him to the starting line. Would she have to destroy their bond so he could grow, so he could become something closer to a First Child, something capable of being her partner instead of her prisoner?

Oh gods, her prisoner. The thought dragged forth memories in an incomprehensible cacophony with one singular shared emotion: sorrow. She pinched the bridge of her nose hard, the discomfort enough to allow her to lock down that bursting baggage.

"The six of us, some of whom already played a part in his existence, were needed to counteract your degenerative influence on him. Try to counteract, at least." Movement bumped her shoulder against Bix's. "Truthfully, none of us know if what we did will work. Never been done before."

"Never been able to get us to agree to one thing before," Music admitted sadly. "But this guardian is special to you, so we tried. All of us."

Bix's eyes burned. She wiped away the tears that snuck up out of nowhere. How could she have been so wrong about everything? Her siblings? Tobek? The motivations? The outcomes? Her meltdowns?

Gah. Her infamous temper and her World-ending tantrums. They happened despite Tobek managing her excesses. She was well and truly emotionally fucked if—no, when—she severed their bond. Assuming he'd let her. She'd offered before, recently even, and he'd adamantly declined. He'd said it would devastate him. She was pretty sure it'd devastate her too. But losing everyone they cared about would be way worse. Way. Way. Worse. Wouldn't it?

"You said you couldn't directly fix the Mids, but you implied you'd made him capable of doing so. How? Clearly not by exsanguination in a root World. Been tried. What does he need? Aside from me to cease interrupting his evolution. And how can I stop the ley lines from blowing everything up while he does his thing?" Bix studied Tobek's frozen expression, the rage visible despite his long beard and wavy hair. She'd been wrong about a lot, but she was fairly certain he had no idea he alone was the key to the Mids' future. The moment time reset, they'd be racing against a doomsday clock. They needed every advantage. She wasn't too proud to ask for help.

"He is what he has always been, only more capable." Movement, with a press of her finger, spun Tobek's tomb as if it was nothing more than a fidget toy. "That means you have to get out of your own way and his. After that, it's all about the timing."

Bix considered that less than detailed instruction. What he'd always been was…what had she accused him of before the ley lines had blown up everything? What was it?

"He's a receiver and a transmitter?" she asked more than asserted as she analyzed recent events. "No. That can't be it. It's not communications that are needed. It's a cure for Devourer toxin that doesn't harm the Mids. The lines and the weave were communicating with him directly, and they still destroyed this World. He awoke with no advanced knowledge of the cure, not even a fragment beyond the foundational elements' desire to talk to the architects. He was as baffled as the rest of us. It must be something he doesn't know he can do. Something new. Something he couldn't do before you upgraded him…"

Her sisters stared at her with anticipation. She stared back, hoping for a stronger clue.

"He is the guardian you chose for the Mids and for yourself," Music prompted. "One wasn't possible without the other, not in the beginning."

"In the beginning," Bix echoed, scratching her Eternal Knot. "In the beginning, he was the receiver for my excess magic. He absorbed and converted it, then transmitted that conversion to the Mids. It's how he evolved. It's how Mids' magic evolved. In the beginning, that absorption happened through our bond, but he hasn't needed that direct feed in ages, not for that purpose. He's absorbency personified…which includes Devourer magic? Each confrontation with the Devourers has been an opportunity for his body to learn how to process their toxic essence. Their blood, their viscera, their magic, he's taken it all. Direct hits. Even though it harms him on the surface, his body still converts it. Only, I've been resetting him before he can feed that modified magic to the Mids."

"The problem with being too good at your calling," Movement drawled.

"Shit," Bix groaned as her heart sank. "To cure the lines and the weave, Tobek has to ingest their poison, amend it, and return it as an immunization. That's what the foundational elements were trying to do on Ariel's World. They failed because the part of me within him wouldn't allow it. That must be why they detoured to the Berserkers. When that failed, they went after Cian and Ashtad. The message they're trying to send is to me, isn't it? A message to let him go."

"You are the penultimate architect, second only to Father." Movement took Bix's hand and squeezed.

"Great." Bix rubbed her free hand over her face as another headache joined her heartache. "Now I just have to figure out when I'm supposed to have ripped out my heart and Tobek's for optimal salvation."

"The future you are trying to structure is one *you* can accept.

We've done what we can to give you that outcome. But, if you go too far back in time, his progress will not be the only one undone." Music took Bix's and Movement's hands, closing the circle of sorority. "Whatever future unfolds, know that we are here for you, little sister. Always."

"You two know how badly I want to save the Mids, so why didn't you tell me how to fix this mess before I made everything worse?" Bix asked, grateful yet baffled.

"Sister, you broke yourself for reasons none of us understand. We don't know how much help you want from us nor in what fashion until you ask." Movement bumped shoulders with Bix.

"Second-guessing you hasn't ended well for us, historically," Music trilled. "You are too much like Father with your complex machinations."

With a wry huff and a shake of her head, Bix opted for a group hug. Music laughed with a joy that sounded like rain upon waxy leaves while Movement danced them in a circle to the beat of Music's innate tempo.

"Thank you, sisters. I'm sorry for assuming the worst about you while being a consummate brat." Bix hugged her sisters tightly, then shambled back to the timeline anchored by the Mids. Returning to the lab hadn't unwound time far enough to stop the lines and weave from attacking. Returning to Ariel's trial would undo too much. Plus, Bix didn't want to erase the teams' collaborative efforts to save the Mids while she'd been putting her marbles in order. They needed to know their efforts mattered, that *they* mattered. From researcher to Berserker, human to dragon, their participation in the salvation of the Mids made them invested in the future of the Mids. Then there were the lives outside her immediate awareness, from Consortium to cockroach, that were influencing outcomes that could make notable differences in the long run. That meant the best place to reset time was the last place she'd reset Tobek.

Man, she hoped she was right.

Waving to her sisters, Bix walked back time, dreading the

impending end of her constant connection to Tobek. How the hell was she supposed to convince her Berserker to willingly break the bond they'd shared for eons? He had to be willing. Had to be. Anything less would wreck her, then she, with her unfiltered emotions, would wreck Worlds. It would be a lose-lose if he said no. But he was a guardian of the Mids. He was *the* guardian. He'd understand their friends and families came first. No matter how painful, he'd agree. Right?

CHAPTER 32

"No."

"Excuse me?" Bix blinked rapidly as her jaw dropped. She stood with Tobek upon the paused timeline of the Mid Worlds. Beyond the line, Feng and David remained suspended midmelt on Ariel's World, still trapped in the frantic tangles of Ariel's ley line.

Bix had chosen to restart the present one minute before she'd arrived on Ariel's World to fetch the frosted heroes. Back at the lab, Cian and Ashtad should've been waging their defense against the foundational elements, but the elements shouldn't have fully retreated from this World yet. She was claiming the few seconds of opportunity between the lines disconnecting from Tobek and the moment they turned their full attention on the lab. She'd learned from previous rounds of Groundhog Day that the scope of repercussions widened with each journey backward. Choosing the right moment to change was critical, even if the changes weren't going exactly as she hoped.

"No, I will not agree to separating from you in any way," Tobek repeated, gently but firmly, tapping the toe of one boot along the illuminated haze as if testing the stability of time. If he let go of her, he'd quickly discover it wasn't structurally sound for anyone other than a First Child aligned to the Cosmos. There was a reason Music had greeted her on the line while Movement had stayed in the present. Same reason Esiw had gathered her bits blasted across time instead of Eko. Time was a function of order.

"Maybe I wasn't clear. The salvation of the Mids and everyone we hold dear depends on you being able to process the poison of the Devourers and feed the purified woo to native magic without any interruptions, particularly from me," Bix clarified.

Tobek kissed her crown, her brow, and her cheek before whispering, "On us. From what you've told me, their salvation relies on our destruction."

"That's a bit of a fatalist's perspective." She leaned back against his strong arm holding her securely against him. "That's not like you at all. Where is the champion of the Mids? The guardian above all other guardians?"

"This guardian suffered three hundred years of forced separation the last time you placed the future of the Mids before the well-being of our family. I know the negative impact it had on me, on you, on those around us, and on native magic itself. So, no. I will not permanently sever our bond. We must find another way for me to purify the lines."

Bix bounced her forehead against his pec. "You're going to make me go all Ghost of Christmas Present, aren't you?"

"It's not necessary. There is nothing you can say or do that will change my mind." He had the gall to chuckle. "I can feel how much you don't want this to happen. Dread, despair, sorrow, it's all coming through."

"So you know I don't propose this lightly." She waved a hand and opened multiple viewing gates to the coal plant where the battalion had yet to rouse from their forced slumber. "This is what you're allowing to happen to your men. The foundational elements couldn't use you as they needed, so they hijacked your connection to your men. For two weeks, the battalion has been in a group coma, acting out a message from the elements in the form of ideograms."

Yes, she'd explained this to him before. Yes, before he'd seen the video compilations. But that was a Tobek from a different time. That Tobek had then been caught in the subsequent explosion. Explosions. Yes, she was banking on the Tobek of this timeline still being horrified.

"Felled by magic." He shrugged. "It's happened to us before. It's not pleasant, but it's the price of being part of the food chain. Stronger magics will have their way. Only thing we can control is our response to it."

Damn it. The present couldn't be recreated in perfection. That apparently included his reactions and opinions. If his men weren't enough to convince him in this timeline, she had to try a different approach.

"Thing is, you *are* the stronger magic," she reminded. "Your evolution? You maxed out phase one and are now entry-level phase two. Only you're going to be stuck here, never achieving your potential simply because you're too chicken to meet the baseline requirement."

A blond brow arched. "Did you just call me a chicken?"

"Bawk, bawk," she mocked.

"Not your strongest argument," he drawled.

"People are in successful, committed relationships without exchanging body parts, right? What we have is a cheat, really." She tapped her knot. "You feel what I feel. You don't have to second-guess anything. You can be supremely confident in not misreading one of my signals because you have a baked-in decoder ring."

He snorted. "Pissing off a cosmic entity who doesn't understand her own emotions is how Worlds end. Cohosted empathy is how you've managed to present as high-strung but mostly normal to those who haven't known you as long as I have."

"It's not about me being publicly palatable," she whispered loudly. "It's about trust and the notable lack of it you have in me."

"Pot, kettle," he countered, flexing his pec so his knot peeked in the vee of his unbuttoned Henley. "I'm abundantly clear on how little you actually trust me."

"Let's not leave out how little you trust yourself, shall we?"

She draped his long hair over his shoulders, then patted his chest. "How about we cut the romantic crap for a moment and admit that we didn't exchange parts to express our love and devotion? I took a piece of you and replaced it with a piece of me because you're my prisoner and I'm your warden. My presence within you is a constant reminder of the demigod you used to be. The destructive, insolent, entitled, angry, lost demigod who had to choose between lifetime imprisonment or execution."

"Remembering things now, are we?" he asked, mockingly aghast and possibly offended.

She gathered his beard and flipped the ends up, as though holding a bouquet. "It was on the glacial land bridge that connected what is now North America to Europe. You, with your silver arm and sword of light, stood on a beach, knee-deep in corpses, mostly humans. A dragon, full natural form, floated a half mile from shore, eviscerated. Your matted locks were caked with its hacked-up entrails. Your fur cloak was from an animal god you'd skinned. You'd lined it with angel feathers. Wrapping yourself in the stolen magics of so many others made finding you easy. Tragically, you stank like pterodactyl vomit. And when you finally saw me, your blood-crusted eyes lit, glowing with the rage that's widely known as Berserker's rage, yet should be called Tobek's Tantrum."

He leaned back and pulled a face. "Pterodactyl vomit? That's a new one."

"I was going to execute you on the spot." She poked his knot on the last three words for emphasis. "But *Gurp* crawled out of a little hole in the ice and pleaded for mercy."

"Surprised the hell out of me too." He grunted and winced as the curse of silence caused his knot to blister. Still, he kept going through gritted teeth, "First time I'd ever laid eyes on the goblin. Hadn't realized he was there, to be honest. Probably would've killed him if I had. I was having a very bad life."

"I'd sent him to follow you. Could he and his great big heart find *any* redeemable aspect of you? He didn't, by the way." She frowned at the knot burning through his shirt, at the colors of her siblings shimmering where it should've been her teal. There would be one advantage of breaking their bond, and it was breaking that damn curse. She hated how that thing kept inserting itself in the middle of their intimate conversations.

"He is a wise goblin." Tobek groaned, throwing back his head and breathing through the pain of the curse. "And you are an obstinate daughter of the Chaos and the Cosmos."

"Whom you wanted to kill." She reached for his knot but stopped. Her touch wouldn't bring him any relief…and his agony probably helped her argument. Maybe. He did have a pain fetish, after all.

"Quite. Badly," he growled and dropped his head forward as his shoulders hunched. The singed bits of his shirt clung to the char and weeping of his knot.

It was her turn to kiss his brow and whisper in his ear, "Now here we are, countless eons later, and again I give you a choice: do you want to become my partner or remain my prisoner?"

He tipped his head to the side, nuzzling her, temple to temple. "You don't understand what I went through for three hundred years of not feeling you. I don't ever wish that hollow, frantic isolation on you."

"And how long have you lived with my constant distrust? How many times did you guess it was born of fear? How long will you punish yourself because you're as afraid as I am?" Her voice quavered. Memories were a funny thing, relational, not linear. Exploring the memory of the day she'd met him also opened the maw of complex emotions she'd felt because of him. It ran the gamut. At one end, radiant, heart-bursting joy; at the other end, that big festering wad of agonies she was *not* going to examine, not when she was in an inhabited area. That introspection required deep space and possibly removal from all timelines just to be safe. But in the now, she needed a beat before she could speak somewhat clearly. "My trust issue with you is that I'm terrified the moment I relinquish my hold on you becomes the moment you run away from me forever."

He jerked his head up. His eyes searched her face. His fingers jabbed in her hair, and he pulled her tightly against him. "Never. Gods, never, ever."

"We're immortal. Never is a long time." She looked away as a tear dribbled over her cheek. Whoa, emotions. If she got what she wanted and what he needed, she would feel all this way more potently because he wouldn't be filtering for her anymore. Equal parts horrifying and about damn time. "I used to justify keeping you tethered because I needed you to be my passkey to the Mids. It was a lie. After the first millennia, you'd sufficiently evolved so a direct connection was no longer required. I simply *liked* having the connection to you."

"Believing you needed me made the power inequity palatable in the beginning and reassuring after that." He doubled over with a groan as the curse intensified. The smell of charred flesh wafted from his knot. His hand trembled as it slid down her back to clutch her hip. "I don't want to let you go. It's selfish, I admit it. I don't care. I've given enough. I've earned my joy."

"It's not letting me go. It's us learning a different way to hold each other." She captured his furry face between her hands, drawing him up. "New beginnings are disquieting until we find our way to the new normal. We've done it before. We'll do it again. You're the one who said that, remember?"

He leaned into her hand, rubbing his cheek against her palms. "If we do this, does it stop the dangers I bring to those around me? Freezing up during conflicts, overdoing spells, putting the men in comas?"

"Because you're a new and improved cosmic sponge, whenever you're exposed to diverse potent magics—like the Devourers' or even Feng's—your evolution progresses. However, the piece of me inside you can't abide the imbalance an evolved you presents to the universe, so it undoes your progress. That causes your body and magic to assume you're under egregious assault; thus, in a feat of self-preservation, you shut down and retreat into what is your native state to heal."

"My native state is a block of ice?" He stilled, then huffed. "That's a bit disappointing."

"If you'd ascended to godhood, you would've been what? A sea god à la Poseidon? Be glad you're not a puddle." She tweaked his beard. "As for screwing up spells, that's all you and figuring out the new parameters for where and how you source and expel the magics to which you now have access."

"Unwilling to take the blame for that, eh?" He winked, straightening.

"I've got too many of my own screwups to claim yours too," she opined.

"And purifying the lines? You're sure I'm the cure?" He eyeballed Ariel's ley line, still frozen in ice, still paused in time. "That line knew why David was bleeding me and still refused to allow us to try the cure. It physically restrained David and Feng."

"It either doesn't know or it realizes you can't because of our bond." She snuggled into his side once again. "The collective consciousness of the foundational elements figured out your role and my interference. I like to think they're aware I'm not intentionally obstructing, and that's the reason they're trying to reach me."

He nodded. "Through the mortals of your inner circle."

"Our inner circle," she corrected.

"Let's say I acquiesce," he hedged. "Any idea how I'm supposed to absorb the toxins from the lines? The most effective way to do it is to take the poison in all at once, but the elements are in a loose weave of multiple intersections. There is no singular point where they all merge."

"You are that singular point." She stuck her finger in the middle of his beard and twirled it until all his hairs touched her skin. "Whenever you are in the Mids, you have only to open yourself to the elements for them to come to you, the hub. Downside, I doubt that much magic all at once is going to be pleasant, at least at this stage of your evolution."

"Phase two, level-one entity. Still going to wind up as Colonel Extra Crispy. Got it."

She cracked a smile despite the weight of the situation. "I would suggest connecting with them on Ariel's unpopulated World. If I'm wrong about the method…well, what's watching another World explode when I can just undo it, right?"

He squeezed her hip. "It doesn't erase what you've witnessed from your mind. For every reset of time, you add another burden to the many you already carry."

"What will it be for us?" She looked up and caught him gazing at her wistfully. "The frightening or the familiar?"

He lifted his hand to her face and stroked her cheek for long moments as they stood in heavy silence. She let him think. It was actually comforting that he was giving the issues serious consideration. They'd been attached at the…well, attached for ages and ages. Continents had broken up in the time they'd been inhabiting each other. No doubt it would be disconcerting, and no doubt they'd have to work on their communication skills, but what couple didn't? It was almost funny. They were afraid of being normal. Ridiculous, right?

"Promise me something," he rumbled at last. "Promise me that when all this is done, when I've hit my peak and finally become your true partner, promise me that we will exchange parts as demonstrations of commitment, love, and mutual respect."

She held up three fingers. "Assuming we don't blow up each other or all existence by doing so, I solemnly vow to permanently invade your personal space."

He pulled her close for a kiss, one that curled her toes.

"Okay," he rasped. "Let's learn how to hold each other differently."

"That's my brave blond bear." This time, she instigated the kiss, wrapping her arms around his neck as her darkness wrapped around his body.

One tentacle of night speared through his Eternal Knot, burrowing beneath the influences of her siblings to find the displaced piece of herself embedded within his essence. He inhaled sharply against her lips. She tangled her fingers in his hair, holding him close as she focused on joy and love, pushing all the good emotions to him, flooding him with optimism and encouragement. Never would she want their final shared feelings to be anything less than positive. Swiftly, without hesitation or second thought, she ripped the piece of herself from him and returned his missing piece in its place. His kiss turned hard as the bray of a wounded beast escaped him. Their shared tears scalded her cheeks and salted their lips.

They clung to each other, outside time, mourning the loss.

CHAPTER 33

Fingers laced tightly with Tobek's, Bix returned to the present on Ariel's World within a shelter of gates and with her Berserker at her side. Feng and David thudded into the muck as time flowed forward. The Phoenix and the dragon roared and struggled against the tangles of the ley line. Ice melted across the lakes. Fragments surged at Bix.

"Now, Tobek, summon the foundational elements to you now. We don't have a moment to waste," Bix encouraged, throwing open more gates to shield the line from her presence.

Grip tightening before releasing her hand, Tobek stepped fully from her protections and planted his big feet on the fading roots of Ariel's ley line. His eyes glowed blue. His magic glowed green. He turned to face her, his jaw clenched.

"Don't leave," he growled. "I need your strength."

"Whatever you want," she called. "You'll just have to tell me. Preferably in words."

"Bix? What's happeni—" Feng cried out, his back bowing as Mids' magic converged on Ariel's World and ripped through its living welfare gauge. The black staining his veins spread into the rachides of his feathers, visible only for a moment before he burst into flames.

"It's too much. They'll destroy this World," David shouted, dragging herself upright. The scrolls within her scales that branded her the daughter of a dragon queen glowed in plums and lavenders as native magic flooded the core in a cacophony of discordant scuds.

"Tobek's absorbing the load. He can handle it. You, however, can't." Bix flung gates around the dragon, burying David in layers while affording a view of the ley lines assailing the evolved hub. There were things happening that a scientist probably needed to see, especially a scientist leading the charge for a cure for lines and mortals alike.

Ominous crackling echoed throughout as the Fates' weave emerged from layers of the World to join the ley lines. Netting of multitudinous threads engulfed Tobek, cocooning him in the blues, purples, and greens of the foundational elements.

Feng keened his agonies at the new arrivals, so Bix boxed him up too. He might be able to handle the influx of Mids' magic in his own fiery way, but the Fates' Other World magic wasn't meant for him.

With the witnesses safeish, Bix focused on Tobek. Her fists clenched, and she bit her lip as his cocoon writhed and undulated. Once upon a time, she would've drawn the excess from him, affording him breathing room to finish a spell before being burned to a crisp by the magic he wielded. Not anymore. Without the part of her existing within him to give her access to his essence regardless of their physical distance, she'd have to go through the foundational elements to reach him. For her to touch a foundational element was to harm it. Downside of being an almost-whole cosmic entity. Plus, her sisters had been very clear that she had to get out of his way in order for him to achieve his potential. She might be obtuse, but she could follow directions when it suited.

Her heart stopped as the cocoon blackened. Gooey slurping resonated along the foundational elements as they pumped their poison into the cocoon. Bix slapped her hand over her mouth and fought down the lurching of her stomach as the sounds amplified. The clashing songs of the ley lines rose to piercing screeches. A foul stench of noxious rot wafted into Bix's shelter, stinging her eyes and making her tongue tingle.

Whatever Tobek was enduring inside that cocoon had to be infinitely worse. She wanted to send him strength and reassurance, but the best she could do was think it. She laid her hand over her heart, over the place her Eternal Knot had once been, letting the chill of the once-warm patch anchor her in the moment. Her mind was such a fickle thing that she swore she could feel Tobek's heartbeat leading the echo of hers.

Wait.

She *did* feel his heartbeat. She'd lived with a piece of him long enough to know his unique rhythms. After all, she'd timed her corporeal pulse to mimic his. His every beat had been a reminder for hers to throb. The familiar bass thumping was not originating within her, despite it sending vibrations through her. She stepped to the threshold of her shelter, leaning ever so slightly over the edge.

Sonic bursts. Emanating from the cocoon. The foundational elements were echoing Tobek's heartbeat. Their clashing songs modulated until every ley line shared the same beat. Melodies tuned to harmonious octaves. What had started as a clowder of cats trapped in a steel drum played as a robust symphony.

The deep tarry hue of the cocoon adopted a green tint. As the music flowed, the foundational elements pushed sonic waves with each downbeat. Blended magics washed through Bix's shelter like a building storm front. The cocoon continued to brighten. Deep forest greens lightened to shades of emerald. Within the cocoon's weave, a marbling of purples and blues emerged.

It was working. Tobek was converting Devourer ick to evolutionary catalysts for the foundational elements. The man was a living, breathing receiver, converter, and transmitter of magics. Pride welled within her. Her smile threatened to take over her face.

The damn man was a fucking miracle. And she had her siblings to thank for it. All of them.

Bix swayed to the song of the ley lines as the foundational elements continued to build their strength and cleanse the Devourer taints from their system. She layered more gates around the shelters she'd made for David, Feng, and herself as the healing storm raged. The mud of the core spun into tornadoes. The roots of the native ley line glowed brightly and swelled from the center to the farthest reaches. Blackish oily slicks drained from the lakes. Sinews grew from south to north and north to south, braiding a lattice that built into an undulating indigo honeycomb connecting the two halves of Ariel's ley line. Within the cells of the comb, images played. Lives being boldly lived across the Mids, within the influence of this line.

Wonder and sorrow and joy and...and a mess of emotions had Bix swallowing rapidly, wringing her hands, and trying to control her breathing. Ariel's ley line was whole again, and it was beautiful. She'd never been close enough to the heart of a ley line to see its many chambers. When she'd arrived here in Feng's protection, she'd assumed the lakes were the origin points. It hadn't occurred to her that they were bleeding stumps. She hadn't understood the breadth of the damage. None of her team had. It'd been new territory for all of them. Now, oh, but now the line's restoration was nothing less than awesome.

Thunder boomed, knocking Bix deeper into her gates.

The cocoon blasted apart. The elements retreated. The storm abated. The symphony reduced to the singular instrument of Ariel's healthy line.

Tobek slumped to the ground, naked, skin lightly charred, hair sparking green magic, inked torso glowing as tattoos moved. A blink, and Bix was on her knees at his side upon a sliver of gate keeping her separated from the ley line's roots. She carefully drew him into her lap and pressed her lips to his crown.

"You did it," she whispered as potent emotions swelled in her throat, threatening to strangle her. "My big blond bear, you did it."

The corner of his lips twitched. His lashes fluttered. Bright blue eyes slowly lost their Berserker's glow as Tobek focused on her face.

"Gurp," he wheezed. "Shower. Lye."

Laughing, she released the Phoenix and the dragon from their protective boxes to do their assessments of Ariel's World and line. They didn't need her gates to get home. Mids' magic would take care of that.

"By all the… This World is balanced," David rasped, slapping her huge dragon's feet along the ground as her wings brushed the ceiling. "It's tangible, the presence of dragons' magic balancing out angels' magic. It's almost like my mother's here again."

"Only the other ley lines could restore balance to this World," Bix explained. "Consider it an advantageous side effect of drawing the foundational elements here."

"Go on, get him home," Feng urged, spreading his wings and shaking out the molt. His veins and the rachides of his feathers were no longer black, his skin no longer tinted gray. Native magic's welfare gauge was well again. With a coo of relief, he compressed into his human form, clad in academic chic. He swept a grand bow and straightened with a wink. "Chief's done more than anyone has a right to ask. David and I will run tests here on the line and the World, see if there's anything to be learned that can be applied to the mortals of the Mids also affected by the Devourers. We'll catch you back at the lab."

"I want more samples from him," David chimed in, manifesting lab equipment with a flap of her leathery wings.

Feng sharply cleared his throat and arched a brow.

"Which can be after his shower and perhaps a rest," David amended.

"Definitely after a long, long rest. We'll see you later." Bix opened gates to Tobek's basement home beneath the coal plant and the very large multijetted shower custom-built for his bulk. Knowing Gurp, the lye would be waiting in the niche and the goblin would be waiting in the hall.

CHAPTER 34

Bix solidified her form into its corporeal state and snuggled against the warmth of her Berserker. Flannel sheets, fluffy pillows, and a fluffier comforter carried his reassuring musky scent of nutmeg, cedar, and sandalwood with a final note of wintergreen. She danced her fingers over the ink covering his Eternal Knot. Even though she'd lost hers, he'd kept his as the anchor for her siblings' influence on his evolution. A bittersweet reminder of their new normal.

"Welcome back." Tobek closed his big hand over hers and brought her palm to his lips for a furry kiss.

"Didn't take you with me?" She hooked one leg over his, drawing his thigh between hers.

"A few times. We've been to see your brothers, your sisters, and Ariel's World. However, you left me here while you prowled the compound. Well, part of you prowled, part of you remained here."

"Must be more worried about the guys than I realized." She stretched. "Did I trigger the wards? Wake everybody up?"

"Turns out I trigger the wards now too, so blame is not solely yours for their restless night. Fortunately, the foundational elements were kind enough to enlighten me on how to improve our security to accommodate the many changes we've all gone through. Gurp, Xipil, and a few of the boyos are upstairs making the modifications. By tonight, we should no longer be grounded to our rooms." He laid his cheek atop her head. "When they're done, you can move back in, permanently."

"We family, yes?" she asked in her best Gurp impersonation. The idea of coming home to her favorite goblin and Tobek again made her essence sing. She missed living below the sea of testosterone.

"Always family." Tobek chuckled. "I want to try something. Ask me a question about our past."

"Testing the curse of silence? It was tied to the part of me that used to reside within you. You should be safe." She leaned back on his bicep to study his face. On the surface, he didn't look any different for all his recent tumult. Only the most observant would notice his pupils had kept an inhuman shade of dark green. Otherwise, he still passed as an inked-up extra on a Viking movie set.

"Your siblings have had their way with me, and, frankly, Movement strikes me as the sort who would double down on that curse." He arched a brow as his lips twitched.

"Yeah, fair. Very fair." She flipped back the covers to see if he was clothed. "If she did, you probably want to be wearing more than your long briefs. Think cross-World journey. Possibly another galaxy. I know how you are about your dignity."

"Modesty is your chosen burden, not mine." He closed his eyes anyway and green magic glowed around his hips and legs as dark jeans manifested on his lower half. "Okay. Hit me."

"There are a billion questions I want to ask you." She traced one of the arcane symbols tattooed on his abs.

"Maybe start small, in case the higher the introspection, the further my propulsion," he drawled.

Snickering, she spun the mental bingo cage for a hopefully innocuous question. "Did you ever try to make me eat real food?"

"Make you? No. Passively encourage it? Often, in the

beginning. Mostly because it disgusted you, and I was keen to make you suffer in whatever little ways I could." He gasped, and his eyes widened.

"Oh, fiend." She tickled his side, earning a flip to her back as he straddled her. "When we re-met, when I was clueless about who you are to me, you offered me food. Steak and broccoli, to be precise. Was that another passive-aggressive move?"

"In my defense, that was common hospitality with a side order of testing to see how well you'd assimilated modern human culture." He planted his hand beside her head and leaned down to brush his nose against hers. "Besides, I didn't want to give you another excuse to dislike me after I'd shot you in the ass with a hose."

"For the record, I don't regret throwing the broccoli at you." She hooked her fingers in his waistband, needing to maintain a physical connection to him. "How'd the confessions feel? You're not on your knees doubled over in agony nor stuck to the kitchen wall, so I'm guessing we can finally have those deep, heart-to-heart conversations that fill romance novels?"

"I prefer the steamier parts of those books." He kissed her neck and growled like a lusty beast against her skin. "Step one in improving our oral communications: establishing the ability to have unfettered oral communications. I think it was a success."

"There is no timeline in which that doesn't sound dirty," she purred, arching her back. "I'm picturing it now. Us, snuggled up on the couch under a fuzzy blanket. Fragranced candles casting long shadows. You trapped, unable to escape my endless interrogation. Sounds like a mighty fine evening…or a thousand evenings."

"Oh, I have plenty of my own questions, sweetheart. We've been separated for over three centuries." He waggled his brows.

"Touché," she quipped.

Sirens bleated and orange lights flashed across the basement. Groaning, Tobek rolled off her and the bed, landing on his feet.

Bix sat up, pushing her hair out of her face. "I thought Gurp was fixing the wards."

"That's not a security alarm. I'm being summoned upstairs." He grabbed a T-shirt from the shelves that doubled as walls in the modern-industrial man cave and stuffed his feet into the biker boots by the foot of the bed.

With a flick of her wrist, Bix opened viewing gates to the only public entrance of the coal plant, the heavy glass and iron door of the body modification shop Dysmorphic. The shop didn't have any customers since the battalion was still on the Consortium-ordered lockdown. Berserkers in stalls tossed aside their sketchbooks and snapped to attention, saluting smartly to a dozen men and women of various mortal races dressed in the Mid World Army's service uniforms.

"Another inspection team?" Bix asked, sliding out of bed, tugging her pilfered MOPAR T-shirt into place. "The MWA can't still think the battalion is guilty of the raids carried out by the Devourers."

"Thanks to the draugr's tenure in Moccus's body, we learned why the Devourers were impersonating us." Tobek drew symbols in the air. Green magic coated his body, changing his casual wear to a fancy uniform with all kinds of colorful bars and stripes similar to the ones worn by the guests in the shop. "Every location on the hit list was part of the Mid World guardians' defense network. People, places, totems, everything taken or destroyed by the Devourers was integral to the gods' plans. Over the ages, we'd helped the guardians establish certain parts of their system."

"Making your guys the perfect patsies." Bix tsked. "And the MWA fell for it, hook, line, and sinker."

"Which is why I'm not surprised to see our visitors." Tobek grabbed a bright blue beret from another shelf before leaning over to kiss Bix's cheek. "Those are my peers from the other branches of the Mid World Army. They should be here for Xipil, but those flashing lights mean I'm the one they want. That reeks of Consortium Oversight Committee, the same committee who conveniently *forgot* when they'd issued orders that conflicted with the timing of the raids."

"Ariel's allies on the committee." Bix laid a hand on his arm. "Wait, you're meeting them in uniform. Does this mean you're going to re-up with the army?"

He paused and looked down at himself, brows knitting. "They happily sacrificed my men to politics. If you and I hadn't returned when we did, the committee would've batch-retired the battalion. There is no way in any hell I let that slide. Forces will be called to account."

"Sic 'em," Bix whispered loudly, smiling. "If you need me…"

She laid her hand against the cold around her heart. Disappointment speared through her swiftly and painfully. No more direct connection to her Berserker.

Tobek grabbed her chin between his finger and thumb. Magics native and Other pulsed through the basement with enough gusto to make Bix's hair dance. Tobek kissed her one more time, then drew back with a playful grin. "As long as you're within the network of the foundational elements, I'll be able to reach you."

"Nice." She furiously wiped the tears that came way too frequently of late. "Sorry about the waterworks. They seem to be my new overflow coping mechanism."

"Cut yourself a break. It's going to take time for you to get comfortable with the fullness of your emotions. Consider me an expert." He caught a tear on his thumb and rubbed it into his palm.

"How are you doing with our new normal? Are you ready to face the Consortium? Especially in the aftermath of this mission?" She genuinely didn't know. She couldn't tap into the thrum of his calm or ride the tides of his temper anymore. She felt like a goof for asking, but there was no other way for her other than ordinary communication.

"Truthfully? I feel hollow. Like a huge chunk of me is missing." He thumped his chest. "I'm analyzing the part of me you returned, sensing that it has developed differently. It lacks the rage that's so intrinsically me but can't compare to the complexity that's you. I have physical changes that I've yet to catalog, and magical boundaries that have shifted and remain undefined. I'm angry, but not at you—at the circumstances that forced our separation. The Consortium's colossal abuse of power is fully within the realm of blame on that latter point. So am I ready to face them? I'm looking forward to it."

She could only imagine. The thrill of evolution was a given for him and his endless thirst for knowledge, but the rug on which he'd stood for so long had been yanked away. His foundations needed repair, possibly a redesign. Strategy and long-term planning were standard components of his thought processes, but hard to do when he wasn't sure of his assets. That last part she totally empathized with. Unloading on the Consortium? She envied him that.

"Then, even if you can't feel my encouragement and pride, know that they go with you." She tipped her head and opened a gate to the morgue. "There's a saying about a man in uniform, and I'd hate for you to get schmutz on your hunksomeness."

"Keep feeding my ego. I love it and you." He waggled his brows, then grimaced at the morgue shining on the far side of the gate. "I expect this to take longer than a while. Would you tell David I'll be around after things shake out, please?"

She nodded mostly to herself as gates closed behind him. She had some loose threads to tidy up with her team, not to mention a desperate need to overwrite the memories of their horrific deaths.

Blended magic zipped through the basement on a strong breeze that made Bix's shirt ruffle and a pillow fall off the bed. A black dress, naughty underpinnings, and a pair of delightfully impractical pumps appeared atop the comforter. Touching the fabric confirmed her attire was capable of surviving her Other Worldly travels far beyond the Mids. A new feat for a Tobek original. Grinning, she headed for the shower and added a tick to the evolutionary advantages column.

CHAPTER 35

Excitement rippled through the lab on constant currents. Researchers hustled and slid from workstation to workstation, eager to share whatever had everyone in such a good mood. Smiles abounded despite deep concentration. Staffing exceeded Bix's first visit, with a notable increase in representatives from the Angelic Host. Bix had no idea if they were Samael's angels or if the "secret" research was no longer secret after Tobek had cleaned the foundational elements.

No one paid her much mind as she made her way to the throng surrounding a transparent containment chamber where Cian's opaque one had been. It sounded like dueling auctioneers at the front of the gathering while an occasional cheer went up from the crowd. Rings of monitors around the chamber flashed molecular models, charts, and data streams. Scattered among the crowd, standing heads and shoulders above the researchers, were Berserkers…who should've been at the coal plant.

"My lady," cheered Hywl, shouldering his way outward from the inner circle. He paused now and again to share a smile with those he was displacing. No one seemed annoyed. In fact, it was all high camaraderie.

"Hywl, I'm surprised to see you here. Happy to see you, but

surprised." Bix edged back as a round of thrilled whooping came from the observers.

The Welshman motioned her toward the circle, ahead of him. "You saw fit to put me here last night along with Runjit and a few medics. We weren't entirely sure why until David showed us this. Oy, oy, give the Chimera some room, yeah?"

Bodies shuffled, clearing a narrow path where more Berserkers crouched or knelt at the front of the circle, likely letting the folks behind them see inside the containment chamber. Within the clear walls, Runjit, David, and two other researchers wearing full biohazard suits scanned, weighed, or measured rocks. Not just any rocks—geodes. Hundreds of them in different colors lined glass shelves, pulsing hues of dark green.

Bix's heart skipped and flipped as she turned to Hywl. "Are those what I think they are?"

"My lady, those are *who* you think they are." Hywl beamed down at her. "Those numbers you're hearing over the speakers? Growth rates. We're talking micrometers for sure, but it's the first sign of change they've shown since being felled by traitors."

Spies, soldiers, and researchers, all magical Mids mortals, had turned into geodes after being injected with Devourer blood. It was the advanced stage of where Cian was headed if David couldn't find a cure. By all appearances, David's team was finally making progress. Maybe the foundational elements were lending a hand. Or maybe David had learned a lot from the purification of Ariel's World and line. Whatever the source of the epiphany, Bix was glad for it.

"A delightful way to be reminded how far collaboration can take us." Bix scanned the crowd. "Don't suppose you've seen Cian or Ashtad?"

"David has the kid hooked to machines, but he's free from quarantine. He's in a medical bay on the other side of this frenzy." Hywl let loose a cheer as Runjit held up a geode and gave his battle buddy a thumbs-up. The rock must've been a fellow soldier.

"I'll leave you to it." Bix patted Hywl's arm and let a gate take her from the throng to the slightly quieter medical section, where hospital beds were lined up and curtains pulled back. Bix paused at the sight of angels in the beds, allowing researchers to take samples.

"Ariel's choir," Feng explained from a bed farther down, situated between Cian and Ashtad. The Phoenix had a white-knuckled grip on a game controller, leaning into every action as if it would aid the speed and accuracy of his avatar in the fantasy video game playing on a large monitor that held his and Cian's unwavering attention. Cian tapped his game controller with equal gusto but added a few grunts for emphasis. In the bed on the far side of Cian, a tragically frail woman with a colorful scarf partially covering her hairless head flipped through bridal magazines. The kid was the only one hooked up to any machines; the rest of the team seemed to be there for moral support.

Joy and pride shot through Bix with enough zing to make her eyes burn. She refused to cry in front of her team. Frankly, the tears were beyond annoying at this point. Oh, but to see her team alive, well, and whole? It was the greatest gift.

"Having her angels here is risky, isn't it?" Bix asked, forcing a modicum of composure as the bald woman lowered her magazine and patted the bed beside her, giving a glimpse of the blue moons in her nails and the death stain on her lips.

"This whole mission's been one long uninterrupted screaming risk." Ashtad chuckled, glancing up from his tablet to toss Bix a grin. "Didn't think bringing down the Chair of the Consortium was going to be part of it, much less the easiest part."

"Like her line and her World, Ariel was infected with Devourer taint." Feng cursed under his breath and hammered on the controller with his thumbs. "Not that it excuses what she's done. For obvious reasons, the Host is unwilling to allow Ariel to participate directly in the research for a mortal cure, so David gets her choir instead."

"We sure that's safe for everyone down here?" Bix hopped up on the bed beside Drew, letting her feet dangle off the side.

"The lines blabbed to their birth mates, so the secret of the lab and its research is out." The breeze carrying the message reached Bix moments before Archangel Samael joined them. "Don't worry, Michael and Raphael are in their heads. The lesser angels will be good little specimens."

"Well, hello stranger," Drew drawled in her best Southern belle accent. "Welcome back to the party."

"Been busy following up on those leads you gave me about Ariel's unsanctioned prisons." Samael jostled the foot of Ashtad's bed. "Thought the demigod here might want in on the liberation of those other Mid World guardians."

Ashtad leapt out of bed. "I could do with a break from the lab. Thanks. Mind if I bring along the demis who helped flush Ariel out of her chambers? The challenge would go a long way in our trials to godhood."

"Round them up. There are plenty of sites in need of breaching." Samael eyed Feng and Drew. "Phoenix, draugr, what say you?"

"I'm full up on crazy gods, but I appreciate the invitation." Drew fired a finger gun at Samael. "I'll stay here with the herb nerd."

Feng cursed again and chucked the controller in Cian's lap. "The kid's kicked my ass repeatedly in this game, so I could use a bit of real-life redemption."

"Good, good. Teams are assembling in the basement of the kid's rowhouse. You should head over." Samael wagged his thumb over his shoulder, waiting while Ashtad and Feng made their goodbyes.

Bix waved to her guys and wished them luck, happiness bubbling within her.

Samael sauntered to Bix, keeping his back to the room. "My line mentioned you and the original Berserker made a great personal sacrifice to cure native magic and to speed its evolution. Didn't say specifically what it was, only that it was significant."

Bix reached for her Eternal Knot but stopped herself. That

was a habit she had to break. There was nothing there anymore. Still, she couldn't bring herself to speak. Not only was this not the place, but the matter was private.

Samael grunted and nodded. "Routing the last of the rot doesn't evict the Devourers from the Mids, does it? Not even upgrading the lines did that, right?"

Bix nodded. "All we did was shore up the foundational elements. The Consortium has work to do before Resen can launch, and we need Resen operational to locate the enemy who is already here while repelling the larger army staging in the ether."

"But Resen's only going to keep the little guy out." Samael looked to Cian when he spoke. "The higher-ranking ones, we still have to fight those."

"That's on the gods. They're the only ones who can kill an anti-god. You guys have to protect your creations and these Worlds from the casualties of war and from the opportunists who inevitably make things worse." Bix didn't mention Tobek or the changes in his men. There was so much she didn't know about their evolution or how Tobek envisioned their future. Could they stand against the Devourer army and win? She didn't know.

There was a pregnant silence before Samael slapped the foot of her bed. "Then you and I are still a team, Chimera. Allies all the way through getting those hangry bastards out of our collective, that's our deal. I'm holding you to it."

"Likewise, Samael, likewise," Bix countered with a smile.

Laughing, the archangel vanished, likely to join the liberation troops.

Bix tapped a foot on the rail of Cian's bed. His crystals were still active, but nowhere as bright and blessedly silent. "So, team leader, are we calling this mission a success?"

"The original mission was just to get samples to David without any of us getting killed." Cian rolled his eyes. "Think it's fair to say we went above and beyond."

"Then congratulations on your first successful operation." Bix grinned as the kid blushed.

"I'd have been dead in a day if you guys hadn't been there for me," he admitted.

"Assembling the right team is the best way to ensure everyone comes home alive." Drew wagged a rolled-up magazine at the kid. "Well, aliveish."

"Hey, did you ever compile those ideograms the Berserkers were forming?" Bix asked. She'd assumed the foundational elements had been trying to send her a message about Tobek, but she'd been wrong a lot on this mission, so maybe proving her assumptions true was in order.

"Yeah, yeah, stripped them down to straight pictures. I can send them to your smartwatch if you start wearing it again." Cian looked pointedly at her wrist.

"Great, thank you." Bix reached through tiny gates to her stash of backup tech, fetching a new smartwatch. She fired it up and keyed in the requisite codes for updates and authorizations. "You know, speaking of nonstandard messaging, you should figure out what it is Ariel's ley line is trying to tell you."

Cian paled, and Drew sat up straighter.

"Uh, Bixie, what do you mean?"

"His crystals. Their light show. It's a message to the only architect who was paying attention at the time the line most needed a friend." Bix tapped her watch as images of ideograms flashed across the screen and projected down her sleeve.

"This is a message from an arcane ley line?" Cian squawked under his breath, gaping at his solid shoulders. "It's trying to talk to *me*? A lowly Sage? A mostly human kid? Man, I am living my best life."

"The fact it's still trying to get through to you, even after it's been healed, makes it all the more intriguing, wouldn't you say?" Bix baited.

Cian snorted and grabbed his laptop from the tray beside his bed. "David recorded all my funkadelia. Where do you think I should start for translations? Signal lamps used Morse code, but the Crimson Market uses colored light to stream wireless data. Maybe I should start by identifying the colors, then worry about…"

Bix and Drew watched as the kid lost himself in a new challenge.

"That's the thing about Sages. Dangle a tidbit of information in front of them, and they go all bloodhound." Drew patted Bix's thigh. "How are you doing, babe? Before you say 'fine,' remember how well I know you."

"You first." Bix returned the thigh pat. "How was it being inside a crow? I know how much you hate occupying birds."

Drew tipped her head and shook it. "What crow?"

"When you vacated Runjit," Bix prompted.

"Nah, babe, no crow." Drew shoved Bix's shoulder. "Suckling pig from the battalion's freezer. It was the best Gurp could do with the plant on lockdown."

Bix started to argue but caught herself. The present couldn't be recreated in perfection. The crow was from a time that no longer existed.

"Suckling pig, how fitting. I'm sad I missed that." Bix shook off the slip of reality and smiled at her bestie. "Dish, girl, I want all the details about your last great occupation."

Drew scooted back and patted her pillow with a twinkle in her dead eyes. "Then you'd best throw up some privacy gates, 'cause I have all kinds of scoop for you."

Giggling, Bix stretched out beside her bestie and opened the requested gates.

CHAPTER 36

Bitter wind skipped along the Potomac River as late autumn cast a fine mist over the waterfront of Old Town Alexandria, Virginia, Primary Mid World. Fragrances of pumpkin spice and mulled cider rolled out the doors of restaurants and shops, stamping their claims on wool coats and loose braids as customers readied for feasts of thanks. Dogs barked in hopeful greeting, while jets roared through landings at nearby National Airport. Coils of smoke from chimneys dotted the skyline of the historic district, then gave way to the gleam of high-rise windows farther upriver. In the distance, the Washington Monument stood unaffected by the political battles being fought beneath the District.

The Consortium had released artfully crafted propaganda to the masses of Chweds explaining the new locations of the ley lines and the resulting changes in native magic as a precursor to the enhanced security that was coming with the launch of the new Mid World defense system. While the Consortium hadn't directly addressed the Devourer panic sweeping through the Chweds, they did leave room for assumptions. Humanity remained in the dark, utterly uninformed and easily distracted. Typical.

Bix huddled deeper in her wine-colored wool coat, clutching a cup of cocoa she held purely for appearances in a quaint little park with a curious art installation just outside the Torpedo Factory. Artworks of every medium shone through the large glass windows of the factory turned studio. Joggers thundered across the wooden docks as tourists embarked on the white-and-yellow riverboat lovingly decorated for the season. A family strung colored lights along the mast of their sailboat tied up in the city marina. Laughter erupted as a stiff breeze caught a string that was rescued by a pack of youths on the pier. Ah, the happiness of cooperation, of lives being lived with hope and belonging.

The artificial wood bench groaned as a big blond Berserker took a seat beside her.

"Were your brothers able to translate the ideograms my men delivered while I was frozen?" Tobek rasped before sipping his steaming coffee.

"It's a warning that by speeding the evolution of native magic, we've invited the heavyweights of the Devourer army into our battle." Bix didn't mention the message had come from a third party who wasn't affiliated with the Mids, the Fates, or her siblings. Esiw was tracking the sender, if only to know how they'd compromised a creation of his creations. When she'd called him out for being the creator of the Fates, he'd noted her mental faculties must be improving to allow her to notice the obvious. Smartass.

"We suspected they'd come once their forward troops got a taste of pure native magic." Tobek scooted closer until their thighs touched.

"I still want to get my hands on the greater goddess who brought the Devourers to Ariel's World. Her access, her connections, they're what we need to infiltrate the anti-gods' hierarchy and gain leverage." Bix stared at the sky, trying to imagine where Indraja was hiding. The damn goddess remained annoyingly elusive. Phobos had convinced the pantheons to unleash their best hunters, yet the hunters had hit as many dead ends as Bix had. Not that Bix had personally stopped searching for the goddess, far from it. Success was just a matter of time.

"Her access to a World's core exposed a weakness in Resen

none of us had anticipated." Tobek swirled the coffee in his cup. "We should probably thank her before you husk her."

"Resen is an aid, not a complete solution to the Devourer problem. Though, it will be interesting to see the system in action if the Consortium ever gets their act together." She looked at him, at his aviator sunglasses, at his black knit cap, at the lengths of blond waves fluttering around his shoulders, at the well-loved oxblood leather coat that creaked ever so slightly when he moved. Warm fuzzies blossomed within her. She'd missed these moments of normal. Of just being two people. Ordinary, if only on the surface.

"Such high expectations you have." He leaned in for a kiss, tickling her face with his whiskers.

She gave him a quick peck and set her head on his shoulder. "How'd your month-long meeting with the Consortium go? The battalion back in their good graces?"

"The men have been cleared of the worst offenses." He nodded. "Hywl and his team are up for an award for taking down the Devourers responsible for the raids on local governments and civilian interests."

"Yay for the boys," she cheered quietly. "The Consortium press you about re-upping with the army?"

He held up his cup. "They offered me a new opportunity."

She had to double-check his expression to make sure he wasn't kidding. A *new* opportunity for the guy who'd been around since the Consortium's earliest days? That seemed…overdue.

"Aaaaaaand?"

"Due to the recent changes in me, coupled with the boots-on-the-ground experience combating foreign invaders, the Consortium would like me to head up the Resen Defense Division. The battalion transfers with me."

"As a new branch within the army?" She wrinkled her nose as a spray of cold water came over the edge of the river wall.

"No. As its own department reporting to the security committee. I would be responsible for building the organization from the ground up, drafting policy, overseeing operations, and owning the blame for all things Resen."

"Pfft. They want you to manage the local rebellions arising from the defense system so they don't have to be accountable for screwing up Resen's launch," Bix scoffed, unsurprised by the superpowers' transparent motivation. "After the Devourers are gone, Resen's day-to-day function will be immigration tracking and enforcement. You'll be tasked with policing gods and Other World entities who visit the Mids because the Consortium wants more leverage over the pantheons. Immigration control will make you really unpopular, which will chip away at your public support, so you'll no longer be a threat to them."

"Having strong opinions about that, are we?" he teased, swapping his empty cup for her full one.

"Sorry. I *am* sorry. That was unkind of me to put a pin in your balloon." She nudged his thigh. "There is no one better qualified to stand up the defense system. You know the science, the magic, and the politics surrounding it. You have a unique relationship to the ley lines and the Fates' weave. You have considerable experience developing successful institutions. Not only are you an architect of the Fates' army, but you also built the Mid World Army into what it is today. You have the connections to do the job right and the balanced perspective to be judicious in how you apply the power of a sprawling law enforcement organization."

"Damn, you make me sound good." He sipped her cold cocoa and cringed. A flicker of green magic, and steam rose out the vents in the lid. "Want to be my PR person?"

"That's Gurp's job," she protested. "Does the Consortium know you're an Other World entity now? Do they fathom you can smite any of them in a fit of rage? On a threat scale, you're an eleven?"

"I suspect that's the reason they're dangling this opportunity in front of me." He set his cup between his thighs and stretched his arm behind her. "I think they're afraid I want the position of Chair of the Consortium."

Bix twisted toward him. "Do you? Do you want to be Chair?"

He inhaled slowly and pursed his lips.

She listened to the tempo of his pulse and how it quickened as he took his time to ponder. "You do, don't you? The election for the new Chair is coming up. If you want it, you need to make it known."

"I don't, not really. Want to be Chair, that is." He slowly shook his head. "Don't get me wrong, I like being a leader. I like the responsibility. I like the challenge. I don't mind the administrivia. I love nurturing talents and affording opportunities. However, I despise the treachery and manipulations that are essential to politics. I loathe pandering for approvals. No, I like the rigid structure of the military. Frankly, I like being high enough up that my opinion carries significant weight."

"So, you want the Resen gig, eh?" She sat back and snuggled into his side. "You know I support you and whatever decision you make."

"Don't worry, sweetheart, I am fully aware that you will subvert me and my organization whenever it strikes your fancy." He squeezed her and laughed. "Balance. It's who you are."

"Have you already accepted the job?"

"There are significant conditions that have to be met before I officially accept. Then there's the haggling over the fine print, and I still have a few personal hiccups to address before I devote all my time and efforts to digging the Consortium out of the disaster they've made for themselves."

"The longer the launch of Resen is delayed, the more footing the Devourers gain," she reminded.

"Resen can't launch until the human populations are deployed to ground the magic around the data centers. How and when it happens is a point of contention among the Consortium that only the new Chair can resolve. Like it or not, bureaucracy is a behemoth even in times of war." He kissed her crown. "I will, however, have to hit the ground running, so I need to start planning what my organization will look like and how it will operate. I would very much like your input."

"When you're ready for it, you need only ask." She toyed with his beard. "But for today, can we pretend that we're blissfully ignorant of what lies ahead? Can we just be normal, happy, and content for a little bit?"

"Can I sit here and savor being in love with the fearless, smart, and beautiful woman next to me?" He straightened his legs and crossed his ankles, holding her close. "Absolutely, sweetheart. Absolutely."

Character Glossary

THE CONSORTIUM

The governing body comprised of representatives from the four superpower races charged with populating and protecting the collective of Mid Worlds.

THE DRAGON HORDE

Led by: The Dragon Queens
Mid World Entities
Provide bodies for lifeforms native to the Mids
Feed on positive emotions
Named Characters: Raspoine, Rummir, Yashanee

THE ANGELIC HOST

Led by: Archangels
Mid World Entities
Provide bodies for lifeforms native to the Mids
Feed on negative emotions
Named Characters: Samael, Michael, Ariel

THE HOUSES OF FATE

Led by: Heads of House
Other World Entities
Sages & Oracles strive to ascend to Fatehood
Provide threads of Fate that secure a soul to a body
Feed on magic expelled by a soul-tethered lifeform
Named Characters: Skuld, Sunan

THE PANTHEONS

Led by: Greater gods who fought their way to the top
Other World Entities
Demigods strive to ascend to godhood
Provide souls for lifeforms native to the Mids
Feed on enriched souls

Named Characters: Phobos, Hel, Jörmungand, Ereshkigal, Nergal, Deimos, and many more.

CHWEDLONOL (AKA "CHWEDS"):

Catch-all term for the myriad magical races native to the Mid Worlds. Created by the Consortium in terms defined by individual Cycle of Soul contracts.

HUMANS:

Do not possess magic, they ground magic; unconsciously drawn to magical hotspots. Created by the Consortium in terms defined by individual Cycle of Soul contracts.

Other Books by K.A. Krantz

Urban Fantasy
The Immortal Spy Series:
THE BURNED SPY
THE PLAGUED SPY
THE CAPTURED SPY
THE HANGED SPY
THE EXPOSED SPY

High Fantasy
Fire Born, Blood Blessed Series:
LARCOUT

THE SHACKLED SPY
Available Spring 2021

Want to be notified when a new book is released? Subscribe to K. A. Krantz's email newsletter at kakrantz.com

If you enjoyed this book, please spread the word and leave a review with the retailer of your choice.

Acknowledgments

To my family, for their consistent patience, support, and laughter. To Jenn Stark, for not letting me wimp out even when the story seemed determined to defeat me. To Linda Ingmanson, my development editor, for never letting me slack on the emotional parts of the story. To Toni Lee, my copy editor and fact-checker, for not only correcting my mistakes but also explaining the reasons and rules. To the team at Gene Mollica Studios, for putting up with my dithering and still making Bix look fabulous.

About the Author

KAK splits her time between Cincinnati and the DC 'burbs with her faithful hairy beast. When not writing, she indulges in a shoe obsession, conducts a love/hate affair with paint, and makes epic messes in the kitchen.

Visit her website at kakrantz.com for free flash fiction, blog posts about her latest fancies, and more. If you're on Twitter, she'd love to hear from you. Tweet @KAKrantz

www.ingramcontent.com/pod-product-compliance
Lightning Source LLC
Chambersburg PA
CBHW052033240626
47153CB00006B/2058

* 9 7 8 1 9 5 2 2 9 3 0 1 6 *